PUBLISHER'S SUMMARY

As Stumpy Fowler sets out to work on one fine May morning in 1956, he's blissfully unaware of what's unfolding around him. At his house, events are being set into motion that will turn his world—the town of River Falls, a place strictly segregated into black and white sections—upside down.

Because Bessie Williams, his wife's "help" and the leader of the Bethel A.M.E. Church choir has decided that this is the year her choir will enter The Sing.

An annual singing competition "open to all," The Sing is the one thing River Falls is known for... and no black choir has ever competed. Bessie's determined to change that, but her decision will have dire consequences: the Klan is active and thriving in River Falls, and they'll do anything to keep The Sing as white as it's always been.

It causes Stumpy to ask questions that he never thought of, arrive at answers he'd never considered, and learn new things about his friends... things he'd really rather not know. Stumpy doesn't really care for change, but suddenly, he's drowning in it.

the Sing

the Sing

CHUCK HOLMES

Deeds Publishing | Atlanta

Published by Deeds Publishing in Athens, GA
www.deedspublishing.com

Printed in The United States of America

Cover design by Mark Babcock

Text layout by Ashley Clarke

Library of Congress Cataloging-in-Publications data is available upon request.

978-1-947309-41-8

Books are available in quantity for promotional or premium use. For information, email info@deedspublishing.com

First Edition, 2018

10 9 8 7 6 5 4 3 2 1

For Linda,
who was with me in 1956 and every year since. I love her
for loving me, thank her for her constancy and admire her for
her endurance.

WARNING

Some readers may find the language in *The Sing* offensive. Lord knows, it offends me. However, it is accurate to the time, and the story would not be nearly so honest without it. I hope the reader will accept it in the spirit in which it is offered.

1

Stumpy Fowler loved waking up beside Mae Beth. It didn't matter that except for a couple of days each year when he was out of town on Kiwanis or CPA business he had been waking up beside her for almost twenty years. And it didn't matter that when Mae Beth didn't see things his way or he didn't see things her way he would wake up with her hugging the other side of the bed like she was trying to get away from him, or that in the worst situations he ended up sleeping on the couch in the living room even though it was about a foot too short to be comfortable. Just about every morning when he looked over at her side of the bed and saw her brown hair spread on the pillow and the smooth skin of her shoulder barely a shade darker than the white sheet, he wondered at just how lucky he was.

Stumpy stretched, but not much, because he didn't want to wake Mae Beth up. It was six o'clock, and there was still another half hour before she had to start her day. He eased the sheet back and slipped out of the bed. Stumpy Fowler had gotten his nickname when he was in high school, not only because he was five-foot eight, but because he was nearly square, with broad shoulders on a solid trunk on short, powerful legs. At forty he hadn't changed much. He looked as strong and immovable now as he did then, a rock of a man and probably nobody's image of a CPA.

He went into the kitchen and carefully measured six cups of water and six scoops of coffee into the percolator. He dropped two pieces of bread in the toaster and took the butter from the refrigerator. Then, he went over to the kitchen table to wait for the coffee to finish perking. As much as Stumpy loved his family, he still valued this quiet half hour in the morning before Mae Beth and Li'l got up, and before Bessie showed up to begin her day's work. He had his coffee, his newspaper, his note pad, and his favorite chair. There was not a thing to complain about.

It didn't take Stumpy long to read the newspaper. A glance at the front page, the sports page, and the comics. What he really wanted to do was start planning his day, making his list.

Ever since Stumpy was in high school, he had begun his day by making a list of everything he had to do that day and everything he wanted to do. He would make the list, then go back and number each entry according to how important it was. When he finished, he would tear the sheet off the pad and put it in his pocket. His day was planned. So far as he was concerned, being organized was every bit as important to an accountant as knowing the tax law.

He had almost finished making his list when he heard sounds at the other end of the house. That would be Mae Beth and Li'l getting up; Mae Beth to start her day and Li'l to get ready for school. Briefly, Stumpy wondered if they ought to quit calling his son Li'l. That was fine when he was a baby, and everybody called him Little Stumpy, then that got shortened to Little and pronounced Li'l. But now Li'l was fifteen and already five ten, two inches taller than Stumpy. It didn't make a lot of sense for Little Stumpy to be bigger than Big Stumpy. Of course, they could do like Mae Beth did. She called them both by their real names: Arthur.

Stumpy added the last thing to his list, Old Mrs. Mc-Ghee's tax return. This year, like every other year, she had shown up with a shoebox full of receipts on April 14th and expected Stumpy to get her taxes done by April 15th. And this year, like every other year, he had filed an extension and spent hours sorting out the receipts and checks. Stumpy finished the list and tore the page from the note pad.

* * *

In her home about four blocks and half a world away from Stumpy Fowler's house on Main Street, Bessie Williams was getting ready to go to work. She had already fixed breakfast for Horace and he had left, walking downtown to his job at the cotton yard. She had made the bed, washed the dishes, and swept the floors in the kitchen and the parlor. She had watered the flowers in the pots on the front porch. Now she could go take care of the Fowlers, just like she had done every day for nearly seventeen years. With one more look around, Bessie stuck her pocket book under her arm and went out the front door. She didn't lock the door when she left. Almost nobody in River Falls bothered to lock their doors.

Leaving home in the morning, Bessie Williams was almost a one-person parade. It wasn't just her size — although she was tall and big in a compact way. She didn't jiggle. She didn't so much walk as she sailed down the walkway, her head up and ample bosoms parting the air before her. Anyone watching would have had to believe she left a wake of bubbling air behind her. Her matte-black skin seldom showed sweat, no matter how hot or humid the eastern North Carolina weather was. Her dress and her apron usually looked as if they had just been washed and ironed.

As she walked down the sidewalk and through the gate in the picket fence, Bessie took a deep breath of the morning air, still cool from the spring night, and started humming *"Just a Closer Walk with Thee."* That would be a good song for today, she thought as she turned down Disciple Street. Although she was not wearing a watch, Bessie Williams knew she would be at the Fowlers by seven. That's the way it should be.

* * *

Not quite five miles outside of River Falls, the road that became Main Street as it ran the scant mile through town and became Highway 55 again when it left crossed over the Oak Grove-Orangeville road. That spot had, at various times, been called Jones' Crossroads or McGhee's Crossroads, according to who owned the general store on its northwest corner, but for the most part, people just called it The Crossroads.

About a mile from The Crossroads, off the road toward Oak Grove down a long two-lane path, was a hundred-year-old house that hadn't been painted in the last twenty of those years. It was what used to be the Sutton farm until Ruby Sutton had married Claymore Thomas. Now it was the Thomas farm, or rather what was left of it. Thirty years earlier, before the Great Depression, the Sutton farm had been the biggest holding in the area. But Ruby's father had lost some of the land in the Depression, and then in bad years Claymore had sold some more to cover the loans that he had made in the spring. Unfortunately for Claymore, there had been more bad years than good years.

This morning, he stood under the big Oak tree in the bare yard, a Chesterfield stuck in the center of his mouth. His round face, his puckered mouth, and the Chesterfield made a series of concentric circles. He pulled the cigarette from his mouth and blew a stream of smoke through his nostrils. He immediately stuck the cigarette back in his mouth and filled up his lungs again. There was nothing relaxed nor leisurely about his smoking. He sucked in the smoke, harshly expelled it, then sucked in some more smoke, all in a rhythm to the thoughts going around in his head.

It wasn't even seven o'clock, and he and Ruby had already had their first fight of the day. All he had said was something about the Klavern meeting that night, and she took off on him.

She had been standing in the kitchen, half in shadow and half in the light from the bulb hanging from the ceiling. She was a big woman, nearly as tall as Claymore and probably heavier. Claymore was sitting at the table, a cup of coffee in front of him and his arms folded. She had just told him that he ought to be thinking about what he was going to do about the crops instead of the meeting that night.

"What I'm doin' is important," he said.

"I'll tell you what's important. Getting the crops planted and cared for. I don't know why you think you have to spend all of your time saving the white race. You and that dozen other do-nothings go out playing in your white sheets, and if you're not careful, we're going to lose this land. Ain't no two ways about it. This was my daddy's and my granddaddy's, and one of these days it'll be Petey's. If it don't go for debt or taxes first."

"I've always got the crops in the ground, and I've always got them harvested," he said. "And they ain't sheets; they're robes. And Petey's going to inherit something a lot more important than just land. He's going to inherit a respect for his race. He won't be told what to do by a bunch of race-mixing politicians and niggers."

Claymore stood up and began pacing. He started to say

something else, but Ruby stopped him with an upraised hand.

"Claymore, this ain't one of your meetings. Don't go making a speech to me. You stay out half the night trying to make like that bunch of yours is really something, then you have to sleep in come morning. Best I can tell, the niggers and whites around here get along pretty good. A whole lot better than our crops do."

Claymore looked at her. "You just don't understand," he said. She turned back to the sink and started pumping water to wash the breakfast dishes.

Claymore had gone out into the yard to smoke under the big tree. He knew better than to try to convince Ruby that protecting their way of life was more important than a few plants in the ground. Women just didn't understand. He couldn't understand why he couldn't have been a lawyer or a teacher and married to somebody who appreciated what the Klan was doing instead of Ruby who was forever telling him what he hadn't done instead of admiring what he was doing.

He leaned against the oak tree, pulled another Chesterfield from the pack and lit it. Claymore felt a heavy sadness pressing on him. If they didn't do something, everything in the south would be different, and white people wouldn't be able to keep their rightful place. Although Claymore didn't think in terms of the social fabric, he could feel that something was about to tear; and for the first time since Ferd Ennis had died and Claymore had taken over leadership of the klavern, he didn't see them as a group of brave men who stood up for the right, but just as a bunch of men who met every week or so and talked. Just talked. And with nothing to back it up. He pulled hard on the Chesterfield again. Sooner or later, they would have to do something besides talk.

He stared at Ruby, still washing the breakfast dishes.

FROM THE RIVER FALLS CURRENT
Thursday April 12, 1956

CHILDREN FETE

THE NORMAN ALLENS' TWENTY-FIFTH

The Norman Allen family celebrated Norman and Alice's 25th wedding anniversary by motoring to Raleigh Sunday and dining at the Canton Inn. Present for the occasion were the Allens' three children: Norman Jr., Doris, and Deborah, as well as Norman Jr.'s wife, Faye. The party dined on fried rice, Egg Foo Young, and other excellent Chinese dishes. It is reported that a good time was had by all.

2

River Falls is a remarkably orderly town. The road from Raleigh becomes Main Street at the city limits and divides the town in half, north and south. The railroad tracks divide it east and west. In its way, River Falls is as thoughtfully laid out as Washington, DC, although it's not quite as old and not nearly as large.

River Falls became a town just a few years after the end of what some people still called "the War of Northern Aggression." The people there had been involved in the war on battlefields as far away as Pennsylvania and as close as their own farms. They weren't fighting to keep their slaves; there were only a few holdings in the county large enough to either need or support them. The largest landowner in what became River Falls made do by having a dozen children. But the farmers did see the need to fight because it seemed like somebody was trying to change the way they lived. And they resisted that on principal.

Most of the families in River Falls — the McLambs, the Johnsons, the Allens, the Jones, the Hallers, and the others — had been there since before the Revolutionary War, and when the town was incorporated, the people in the first census — both black and white — had the same names as the people in the 1950 census. Nobody in River Falls had a last name that ended in a vowel.

And nobody in River Falls knew exactly why it was named River Falls. Some of the older citizens talked about how there had been an argument between two of the bigger landowners, each claiming the right to the town's name. It could have been Johnsonville or Jonesboro. But it was finally named River Falls, despite the fact that it was a dozen miles from the river and more than thirty miles from the falls. It was a puzzle, but like so many other things, people just accepted it.

There was a predictable pulse to the week in River Falls. Five days a week, the two thousand inhabitants went leisurely about their business. Some stores saw just two or three customers all day, and in the barber shops, the barbers and the shoeshine boys spent more time sitting in their chairs reading *Sports Illustrated* or the *Saturday Evening Post* than barbering or shining.

But on Saturday the population swelled as farmers and their families made their weekly trip into town. The men went to the seed and feed store, the women got clothes for the children, and the children begged to go to the dime store. In the summer, the sidewalks were clogged with knots of people until eight or nine o'clock at night when they went back to their farms, leaving the two thousand citizens of River Falls to rest on Sunday and get ready for the next Saturday.

That was true every week of the year except one: the week of the second Sunday in June, also known as "Sing Sunday." The Singing Convention had been an annual event in River Falls for nearly thirty years and soloists, duets, quartets, family groups, and choirs came from all over eastern North Carolina, South Carolina, and Virginia to compete. The Monday through Friday before Sing Sunday were, to all appearances, almost exactly like any other Monday through Friday, but the ordinariness of these day was deceptive. All over town there were pockets of unusual activity. The storeowners along Main Street from Country Carl Cagle at his grocery to Doc Benson at his corner drug store were making certain they had enough stock. The garden clubwomen were holding a final meeting to recount the corsages and bouquets they needed. The Boy Scouts, charged with directing the streams of traffic, huddled over Chamber of Commerce maps of River Falls bargaining for the best corners; twelve and thirteen-year-old boys anticipating the excitement of telling adults when to stop and when to go.

By Saturday, all this activity had broken the surface. Workers were putting benches in the singing grove. Lemonade and hot dog peddlers were setting up their stands, and River Falls' three policemen were gritting their teeth and dreading Sunday.

On Sunday, the population quickly swelled by nearly ten thousand souls. They were mostly families who — at least the parents — simply loved gospel music. There were some who enjoyed the carnival atmosphere the crowd brought to the town. Afterward, when the crowd dispersed in the evening, there were always a few left behind in the city jail because they mixed the gospel music with too great a quantity of white whiskey, or because they tried to take something—a purse or a wallet—that wasn't theirs.

On Monday, River Falls had for all appearances returned to normal. The population again was two thousand, and those people went about their weekday business preparing for the next Saturday.

It was that kind of order that Stumpy Fowler prized, predictable and unchanging. On this cool April morning, he was enjoying his walk down Main Street to his office in the second of the business district's three blocks. The trees that reached across Main Street from either side had about finished leafing out and were already casting a greenish shade over the sidewalk. In another month, this same walk would be a struggle through the wet heat that settled on River Falls and lasted from June to early September, but Stumpy didn't think of what would happen next month. He was happy to enjoy the morning as it was.

It took Stumpy less than ten minutes to walk from his house to his office, but in that ten minutes, he had prepared himself for his business day. He unlocked the door and went through the front office to his office in the back. In his office there were piles of folders neatly stacked on the side of the desk, in the chairs, and on the side table. These were the financial affairs of most of the substantial people in River Falls. Stumpy settled down in the worn leather-bottomed desk chair, took a deep breath, and pulled his list from his pocket. He was ready to go to work. The item with the one beside it said: *Sng stmnts to A.Y.* Translated from Stumpy's shorthand, it said that he was supposed to take the financial statements for the Singing Convention over to A.Y. Pollard's so the committee chairman could review them over before the meeting tomorrow night. Stumpy reached into the stack of folders on the right side of his desk and pulled one out. He looked at it to make sure it said 29th Annual Singing Convention. It did.

Stumpy looked at his watch. It was eight-thirty. He decided he ought to give A.Y. a half hour or so to start his own day; so he pulled another folder from the pile and opened it up.

* * *

River Falls High School was, for River Falls, a big building. Dirty, dark red brick, three stories high. The older part had been built in the twenties, and the back part had been added as a WPA project in the thirties. The front had classic columns and broad granite steps leading to a set of double doors, a very formal presentation for a boxy building sitting on a block of bare ground. The PTA had tried to grow some grass, but as hard as they tried, they never succeeded, the grass being no match for the hundreds of feet that walked across it to the front door of the school every day. Like the town itself, the school had a name that really didn't fit the facts. River Falls High School had about five hundred students, starting with the first grade and going through the twelfth. It was the only school, high or otherwise, for the white children in that corner of the county.

Of the hundred or so high school students, eighty or more were gathered in front of the school on any school morning when it wasn't pouring rain or freezing. There were the city kids — those from River Falls—in their bunches, and the country kids in their bunches, standing, and talking, and waiting for the sound of the first bell. Li'l Fowler and Billy Royce Pollard were just about to join one of the knots of city kids when they heard yelling from across the schoolyard, at the long row of yellow school busses. It wasn't the yelling that caught their attention, but the mix of excitement and fear in it.

"Wonder what that's about?" Li'l said. All he and Billy Royce could see was a bunch of boys, some shoving and others jumping up and down, trying to see what was happening in the middle of the circle. They started walking toward the noise.

"What'cha want to bet that it's Petey and his gang," Billy Royce said.

"Probably. Wonder who they got this time?"

"Let's go see."

When they got to the outer edge of the mob, they saw that it was Petey Thomas and his gang, and their victim was Wendell Gibson. Wendell was a big boy, well over six feet tall, but because he was slow, he was still in the sixth grade. Wendell had never been known to hurt anybody; he was almost embarrassingly grateful for any attention paid to him, except for the kind of attention Petey Thomas and his friends were giving him now. They had backed him against the bus, poking and prodding him with their fingers.

Petey kept grabbing at Wendell's belt, threatening to take his pants down. Wendell flinched from the poking fingers and tried to hold on to his belt at the same time. Tears were streaming down his face. He tried to bolt through the boys encircling him, but they kept pushing him back. His tormentors were laughing and hooting. Wendell tried to burrow into the side of the bus. Li'l noticed that there were a lot of kids watching and very few of them were laughing; and none of them were interfering with Petey and his three friends.

Billy Royce pushed into the ring and stepped in front of Wendell. "I think that's enough, Petey. Leave him alone."

Petey Thomas took a step back. He was smaller than Billy Royce, only about five-nine, and maybe a hundred and thirty pounds. Unlike his daddy, who had a round face and a round mouth, Petey had a long face, slashed across the bottom with a near-permanent sneer. Petey also had three or four boys who were bigger than he was who were always with him.

"What's this to you, Pollard? You want to get out of the way before you get hurt?"

"I don't think so, Petey. You and your boys just go play somewhere else. Wendell and I have to go to school."

Petey looked over his shoulder to make sure his friends were still there, and took a step closer to Billy Royce and Wendell.

"If you want to take up for the dummy here, I guess you can. And you can get the same thing he's going to get."

Li'l hesitated at the edge of the circle. He didn't want to get into a fight. But he didn't want to leave Billy Royce standing there facing Petey and his buddies. In an instant, he weighed the possibilities of a black eye or bloody nose against watching his best friend get beaten up and having to live with himself as a coward. He decided that taking a punch — or even several — would be easier than the alternative, so he took a deep breath and pushed his way through the circle of boys. Billy Royce looked over at him and grinned. Li'l moved over beside Wendell, and Billy Royce moved on the other side. Standing beside Billy Royce and Wendell, both over six feet, Li'l knew he looked small, but there was nothing he could do about it now. Neither Li'l nor Billy Royce was known for fighting. Billy Royce was even less likely than Li'l to be called out to fight because, according to the traditions of the school yard, Billy Royce didn't fight exactly fair. It was a long-standing tradition that there was a lot of talking before anybody threw a punch. Somebody stuck his chin out and said, "Go ahead. Just hit me." With most of the schoolyard fights, that went on for some time. The problem was that Billy Royce didn't observe that tradition. When somebody said, "You go ahead. You just hit me." Billy Royce did, and whoever said it would wake up sometime later, the print of Billy Royce's knuckles somewhere on his face.

Li'l and Billy Royce stood there with their backs to the yellow school bus, their hands hanging at their sides, just waiting. So far as anybody could tell, it didn't bother them a bit that Petey and his bunch had them outnumbered five to two. Li'l reached over and patted Wendell on the shoulder. Wendell wiped his nose on the sleeve of his shirt. He had almost stopped crying. Around the edge of the crowd, the city kids and country kids waited to see what would happen next. Then the bell rang, and without saying much, the crowd started heading for the door of the school.

Petey took a couple of steps back. "I gotta go. I ain't going to have to see Morgan because of three dummies." He turned and walked away, trying not to look like he was walking as fast as he was. His gang immediately fell in behind him. Li'l grinned at Billy Royce.

"I guess somebody was saved by the bell," he said. "Wonder if it was them or us."

"Petey, for certain," Billy Royce said. "He's the first one I'd have punched, but after that I'm not sure. Some of his buddies can be pretty rough. I saw Jamie hit a mule in the head with his fist one time. Didn't seem to hurt the mule, but it didn't bother Jamie either."

Li'l took Wendell by the arm. "Let's get in. We don't want to go see Morgan either."

It is possible that River Falls had the lowest incidence of tardiness of any school in North Carolina. Being tardy usually meant writing 500 sentences, but worse than that it meant a visit to the principal, "Moanin'" Morgan. He never scolded or shouted at you, but he whined on and on about your lack of respect, lack of discipline, and lack of whatever else he could think of. It was an awful experience. Juniors and Seniors had been known to interrupt their necking behind the boiler room chimney just to keep from being tardy for class.

With Li'l on one side and Billy Royce on the other, they escorted Wendell into the old school building.

* * *

At exactly nine o'clock Stumpy picked up the Singing Convention file and started to A.Y. Pollard's office. As he walked the short block, Stumpy noticed there were still nearly no cars on the street. In yesterday's News & Observer there had been an article about Raleigh's rush hour traffic, cars sitting bumper-to-bumper trying to get downtown in the morning, and the same going the other way in the afternoon. He couldn't imagine living in a place like that. In fact, he couldn't imagine living anywhere he couldn't walk wherever he wanted to go. He owned a nice car, a 1955 Oldsmobile 98, but the only time he used it was for Sunday drives or when the weather was too bad to walk. Stumpy had walked up and down the streets in River Falls almost all his life, and he didn't want to have to do anything else.

The brick and marble bank building sitting on the corner was squat, just two stories high, but everything about it — the marble columns on the front, the shining double glass doors, and the odd colored corner stone with "1939" chiseled into it — tried to scream "substantial." It had been built at the tail end of the depression when there were still a lot of bad memories. Now, in better times, it just looked a bit pretentious. Stumpy walked past the double glass doors, around the corner, into the slightly smaller side doors, and up the sweeping staircase to the second floor. As he looked at the marble around him, it occurred to Stumpy that A.Y. enjoyed some advantages as the wealthiest man in River Falls. He owned the bank, the feed store, and an appliance and hardware store, as well as his law practice. Since he owned the bank, he could have his offices over the bank, which was much nicer than having them over the seed and feed store. It also occurred to Stumpy that even though A.Y. Pollard was the richest man in town, it had never changed his attitude toward anybody, and that was a check mark for him in the character column.

As he opened the heavy glass-paneled door with A.Y. Pollard, Attorney stenciled on it, Stumpy saw that Gladys' desk was deserted and the door to A.Y.'s office was closed. He guessed that meant that A.Y. was conducting lawyer business with somebody, so he took a seat on the sofa and picked up a week-old copy of the *River Falls Current*. He couldn't hear anyone talking in A.Y.'s office and wondered if Gladys and A.Y. had left and forgotten to lock the door. He was trying to decide whether to leave and come back when the door opened and Gladys came out. When she saw him, she stopped, smoothing her dress down. Although Stumpy knew that Gladys was over forty, he had to admire the way her looks kept denying it. Having her around was another advantage to being the richest man in town.

"Oh, Stumpy. I didn't know you were here. You've come to see Mr. Pollard?"

Stumpy stood up. "Hello, Gladys. Yeah, I need to see him for a minute if he's here."

"He is. Let me see if he's off the phone yet. He's been talking to a lawyer in Charlotte for about twenty minutes."

She turned and disappeared into A. Y.'s office, closing the door behind her. He could hear a mumbled conversation, then Gladys came back out and headed to her desk. "Just go on in, Stumpy. He's off the phone."

A.Y. was sitting behind his big dark wood desk, flipping the pages in a blue file folder. He was the same age as Stumpy, but so much sitting and Leola's cooking had added visible pounds. His face was full, and there was the beginning of a second chin hanging under what had once been a sharply chiseled first chin. Now, the chiseling was indistinct, like the sand damage to Egyptian Sphinx. Stumpy noticed that A.Y's face was a little redder than usual. His tie was pulled down, and his sleeves were rolled up. Stumpy wondered just how much effort A.Y. put into looking so much like a busy lawyer.

"You got the statements?" he asked.

"Good morning to you, too," Stumpy said. "Yeah, I got the statements, just like I do every month." Stumpy dropped into a chair in front of the desk, pushing the file folders over to A.Y. A.Y. picked up the folder and leaned back in his chair. He flipped through the pages, not spending much time on any of it until he got to the last page. He nodded.

"That's good," he said. "We're going to finish with at least as much in the bank as we had when I became chairman. And that's even including all that tree work we had to do at the grove. All I ask is to finish this thing up in good shape. I never thought three years would be so long."

"That's what you get for letting them make you chairman. About the same thing I get for being treasurer. A lot of criticism and questions, and no money at all."

A.Y. laughed. "But think of the honor."

Stumpy smiled. "I guess." Pushing up out of the chair, he said, "I suppose I better be getting back to some paying business. You need anything else for the meeting tomorrow night?"

A.Y. shook his head. "I think this will do it. I'm looking forward to a short, uneventful meeting, and then I only have one more to worry about before the Singing Convention. After that, somebody else can have this."

* * *

Back at Stumpy's house, the day had begun in a normal manner. Stumpy had gone to work. Li'l had gone to school. Bessie had come to work. And she and Mae Beth had gotten their day started by stripping all the beds and beginning several loads of laundry. While the washing machine rumbled in the background, Bessie and Mae Beth sat at the kitchen table sipping coffee and shelling peas, talking about nothing in particular.

"You know, Mrs. Fowler. I can't help but think it's a shame," Bessie said, not relating her statement to anything that had been said before.

"What's a shame, Bessie?" Mae Beth said, dropping a hand full of pea shells in the trashcan.

"Well, the fact that there's some real good choirs around here that don't get to sing in the Singing Convention."

"You know that any choir that wants to sing and has ten dollars for an entry fee can sing, Bessie."

Bessie's rhythm of splitting the peas, dumping the peas from the shell, and grabbing another didn't vary. She continued shelling for a full minute before saying anything.

"No, ma'am. They can't."

Mae Beth looked over at Bessie, sensing this was more than typical pea-shelling conversation. She pulled another handful of peas from the basket on the floor.

"Just which choirs can't sing at the Singing Convention, Bessie?"

"Well, my choir. That's one," Bessie said. And she looked at Mae Beth Fowler as if the whole thing were her fault.

Mae Beth started to say something, to remind Bessie that she didn't decide which choirs could or could not compete in the Singing Convention, but Bessie had picked up the trashcan and taken it out the back door to dump it. Mae Beth didn't feel like talking to the imposing back of Bessie Williams. Nothing more really needed to be said. Mae Beth understood that Bessie had left the ball squarely in Mae Beth's court.

* * *

That evening, back on Disciple Street, at the upper end where the houses were a little bigger and the yards were generally better kept, a lot of the people were outside, enjoying the cool May air. Neighbors waved and called to each other, and some walked along the dirt street. Bessie Williams went from plant to plant in her front yard, pouring water from an old, nearly rusted-out sprinkler can. She moved serenely between the plants, occasionally stopping to pull a bug or a dead leaf from one. She came to a straggly rose bush, three mostly bare sticks with three roses at the end. She leaned over and smelled the flowers. "You ain't got much," she thought as she looked at the bush, "but what you got is real nice." She moved on to the next plant.

Horace, her husband, came down from the porch. He was taller than Bessie — nearly six feet five — and about as broad. He was blacker than Bessie, a deep, shiny coal-colored black. And even beneath the blue chambray shirt his muscles were obvious. It was known that Horace could throw a cotton hook over his shoulder and pull a five-hundred-pound bale onto his back and walk away. Sometimes groups of boys would congregate at the edge of the cotton yard just to watch Horace work.

From the corner of her eye, Bessie could see him watching her, and the fact that he obviously took some pride in what he was watching made her feel good. It also made her hesitate to tell him about her conversation with Mrs. Fowler that afternoon. She hadn't told him when they both got home that afternoon. She had started to tell him at dinner, but hadn't. She went back over to the faucet to refill the watering can, wondering why, when she had never really worried about telling Horace anything, she couldn't bring herself to talk about this.

She put the can down and turned around. "I talked to Mrs. Fowler today," she said. She resisted the impulse to put her hands on her hips. She knew that Horace would take that as a signal that they were about to have an argument. And she really didn't want an argument about this.

"Uh-huh," he said. "What about?"

"The Singing Convention," she said. She walked over and sat down beside him, waiting for him to say something. It didn't bother her a lot when he didn't. She knew that Horace Williams enjoyed long silences and spent his words like gold. So she just sat there with him for a minute before going on.

"I told her I thought it was a shame that everybody couldn't sing in the Singing Convention." She looked at him from the corner of her eye to see his reaction. She didn't see any.

"She said she thought everybody could," Bessie said, "but I told her that my choir couldn't."

"What'd she say?" Horace asked.

"Wasn't nothing she could say. She knows no colored choir ever sang in the Singing Convention before."

They sat there, side by side, listening to the neighborhood sounds around them.

"You were right," Horace said.

Bessie turned and looked at him. This wasn't what she was expecting, although truth be told, she didn't really know what she was expecting.

"You think so?"

"Yes. You said you talked to Mrs. Fowler. Sounds like you talked to her, but she didn't talk back much."

"That's the truth. But I think Mrs. Fowler knows what we were talking about. She's a right smart woman."

"You think she'll do anything about it?"

Bessie squinted at the plants in the front yard. It was getting darker, and her eyes weren't what they used to be.

"I don't know," she said. "What do you think?"

"I think things are real slow to change in a place like River Falls."

* * *

A.Y. Pollard had been raised with a big family in a big house. There was his mother and father, two brothers, and a sister. His father had been one of River Falls' most prominent citizens: a lawyer, a businessman, a Sunday School teacher, but most of all, a man given to knee-slapping laughter, and that set the tone when A.Y. was growing up. Now, both his brothers were dead, killed in Europe during the war and his mother and father had passed not long after that, leaving A.Y. with just his sister, who had married and moved to the middle part of the state. A.Y. still lived in the big house, but it was sadly different. He sat in his leather chair, staring at the television set. Virginia was physically in the same room, but A.Y. really didn't know where she was. She flipped the pages of a magazine, neither stopping to read what was on the pages or even to look closely at the pictures. The twins, Zona Faye and Billy Royce, were each up in their rooms; they didn't spend any more time together than they were forced to. A.Y. thought about how it used to be in this house, and how it was now, and he wondered if it was all his fault.

Virginia had come to River Falls as a schoolteacher, the independent daughter of one of the better families from a community on the coast. In her first year there, A.Y., a newly graduated lawyer, began courting her, and it seemed like a natural thing for them to get married, with good families, good blood lines and all, but A.Y. hadn't counted on the insular nature of the women who counted for society in River Falls. Even being A.Y. Pollard's wife wasn't enough to overcome the fact that she had come to River Falls as a woman with a job and without a husband and had made it known that while she might want a husband, she really didn't need one. For women who had been passed from father to husband and enjoyed their positions, this attitude was insulting. Except for a few occasions when A.Y.'s money was needed for a charity event or volunteers were required, Virginia was never included. After several years in River Falls, her independence faded, along with her bright eyes and sparkling wit. Now they just sat in the parlor alone together.

He was proud of Billy Royce. Although he was a mediocre student, Billy Royce seemed happy enough and seemed to land on the right side of things more often than not. He was somebody that A.Y. could count on and, just as important, he was somebody who could laugh. Zona Faye, on the other hand, seldom laughed, and all she could be counted on to do was what was in Zona Faye's interest.

Despite that, A.Y. showered love on his daughter, seeing in her a bit of what he had once seen in her mother.

He looked back at the television set, its lighted rim glowing around the black and white picture. He was surprised that the program had changed. He hadn't even noticed the other one ending.

* * *

Stumpy Fowler was sitting on the edge of the bed watching Mae Beth brush out her hair. She was one of the few women her age who kept her hair long and put it up every day. Stumpy reflected that for a woman in her late thirties, Mae Beth had certainly kept her looks and her shape. The shorty pajamas she was wearing showed most of her shape, and he wondered if she was wearing them for a reason. The thought crossed his mind that maybe she thought tonight would be a better night than Saturday night for making love.

"Arthur, what would happen if we had a colored choir in the Singing Convention?" She said it just like it was a normal, everyday question. In fact, her tone was so normal Stumpy thought that he had misunderstood her.

"Huh, what do you mean?"

"I mean, why can't Bessie and her choir compete in the Singing Convention."

This time Stumpy understood her. He quit watching her brush her hair and focused intently on her face.

Stumpy knew to take any conversation that included Bessie Williams seriously. Bessie was Mae Beth Fowler's help and had been almost since they got married. She cleaned the house, cooked most of the meals, and participated in raising Li'l. As much as anything, she was somebody Mae Beth leaned on; so anything concerning Bessie was not to be ignored.

"What is it we're talking about here?" he asked cautiously. He remembered that at least once in their twenty years of marriage a quiet conversation with Mae Beth had ended up with him sleeping on the sofa for nearly two weeks.

"Just that. Why is it we don't have any colored choirs in the singing convention?"

"Well, it's the same reason we don't have any colored trios or quartets or solos or duets. We just don't have any."

Mae Beth nodded like she understood the logic of Stumpy's answer, then she said, "And why's that."

"Mae Beth, you know that we have never had any Negro choirs or any other Negros at the Singing Convention. That's just the way it is. Their music is different from ours. They probably don't want to be in the Singing Convention anyway."

"Yes, they do. And I think they should."

By now, Stumpy had gotten in bed and was lying on his side with his back to Mae Beth, hoping to discourage any more conversation. She came over to the bed, sat down beside him, and ran her fingernails down his arm, very lightly. Stumpy looked up at her and saw that she was smiling. Maybe, he thought, that's the end of that.

He reached over and patted Mae Beth's leg and her

stroking on his arm became more insistent. His hand slid up her leg, and she turned slightly toward him, rubbing her palm down his chest, pulling at the hairs. Stumpy turned over on his back and reached up to pull her down.

Mae Beth smiled and stood up. "I think I'm going to go read a while," she said. She turned and walked to the door. "You know, I still don't quite understand why we don't have any colored choirs in the Singing Convention." And she went downstairs.

Stumpy lay on the bed, knowing that tonight — and probably Saturday night — were not good nights for making love.

* * *

But for some people, the night wasn't over. About three miles out of town, down the Raleigh highway and off on a little dirt road, about a dozen men sat inside a tobacco barn. It was hot even though the doors on both ends were open, and the barn had the dusty dry smell of last year's cured tobacco.

Most of the men leaned against the walls or on the flues, but in the middle of the barn, pacing around on the sandy floor, Claymore Thomas was working himself into a lather, having passed the sweating stage an hour or so before.

Claymore Thomas could have been a preacher. His chubby round face was often given to a slight beatific smile. His body matched the face, chubby, round — like somebody who might play Santa Claus at Christmas. But Claymore Thomas had good will for only some of his fellow man. Claymore truly hated niggers, and they were the subject of his harangue tonight, just like they always were.

"I tell you," he whispered fervently to his congregation of a dozen, "first it's the schools, next it's your daughters, then y'all going to have mongrel grandchildren. Ain't white. Ain't black. Ain't no good for nobody."

He stopped and glared around the group. Nobody moved except to nod agreement. Over in the corner, Otha Forster, nodding like the rest, wished Claymore would spit it out and get it over with. It was already eleven o'clock, and he had to be back in the fields at sun up. But he didn't want to be the one to try to stop Claymore. That could be dangerous.

"If the Klan is going to stand for anything," Claymore was saying, "If we're going to be something more than somebody's quilting society, if we're going to stand up against the Yankees stirring up the niggers —" He stopped, narrowed his eyes, then he lowered his voice until it was nothing more than a hiss — "We've got to do something. Do something."

"What we going to do, Claymore?"

Claymore Thomas whirled around to see who had broken the spell. It was Aaron Smelt. Everybody relaxed. Nobody, even Claymore, took offense at Aaron. He was a little slow, a good man but apt not to keep up. Claymore wiped his face on his shirtsleeve and smiled his beatific smile at

Aaron. "I don't know, Aaron. Not right now. But we'll do it and it'll be big."

Aaron looked pleased. He'd like to do something big, something that would send the Yankees back where they belonged, although he wasn't sure exactly where that was, even though he did know that the niggers ought to go back to Africa where they came from. "Yeah, Claymore," he said. "Something big."

"Well, let's call it a night, boys. We all got some thinking to do," Claymore said. He ducked out of the little tobacco barn door into the cooler air of the night. It felt good, but it always felt good when they struck a blow for the south and against the nigger loving, race-mixing government. He stopped beside his International pickup. "One of these days," he thought, "we will do something big, something that matters."

* * *

Li'l lay on top of the sheets reviewing his day. Not much had happened at school, except for the almost fight with Petey, and that turned out to be nothing. He thought about running into Zona Faye in the hall. Despite what Billy Royce said about her, Li'l's thoughts about Zona Faye were much like his night-time prayers; they were his way of trying to approach a higher being. Tonight, like many nights, Li'l thought about the moment at Zona Faye's house when, accidentally or on purpose, she had leaned against his arm and for that moment he had felt her breast against his body. It seemed to Li'l she had leaned there a bit longer than necessary, and in that split second, there was a message with a promise. But it had never happened again except in Li'l's mind.

On the bedside table, there were a North Carolina Driver's Manual and a King James Bible. Under his bed was a Mickey Spillane novel with about thirty pages dog-eared. These were his instruction books for adulthood.

3

For Stumpy, the walk from his office to his home was no different from any other spring day. As he turned up the front walk, he noticed the paint on the eaves was beginning to peel. Not much, but enough that they needed to start thinking about painting again. He looked at the front of the house and the doorframe and thought maybe just a touchup would do.

It was a satisfying house, built over fifty years earlier. Stumpy and Mae Beth had bought it right after they were married, and over the years they had made a few changes like adding the picture window in the front of the house and a shower over the bath tub but basically it was still the house Dr. Robbins had built before Stumpy was born.

When he opened the door, he noticed that the table was already set for dinner. Mae Beth threw her arms around him, kissed him on the cheek, and hurried off, returning almost immediately with a glass of iced tea. He took the tea and went into their bedroom to get rid of his tie. He looked at his watch to make sure it was just five-thirty. It was, just like about every other weekday when he came home. He went back into the living room and sat down in his Lazy Boy, picking up the *News & Observer* from the magazine rack behind the chair. Mae Beth came in from the kitchen.

"Don't get too comfortable. We'll be eating in just a few minutes," she said.

"Okay, but why?"

"Because you have a Sing meeting at seven o'clock."

"Yeah, but I've had a Sing meeting every other Tuesday for about two years now, and we never ate particularly early before."

"I just wanted to make sure you got there in plenty of time. You are going to find out why Bessie's choir can't sing in this year's singing convention, aren't you?"

Stumpy could hear Bessie in the kitchen, and he was sure that she could hear anything they said in the living room. He glanced in the direction of the kitchen. Mae Beth just stood there, a small smile on her face.

In as low a voice as he thought would reach Mae Beth, he said, "Like I told you, that's just the way it is. It's always been that way."

There was a clatter in the kitchen as Bessie put pots in the stove. Mae Beth looked over her shoulder.

"Well, maybe it doesn't have to be that way. I know you want to find out."

Stumpy just tried to sink down into the Lazy Boy. He didn't really want to find out, but he didn't want to have this conversation every other Tuesday night either. He decided he would bring it up; A.Y. would shoot it down, and then it would be done. He went back to reading the sports section.

Bessie left at six o'clock, just as they were sitting down to supper. Stumpy wasn't sure whether he really saw Mae Beth give Bessie what he would have called "a meaningful look" or not, but as Stumpy, Mae Beth, and Li'l ate, he tried to talk about anything except the Singing Convention.

"Somebody told me that you took up for Wendell Gibson yesterday," he said to Li'l. "I was talking to Frank at the drugstore, and he said his daughter told him that Petey Thomas and his bunch were messing with Wendell, and you stopped them."

"Wasn't really me. It was mostly Billy Royce. Then the school bell rang. I didn't really do anything."

Stumpy looked at his son. He was proud that Li'l had stood up to Petey and his bunch. He was even prouder that Li'l didn't think it was a big thing.

"Either way," Stumpy said, "I'm glad you took up for Wendell. He's got a hard enough life without somebody making it harder. Besides, Frank's daughter thinks you're a hero, now."

Li'l's expression looked like he had just tasted something bad.

"Dad, Frances is in the eighth grade."

Stumpy didn't bother to continue the conversation, but it occurred to him that in three years, Frances would be in the eleventh grade and Li'l would be starting to college, and since Frances was getting to be as pretty as her mother, Li'l might not make such a face when he thought of her. Mae Beth asked him how his day had been, and he asked her how hers had been, and they talked about nothing through the rest of supper. When they finished, Mae Beth started clearing the table, Li'l went to his room to do his homework, and Stumpy went to their bedroom to get a short-sleeved shirt to wear to the meeting. As he was changing, Mae Beth came up behind him and put her hand on his shoulder. "I hope you have a good meeting tonight, honey. I'll look forward to hearing about it."

Stumpy kissed her on the cheek and left. The May evening was just as pleasant as the morning had been. He passed Mackaby's Funeral Home and noticed the big white wreath beside the door. He wondered who had died that day. The big old mansion had once belonged to a doctor, and now it was the town's funeral parlor. Beside it, perhaps symbolically, was Dr. Raynor's house. He was one of two doctors in River Falls and had just built a nice brick clinic. As Stumpy walked down Main Street, passing one familiar house after another, he was enjoying the peacefulness. The houses looked rooted there, not like they had just been put up to make scenery along the street, and most of the houses had some kind of connection to Stumpy's life, as far back as when he was in grade school. At the Owen's house, the big pear tree still stood at the edge of the driveway. Stumpy and his friends would sneak into the yard and steal green pears off the tree. And there was Mrs. Smith's house. She was a widow and had been an English teacher at the high school until her crippling arthritis fixed her so she couldn't teach. She could hardly hold a book, but she always had two or three children in her reading program. It had been going on since Stumpy was in high school. She gave each student a list, and when the student had read the books on the list, he'd get a reward. When he was in high school, Stumpy had gotten a baseball glove for reading Moby Dick and David Copperfield and two or three other books. She still did that, even though she was in her eighties and could hardly get out of her bed.

When Stumpy got to the bank building, Pete Jennings and Gerald Raney were already there, standing on the sidewalk. The three men nodded at each other, and Pete went on telling his story.

"She couldn't understand why it wouldn't run. She kept saying that it had plenty of gas in it. I almost didn't have the heart to tell her that the gas was fine, but the problem was it didn't have any oil in it. That motor was froze up tighter than an old maid's crotch."

"Well, she probably doesn't even know what's under the hood of that old car. She's always had somebody take care of that for her, until Al died."

Now Stumpy caught up with the story. Al Campbell had died about two months ago. He had been in his eighties, and his wife, Flora, wasn't far behind. She still puttered around River Falls in a 1948 Pontiac, and based on what Pete had just said, she probably wouldn't be doing much puttering any more. Pete owned the Pure Oil station, the town's only tow truck, and he was almost everybody's mechanic. Pete had come to the meeting dressed just like he had been all day, in his khaki uniform with the Pure Oil emblem over the right pocket and "Pete" embroidered over the left. His face and hands were clean except for a rim of grease around his fingernails. Anybody who knew Pete expected him to look that way. He was still as trim as he had been in high school, and he still kept his hair cut short all over. He said that made it easier for him to get the grease out of it.

Gerald Raney, on the other hand, hadn't been fit in high school and was even less fit now. Stumpy figured that Gerald must weigh about two-fifty, spread widely over a short frame. He didn't get a lot of exercise, just sitting at his desk or in somebody's living room, selling insurance policies. If being overweight was bad for you, Gerald would probably die young, but it would certainly be with a smile on his face. He could find something funny in about anything, and if he couldn't find something funny, he'd make it up.

Gerald started telling them about his conversation with Nub Browning. Nub was the area's most successful bootlegger, and his son, known as Nubbin, was about to follow in his footsteps. "Old Nub just couldn't understand why Nationwide wasn't going to insure Nubbin, just because he'd had three speeding tickets before he ever got his driver's license, and all three of them were in that souped-up 98 Olds that Nub hauls his liquor in. He took it real personal."

A.Y. walked up just as Gerald was finishing his story. He looked at his watch.

"It's five minutes to seven. You're early. You fellows must not have anything to do at home."

"That's the problem," Pete said. "I stay at the station and I got work to do. I go home and I got work to do. Coming here's the only place I don't have to work."

They walked up the staircase to A.Y.'s office. Stumpy noticed that they were climbing the stairs slower than they used to. He guessed that when you hit your forties, you start slowing down.

A.Y. unlocked his office door and switched on the light.

"Y'all go on in the conference room. I'm sure the rest of them will be along in a few minutes," he said. He went on into his office. By the time they had settled around the conference table, A.Y. was back carrying a stack of manila folders. A.Y. took his seat at the head.

Callie Turlington came rushing in, apologizing for being late. "I just don't know where the time got to. I was all ready to leave in plenty of time, but I guess it just took me longer to get here than I thought." She dropped her purse, a big three-binder, a legal pad, and a bunch of pencils on the table. "I don't know what I'm going to do about me. I just can't seem to get anywhere on time."

All four of the men tried to hide their smiles behind their hands. This was the same speech that Callie made at every committee meeting, and she was never late. She just seemed to think she was.

"Calm down, Callie," A.Y. said. "Emil and Kenneth aren't here yet. In fact, you're right on time."

Callie nodded and started arranging her notebook, legal pad, and pencils in front of her. Callie was almost exactly the same age as Stumpy, and except for the big glasses she had to wear because of her near-sightedness, the years had been kind to her. Her face didn't have many more lines in it than it had when they were in high school. Her features — the blue eyes behind the glasses, the small straight nose, and the slightly wide mouth that was only rarely engaged in a full smile — were still pretty. She wore her hair up in a bun. Stumpy guessed that was how she thought the town librarian should wear it. For a while just before Stumpy had started dating Mae Beth, he and Callie had dated. Not much had come of it.

Emil Barnes came in, still wearing his coat and tie. Emil sat at his watchmaker's bench all day wearing his tie, and when he got up to show somebody some jewelry, he always put on his coat before he came to the front of his jewelry store. Emil just nodded to everybody and sat down beside A.Y. He hadn't even settled in his chair before Kenneth Adams strolled in. He looked around the room, nodded to A.Y. and sat as far from Stumpy as the conference table would let him. That was the way it always was. He guessed that Kenneth was never going to get over what Stumpy had done to him nearly thirty years ago. A bunch of the boys had gone skinny-dipping down at Woodall's pond. Stumpy had gotten dressed and run off with Kenneth's clothes. It had taken Kenneth hours to sneak home, hiding behind trees and shrubs, and then when he got home, he got a whipping for losing his clothes. He was usually civil to Stumpy, but barely. Stumpy figured that Kenneth wouldn't throw water on him if he was on fire.

"Al won't be here tonight," A.Y. said. "He had to go on a trip. We're probably not going to do anything important anyway. Let's get started."

Callie read the minutes of the last meeting, and everybody agreed to approve them. A.Y. went over the financial statement that Stumpy had brought him, and they approved the application of a man from Oak Grove who wanted to sell cotton candy across the street from the singing grove. Stumpy looked at his watch. It wasn't even seven-thirty, and it looked like the meeting was about to wind up. He could hear Mae Beth's last words to him as he left the house: *I'm sure you want to find out why.* That meant the first thing he would hear when he got home was what he found out and what he had done about it. But really, she hadn't said anything about him doing anything about it. She just said to find out why. Inside his head, he shrugged. He guessed that was exactly what he was going to do.

A.Y. was closing his manila folders. He looked around and asked if there was any new business. Before he put the question mark at the end of the sentence, he was pushing his chair back. Stumpy raised his hand.

"I don't know if you'd call it new business or not, A.Y., but I have a question."

A.Y. leaned back to the conference table and waited for Stumpy's question.

"I was just wondering why it is that we have all these choirs and other folks coming from all around to sing in the Singing Convention, and the Bethel A.M.E. Choir from right here in River Falls hadn't ever sung there."

A.Y. sat there a minute. "I don't know. I don't imagine that they want to sing in the Singing Convention. They're colored."

Stumpy shook his head. "No. I know they'd like to sing there. Bessie said so. Is there any reason they shouldn't?"

A.Y. pulled his chair back up to the table and sat up straight. Stumpy looked around at the rest of the committee. Everybody except Callie looked confused. She had her head down, writing on her legal pad as fast as she could.

"I guess it's just never been done. It's tradition."

"Well, what would happen if we changed the tradition? What would happen if we let Bessie's choir sing?"

"Maybe we could take this up after we get all the pressing business from this Singing Convention taken care of." He looked around the room. "Do I hear a motion that we adjourn?"

Before anybody could say anything, Stumpy jumped back in.

"No. I think we should take a minute now. Is there a reason that Bessie's choir shouldn't be in the Singing Convention?" Stumpy was surprised at the strength of his own voice. He was leaning as far as he could toward A.Y.

A.Y.'s face began to change colors. A pink flush began at the base of his neck, turning into a bright red as it climbed up around his ears, and developing a dark tinge of purple as it spread onto his face. A vein the size of a chubby little finger began to throb in his temple. His eyes bulged, big and white, like they were about to pop out. He had his hands pressed down on the table like he was trying to keep it from flying away.

"Because it's never been done. And it probably won't ever be done. That's not the way the Singing Convention's been set up."

Stumpy leaned back in his chair. "No need to get so hot, A.Y. I told Mae Beth that I would ask. I asked."

A.Y. Pollard began to return to his natural color. He wiped his face with his handkerchief and nodded. "All right. But I'd think you'd already know the answer to that.

I'm a fair-minded man, but there're some things we can't do. And that's one of them. Do I hear a motion to adjourn?"

"Move t'ajourn," somebody mumbled.

"Second," somebody else said. Stumpy didn't even try to figure out who said what. He had asked, and he had gotten A.Y.'s answer. That should be good enough.

The meeting broke up like it usually did. Kenneth Adams leaving without saying much of anything to anybody. Callie continuing to make notes on her pad. Emil and A.Y. talking at the head of the table. Pete Jennings pushed Stumpy toward the door. He didn't say anything until they were walking down the stairs.

"What was that all about, bud? You nearly gave ol' A.Y. a heart attack."

"Wasn't about anything," Stumpy said. "Mae Beth asked me to find out why Bessie's choir couldn't sing in the Singing Convention. I told her about the same thing A.Y. said. It's always been that way. But I guess she wanted to hear it from somebody besides me. When Mae Beth gets something in her craw like this, she's not going to let it go until she's satisfied. So I asked. I don't know why A.Y. got so hot. I just asked a question."

Pete grinned. "Not exactly. You asked it three times, and A.Y. really didn't want to answer it. I think he boiled over because you wouldn't let him off the hook. When you think about it, not doing it because you've never done it ain't much of an answer."

"Well, it was good enough for me. I hope it's good enough for Mae Beth."

"Good luck on that."

Pete gave a little salute as he crossed the street, heading back to his service station. Stumpy walked up Main Street, trying to decide just how he was going to replay the committee meeting for Mae Beth. Pete was right; it wasn't a very good answer, but that was the way it was. This was the twenty-ninth Annual Singing Convention, and for twenty-nine years the rules — both written and unwritten — had been the same. There had never been any saxophones or trumpets, and there had never been any Negro choirs or solos or duets. As he recounted the meeting to himself, he had a gnawing fear in the back of his mind that this wasn't going to be the end of it. Mae Beth might not be as willing to accept A.Y.'s answer as he was. At the end of the three-block walk up Main Street to his house, he was no more confident than he had been when he started.

Mae Beth was sitting in the living room darning some socks when he got home. Li'l was stretched out on the sofa watching some cowboy show on television. Stumpy kissed Mae Beth on the cheek, pushed Li'l's feet off the sofa and looked at the television screen.

"Tell me about the meeting," Mae Beth said. That wasn't unusual.

"Not much happened. Pretty much the usual."

"What about Bessie's choir? Did you bring that up?"

"Yes. In fact, I brought it up and when A.Y. didn't want to talk about it, I pushed it until he about exploded." Stumpy hoped that he would get some points for effort, even though the end result wasn't what Mae Beth wanted.

She just sat there, looking at him, a small smile on her

face. He had seen that expression before, and he knew she wasn't going to say anything. It was still his turn.

"A.Y. said that it was a tradition with the Singing Convention, and that in the twenty-nine years it had been around, we had always followed that tradition, and we still would." He got the words out as fast as he could. Before she could respond, he added: "But this is the last year A.Y.'s going to be on the committee. We might get somebody next year who would see it different."

"I see. I'm not sure how Bessie's going to take that. She thinks it's important for her choir to get to sing. I would sure like to tell her something besides 'it's tradition.'"

She went back to darning the socks. Stumpy sat there looking at the television set, wondering if this was over and what he would do if it wasn't.

4

Small towns have some sort of capillary system where — once news is spilled somewhere — it immediately spreads. River Falls had a weekly newspaper, nearly fifty years old, that served to provide social reports and confirm some of the milder rumors, but the real news medium in River Falls was gossip. It was very efficient, and it was most efficient when the news was either bad or spectacular. The news of Stumpy's question at the committee meeting the evening before came under the heading of spectacular.

Had the system been as accurate as it was efficient, it wouldn't have been so spectacular, but when Kenneth Adams got home, he complained to his wife Louise that he'd missed almost all of *"The Phil Silvers Show"* because of some nonsense Stumpy Fowler had brought up about Bessie Williams' choir singing in the Singing Convention, and as soon as he had settled in his Lazy Boy and gone to sleep in front of the television set, Louise called Mrs. Ada Watkins and told her what she had heard — or thought she had heard — from Kenneth.

The fact that Mrs. Ada was nearly eighty years old and had lost much of her hearing and sight didn't keep her from enjoying her lifelong hobby. A juicy piece of gossip to Mrs. Ada was better than pork chops, and it got even better every time she shared it. As soon as she got off the phone with Louise, Mrs. Ada called eight or nine of her closest friends and told them about Stumpy Fowler making a motion to let Bessie Williams' choir in the Singing Convention. And no, she didn't know if the motion passed or not, but you just couldn't imagine somebody like Stumpy doing something like that. Then most of Mrs. Ada's friends thought of somebody they ought to tell. Before bedtime, it had been passed from mouth to ear, and Stumpy's question had become a motion that was, according to several accounts, rapidly becoming a movement. The news had pretty well covered River Falls and had made it all the way out to the Crossroads.

* * *

When Claymore Thomas hung up the phone, his face started turning red and his lips pursed in a tight circle. He stomped out of the house and went out under the big tree in his front yard. He walked around the tree three or four times, wondering just what things were coming to that a white man would try to do something like get a nigger choir in the Singing Convention. That was gospel music. God's music. And no sons of Ham were going to mess that up. But by the fourth circuit around the oak tree, Claymore began to see this might be just what he had been waiting for. The Klan had gotten soft. They really didn't do anything but stand around and talk. Something like this could spur them to action. He leaned against the tree and pulled a cigarette out of his overall pocket. This was something they could get their teeth into. Claymore let his back settle into the bark of the old tree and pulled the smoke through the Chesterfield and deep down into his lungs. And he expelled the smoke through a very small smile.

* * *

When Li'l and Billy Royce walked onto the school ground the next morning, the first thing Li'l noticed was Petey Thomas looking at him and laughing. The boys who always hung around Petey were laughing, too, not trying to hide that they were looking straight at Li'l while they were doing it.

Li'l stopped at the steps going up to the broad front doors. "I think I need to go ask Petey what's so funny," he said.

Billy Royce shook his head. "Who knows? I don't really care."

"You're right. He'd think pulling the wings off birds was funny." The two of them started up the steps. Then they heard Petey yell, "Hey, Li'l, you going to go sing in Sister Bessie's choir this Sunday?" Then Petey and his friends almost fell down laughing. As Li'l turned around, Petey said, "You know, I always thought you were a nigger lover. But I didn't know your daddy was, too."

Li'l looked at Petey and his friends. He knew they were looking for trouble, just like they usually were, and he wasn't looking for any trouble. Li'l didn't know what this was all about yet, but connecting the words "daddy" and "nigger lover" in the same sentence was enough to make it obvious he should be doing something, so he put his books on the ground and walked over to where Petey and his gang were standing. He checked over his shoulder to see if Billy Royce was still with him. He felt better when he saw that Billy Royce was right behind him.

"What'd you say, Petey?" he said, as he walked up to the little knot of boys. "I don't think I understood you."

Petey took a small step back toward his gang. "You heard. You just a nigger lover."

Li'l stopped about two steps away from Petey. "Okay. I thought you said something about my daddy."

Petey grinned. "He's a bigger nigger lover than you are. Maybe your whole family ought to go sing with Bessie Williams' choir."

Li'l really didn't know what happened then. He just felt a flush of rage. Petey didn't even have a chance to get the grin off his face before Li'l stepped across the four or five feet separating them and planted his right fist in Petey's face. Petey went down, blood coming out of his nose. His friends looked at each other, not quite sure what to do until Petey yelled up from the ground, "Get him. Kick his ass." The boys quit looking at Petey and moved toward Li'l.

Billy Royce came up behind him, and a circle of students gathered around, yelling, "Fight!"

Billy Royce stepped in front of Li'l and smiled at the biggest of Petey's friends. "You boys really want to look like Petey down there," he said. "That's fine with us."

"Y'all get on'em," Petey yelled, but he was giving his orders from the ground, and the blood was still running out of his nose. The boys didn't move. Finally, one of them reached over to help Petey up. Petey shook off his hand and scrambled to his feet. "I'll get you for this, Li'l Fowler," he said, but because he had his hand over his mouth and was holding his nose closed, it came out "I diddo ferdis." He looked at Billy Royce, and said, "You, too."

Billy Royce just smiled at him and tugged at Li'l's arm. "Come on, Buddy. There's a lot better people we can have fun with."

They walked back toward the door, not looking over their shoulder at Petey and his gang.

"I wonder what that was all about," Li'l said. "Petey's always a jerk, but he seemed to be trying to be a jerk in some kind of special way today."

"It's about the meeting last night, the Singing Convention committee meeting," Billy Royce said. Li'l noticed that he said it very softly, like he would be just as happy if Li'l didn't hear it. Li'l stopped and picked up his books.

"What about it?" he asked.

"I heard daddy talking to Leola this morning about it. Seems that your daddy wanted to know why Bessie's choir couldn't be in the Singing Convention. He asked the question, according to daddy, like he was trying to do something about it. Leola's a member of Bessie's church, and Daddy was asking her to see if she couldn't quiet Bessie down. Daddy said he didn't want any trouble at the Singing Convention this year."

As they trudged up the steps to the double doors, Li'l kept turning this over in his mind. Would his daddy do something like that? If he did, why did he do it? Then he wondered what would be wrong with it if Bessie and her choir did sing. Li'l had pretty much been raised by Bessie; she had been around all of his life, and he couldn't think of anybody that was a more sincere Christian than she. Finally, he decided he didn't know what to think.

"How'd it end up?" Li'l asked.

"Best I could tell, daddy told your daddy that it hadn't ever been done, and that was good enough reason not to do it."

* * *

In River Falls, the first street off Main Street is Church Street. The Missionary Baptist Church, old dark brick and full of angles and coves sits on one corner. About two blocks down, on another corner is the Methodist Church. These are the two important churches; if God worried about business, civic affairs, and keeping the lawns and gardens in River Falls lovely, He was certainly either a Baptist or a Methodist. Or maybe both.

On down Church Street, each one sitting on its own corner are the Pentecostal Holiness Church and the Catholic Church. Sometimes Li'l and Billy Royce would walk down Church Street on Sunday evening past all the churches. There would be cars around the Baptist Church, but the light would barely make it through the stained-glass windows, and even if you walked almost up to the door, you couldn't hear anything happening inside. At the Methodist Church, there would be some cars, and the lights would be on, but from the sound, you couldn't tell if there was anybody there. But at the Pentecostal church, it was different.

The Pentecostal Church didn't have stained glass windows, so the light poured through onto the church yard, and on most warm nights, the windows were up, so the sound of the singing and preaching and praising was just as loud outside the church as it was inside. Sometimes Li'l and Billy Royce would sit on the curb outside the church and listen for most of the service. They heard the preacher tell the congregation they were all sinners and were likely to be going to hell. The congregation Amened the preacher and seemed pretty happy about it. To the boys, the music at the Pentecostal Church seemed a lot like the music at the A.M.E. church, but not as good. But it had a beat, and the Pentecostals sang like they believed it.

The tiny Catholic Church across the street didn't have its lights on at night or, for that matter, on most Sunday mornings. There were only nine Catholics in River Falls and three Sundays a month they had to go to Springdale to church. One Sunday a month, a young priest would come to the little church.

One of the things Li'l and Billy Royce had talked about as they walked down Church Street, or sat on the curb outside the Pentecostal church was which kind of church God liked. It seemed strange that God would be so serious and proper for two blocks, then about three blocks later He would get hand-clapping happy and noisy. They agreed they liked the Pentecostal church best. At least it didn't put you to sleep.

On the morning after the Singing Convention committee meeting, there was something going on in three of the four churches on Church Street. In the Baptist Church, the young Reverend Jerry Stone was attempting to look like the spiritual leader of his flock while Mary Alice Blackmon leaned further and further over his desk, talking louder and louder. Mary Alice was the organist and choir director at the Baptist Church and had been since about six years before the Reverend Stone was born.

"—and if you preachers don't do something about it, they'll let just anybody into the Singing Convention, and there won't be any honor at all to winning the choir division."

When Mary Alice stopped to suck in her breath, Jerry Stone jumped into the silence.

"Now, Mrs. Blackmon, I don't believe that..."

Unfortunately, Mary Alice had recovered her breath.

"This is a tradition, Reverend Stone. A tradition! And somebody has to stand up to all those people who want to destroy our traditions."

The Reverend Jerry Stone sat there, pinned by Mary Alice's voice to the back of his chair, wishing he had become a missionary to the Congo.

At the Methodist Church, Carl Edmondson was packing his books into cardboard boxes. After four years in River Falls, Carl was moving to a larger church. When the assignments had been published, the congregation at the River Falls Methodist church had been disappointed, and Carl Edmondson delighted. Not that there was anything wrong with River Falls, as he had told the new pastor on the phone that morning. It was a nice small town with good people. To himself, he thought, the operative word was "small." There was not a soul in his congregation who could really appreciate good preaching. And there was certainly no room to grow.

So, thought Carl Edmondson, I'm going to a better place.

As he dusted off a copy of "The History of the New Testament Church," he managed a small grim smile. If what he had heard at the café this morning was true, River Falls would be in turmoil for weeks, maybe months to come. Carl Edmondson didn't spend all those years in college and seminary to deal with questions like whether a Negro choir could sing in some sort of small town gospel convention.

In his office at the Pentecostal Church, Grant McLamb was just about to begin his morning prayers. It took him longer to get on his knees these days, he thought. And it took him even longer to get up. But, at 75, what did you have a right to expect? He steadied his big frame with a hand on the edge of the desk and slowly and loudly sank to his knees.

"God," he thought as tried to shuffle his bulk into a

tolerable position, "I don't know what you've got for me in Heaven, but I sure do hope it includes a new pair of knees."

Grant McLamb tried to empty his mind, but the picture of thousands of people sitting at the Singing Grove kept coming into it. He could see the men wiping the sweat from their faces with their handkerchiefs, and the women trying to keep the children in line. He could hear the noise and the gospel songs over the speaker system. Then in his mind he heard Sister Bessie and her choir. Grant McLamb smiled. "Come ye who love the Lord," he thought. And God knows Sister Bessie loved the Lord. "God, help 'em all," he prayed. "And God, if it's your will, especially help Sister Bessie."

* * *

Stumpy noticed that Mae Beth had put on her long cotton nightgown, even though it was every bit as hot as it had been last night. She hadn't really had a lot to say to him since he came home from the office. It was like he was a visitor, maybe a relative that she knew she had to put up with, but didn't much want to. Stumpy sat on the edge of the bed, trying to figure out what to say to her.

"I told you I tried," he said. "A.Y. just isn't going let anything upset his applecart the last year he's chairman of the Sing. Can't you just tell Bessie that we'll try it again next year when there's another chairman. I mean, after all, it's already been twenty-eight years. One more shouldn't make that much difference."

Mae Beth turned to face him. "I've been thinking about this, Arthur. I don't know why we've waited twenty-eight years to do something about it. Bessie's like family to us, and you don't let your family get insulted every year by having a bunch of people tell them that they're not good enough to be a part of something."

"You know it's not like that. Most likely nobody ever thought to do anything different, neither them nor us. It's always been that way."

"I don't think we should just let A.Y. Pollard decide that it's always going to be that way. You're the treasurer for the Sing; you're as important as he is. You should be able to get something done."

She was shooting the "you's" at him like they were coming out a machine gun. It was all Stumpy could do not to flinch as they went by. He knew it wouldn't do any good to try to explain that the treasurer doesn't have the same standing as the chairman, and—at best—he was just one vote. He also knew that arguing with Mae Beth was a losing proposition. She ranged all over the place, sometimes throwing things out that took him a minute or two to connect up to the thing they were arguing about. One thing he kept reminding himself was that, unlike his mama, she was not a woman given to arguing about everything. He didn't have to go through this too often.

Before he was able to actually say anything else, he heard a crash. It sounded like it came from the living room. Stumpy jumped up and ran into the living room. He saw a jagged hole where the picture window had been. He took a step into the living room and felt a piece of glass stick into his foot.

"Stay out of here," he said. "There's glass on the floor." He backed up a step, backing into Mae Beth and Li'l who was standing right behind her.

Stumpy threw open the front door and ran into the yard. It was empty. He ran to each side of the house, looking for whoever had crashed something through his window. He thought he saw some tail lights going down Main Street. Stumpy stood in the front yard, his fists clinched. But whoever had broken the glass was gone. He looked at the gaping hole where his picture window had been. Then he turned around and walked slowly back into the house.

"Li'l go through the kitchen and turn on a light," he said. "We don't want to go in there until we can see where we're walking." He hobbled into the bathroom to see if he could stop the blood that was coming out of the sole of his foot. The puncture was very small, with just a trickle of blood oozing from it. What bothered him more than the little cut was the gaping hole where his picture window had been. He got a Band-Aid out and put it on the bottom of his foot, then went back into the living room.

In the light, he could see shards of glass scattered on the drop-leaf table in front of the window and over most of the floor. The lamp that had been sitting on the table was on the floor, its globe broken. In the middle of the room was a piece of metal with paper tied to it. Stumpy picked his way across the room and picked up the metal piece. He saw it was a weight like they used for weighing cotton in the field. This one had "two lbs." stamped on the side. He ripped the paper off and opened it up. It said: "Nigger lover. Go back where you belong."

Stumpy felt anger wash over him, first at being called a nigger lover. Nobody called you that and got away with it. Then he thought how silly that was when what he should be mad at was that somebody thought they could break his picture window just because they didn't agree with him. The next thing he thought was what kind of dumbass threw this thing and thought Stumpy belonged somewhere besides River Falls. His family had been around here for more than 200 years. This was, by God, where he belonged.

He carefully put the weight down on the floor and slipped the paper under it.

"Li'l, go and get an old blanket. We need to cover up this window or we'll have all sorts of bugs by morning. Your mom and I'll get the glass up. Let's get it done so we can go to bed."

Li'l left to get the tarp, and Mae Beth came back in with the broom. Stumpy started picking up the bigger shards of glass. "Looks like you're going to get a new window treatment, at least for the night," he said. He looked at Mae Beth. She didn't smile.

"This is about Bessie, isn't it?"

"Uh huh. Some ignorant SOB doesn't agree with what he thinks went on the other night."

"You think it was Claymore Thomas?"

Stumpy kept picking up glass. "Could be. But there are a lot of ignorant SOBs around here. Doesn't have to be Claymore."

"Do you think we shouldn't have started this?"

Stumpy noticed that Mae Beth's voice was getting smaller and smaller.

"Doesn't really matter what I think about that. We started it, and somebody took offense."

"I'm sure Bessie will understand anything we decide. She doesn't want anybody hurt over this."

"Me either," Stumpy said, standing up with a six-inch piece of jagged glass in his hand. "I don't want any of us hurt, but I sure as hell would like to hurt whoever threw this thing into my house. I don't like this even a little bit."

For a man who almost never got angry, Stumpy Fowler did a good job of it then. Somebody had threatened his home and his family, and he figured that couldn't be the end of it.

"Why don't you go to bed, Mae Beth. Li'l and I'll put up the blanket, and I'll be in there with you in a minute."

Stumpy and Li'l rigged the blanket over the picture window, tacking it at the top and taping it along the edges. When they finished, Stumpy told Li'l to go on to bed. Then he turned off the living room lights and sat down in his recliner, staring through the blackness of the room at the gray patch over the window. Stumpy couldn't remember when he had ever been the victim of violence, especially something as stupid as this. Nothing had really happened at the Sing committee meeting that meant anything. He'd asked a question. A.Y. had about had a stroke, but he answered it, and so far as Stumpy had been concerned, that was the end of it. Now he had to decide whether it was or wasn't. If this was worth throwing a cotton scale weight through somebody's window, it must be more important than he thought it was. Stumpy sat there in the dark glaring at the darkness for another hour before he got up and went to bed.

5

About eight o'clock the next morning, a black-and-white Ford with "River Falls Police Department" painted on the door pulled up the curb. Earl Holland sat for a minute watching Stumpy staring at the splintered window. Since the blanket was still taped over the inside, Stumpy's picture window was just a gray hole with a small area of reflection around the edge. Earl got out the car and ambled over to where Stumpy stood. He was a rail of a man, tall, narrow, and topped with an unruly head of red hair. As always, a cigarette was hanging out of Earl's mouth, the rising smoke making him see the world through a narrow squint.

"Sure made a mess, didn't they?"

Stumpy nodded. He really didn't feel like spending a lot of time on something that obvious. "Perry said that he could get over here today to fix it, but I've got to have a police report before I file my insurance."

"You think your homeowner's is going to pay for this? Don't look like an accident to me."

"Yeah, they pay for vandalism. And if this isn't vandalism, I don't know what is"

Earl pulled the inch-long butt of the cigarette out of

his mouth, dropped it on the ground, and ground it out with his foot. He pulled a small notebook out of his pocket. "Okay. Tell me what happened?"

Stumpy gave him an outline of what had happened the night before. When he finished, Earl asked him if he had any idea who did it.

"I've got an idea, but I don't have any proof. I think it was either Claymore Thomas or one of his buddies. But I don't think you can arrest any of them just because I think so."

"Uh-huh," Earl grunted. "But we can sorta keep an eye on them. Best we can, of course."

Stumpy knew what that meant. River Falls' three-man police department wasn't very busy, but a wreck or some kids knocking down mail boxes could tie up the entire force. Stumpy nodded.

"I'd appreciate whatever you can do. I don't want to have to buy a new picture window every week."

"How come you started this, anyway, Stumpy? I never figured you for a rabble rouser."

"Damn, Earl. All I did was ask a question in the meeting. And I did it to make Mae Beth happy. Seemed to be something she really wanted to do for Bessie. I guess you can understand that."

Earl lit another cigarette, nodding. The police chief was known to be one of the most hen-pecked men in River Falls. His wife, Velma, had a sharp tongue and probably outweighed him by thirty or forty pounds. Stumpy had often wondered why Earl didn't use his gun on Velma, at least enough to scare her a little bit.

"It wouldn't bother me if Bessie and her choir did sing in the Singing Convention. If it wasn't for Horace and Bessie and some of their friends, we'd have a lot more trouble up on Disciple Street than we do. They're good people, don't care what color they are."

"Yeah, but I don't think everybody agrees with you and me on that," Stumpy said.

Earl put his notebook back in his pocket. "I don't know. Probably more people than you'd figure," he said. Stumpy walked back over to the police car with him.

"I appreciate your help, Earl."

"Uh-huh," Earl said, and got into the car.

It occurred to Stumpy that he hadn't even had a chance to make his list for today. He headed back into the house.

* * *

In the old country house down at the Crossroads, Claymore Thomas was just hanging up the telephone, trying to sort out his feelings about what he had heard. He was glad somebody put something through Stumpy Fowler's living room window, and he would have been happier if it had hit Fowler or at least his boy. But he was embarrassed that he hadn't done it or couldn't even find out who did. It seemed like somebody actually did something, and as best he could tell, they didn't have anything to do with the Klan. Seemed like they were always a step behind. Now they needed to do something bigger than that, or nobody would pay any attention to the Klan at all. As Claymore walked out into the yard and lit a cigarette, he wondered what that could be. Right now, he didn't have any idea.

He needed to go into town to find out what was going on, but he knew he'd catch hell from Ruby if he didn't get back to the field. He'd been out there since six o'clock, at first light, and he'd already put in a couple of hours. That ought to be good enough for a while. He walked back to the front door of the house.

"I'm going in to town," he yelled in no particular direction. Then he jumped off the porch and walked to his pickup before Ruby had a chance to answer. It made him feel nervous to know that somebody had struck a blow for the white race in River Falls, and he didn't have anything to do with it.

* * *

When Bessie had come to work that morning, she saw the cotton weight, the note, and the glass on the floor. She muttered to herself while she got busy cleaning up the glass, but it wasn't until after Stumpy had gone to work and Perry Ellis had gotten there to put in the new picture window that she said anything about it to Mae Beth.

"All this is because Mr. Stumpy asked about my choir, ain't it?"

Mae Beth nodded. "Arthur says that he asked, and that A.Y. Pollard wasn't about to make any changes in his last year as chairman. Arthur says that the next chairman might be willing to do something."

"You know I didn't mean for this to cause you and Mr. Stumpy any harm."

"We know that. And we don't blame any of this on you. There are just some people who'll take any excuse to raise some cain. It'll all blow over."

Bessie nodded and went back to cleaning up. That new picture window would have to have the labels scraped off, and then all the handprints would have to be washed off. She needed to vacuum the living room again just to make sure that all the glass chips had been gotten out of the rug. There was plenty left to do to make things right, but as she went about her work, Bessie couldn't decide what to feel. She sure didn't want anything bad to happen to Mr. Stumpy and Mrs. Mae Beth or Li'l, but she didn't want to be put off another year or maybe forever before her choir could sing in the Singing Convention.

Horace couldn't understand why this was so important to her. He didn't really disagree with her as much as he was just puzzled that it mattered. "You're fifty-six years old," he had said, "and all your life it's been the same thing. The white people have some things they don't want to share with us. Their churches. Their restaurants. Their schools. They'll share their dirty clothes and their dirty dishes and lifting their cotton bales. And sometimes they decide they want to do something nice for some people on Disciples Street, so they come down here and give some people some food or old clothes. And that's the way it's been ever since you been born. I don't know what makes you think it's going to change now."

Bessie knew that for a man of very few words, a speech like that required a lot of effort of Horace, but she couldn't help thinking that maybe just because something had always been a certain way, it had to stay that way. The Supreme Court had said just because the southern states called their schools "separate, but equal," it wasn't right, and sooner or later all the schools were going to have to let Negroes in. It was already happening in some places. Bessie raised both her boys to believe they could do anything they set their minds to, and now they both were out of college and a long way from River Falls. They had believed her when she said that there was life beyond keeping white people's houses and hauling bales of cotton around the cotton yard. Now she wondered if she really believed herself, and if she did, what she should do about it. She knew she didn't want to cause Mr. Stumpy any more trouble. He was a good man. But maybe there was something else she could do.

* * *

After he had taken care of the first three things on his list, Stumpy decided to walk down to A.Y. Pollard's office. As he walked down Main Street, he looked carefully at every person he passed, wondering if they were thinking about somebody putting a brick through his window, and if they were thinking about it, were they for it or against it. But everybody he met looked just like they usually did — until he almost bumped into Claymore Thomas as Claymore came out of the feed store. Claymore stepped back and grinned, at least as much of a grin as his round mouth would allow.

"Well, Stumpy, I hear you got some new home decoratin' last night," he said.

Stumpy just looked at him and started to step around him.

"I'm all in favor of that sort of thing myself," Claymore said. "I'm just sorry I couldn't have helped."

"Claymore, I'd appreciate it if you'd get out of my way. I'd rather talk to somebody who has some sense."

The grin flickered on Claymore's face, but he got it back in place. "I don't know if I'd be talking about having sense if I was you. Not after you trying to stir up a bunch of race mixing here." Claymore took a step closer to Stumpy. "I guess you found out what happens when somebody goes against the natural way of things."

Stumpy put his hands in his pockets, just to make sure one of them didn't go out on its own and knock that grin off Claymore's face. He looked carefully at Claymore, as if he were memorizing the round face and round mouth and slitted eyes. Then he smiled and said, "Claymore, I don't think you know anything about the natural way of anything. I think you're about as unnatural as anything I've ever seen. Now, if you'll step out of my way, I'd appreciate it. Otherwise, I'll just knock you on your ass right here on Main Street."

Claymore's mouth opened and closed twice, but nothing came out. Finally, he muttered something about "you'll get some more of the same thing" as he stepped around Stumpy and went on down Main Street.

Stumpy watched Claymore for a minute, then started walking to A.Y.'s office. He thought about Chief Holland's comments, then about Claymore Thomas's. It was hard to believe that Stumpy, Earl, and Claymore — as well as A.Y. Pollard and most of the other folks — had all come out of the same pond and ended up as different as they did. After thinking about it for a minute, all he came up with was that he'd rather have Bessie and Horace as neighbors than Claymore, and that wasn't a particularly startling thought.

He climbed the wide steps up to the second floor of the bank building and walked to the end of the hall where A.Y.'s office was. Gladys was sitting at her desk typing file labels for a stack of manila folders she had on her desk.

"Mornin', Stumpy. You need to see Mr. Pollard this morning?"

Stumpy nodded. "Just for a minute or two. Some Sing business."

"He's supposed to be in court about ten, but I imagine he could spare you a couple of minutes. Let me see." She got up and walked briskly into A.Y.'s office.

In less than a minute, she was back, motioning him through the door to A.Y. Pollard's office. A.Y. was standing behind his desk, stacking files, and occasionally putting one in the big briefcase that sat on the desk. He looked up and nodded to Stumpy.

"Morning, A.Y."

"Morning, Stumpy. Heard you had some excitement over at your house last night."

"I guess bad news travels fast."

A.Y. quit stacking files. "Hell, in River Falls all news travels fast. Then some things that aren't news at all. You know this is about that Bessie thing you brought up at the meeting, don't you?"

"Yeah, I figured that out pretty quick."

"So, you going to give that up? At least for now?"

The two men stood across the desk from each other, A.Y. waiting for an answer before he went back to stacking his files; Stumpy trying to decide what the answer was. Finally, Stumpy shook his head.

"I don't know, A.Y. Before last night I was just doing something Mae Beth had asked me to do, and I figured that was enough. Now, after somebody put that cotton scale weight through my picture window, I don't know."

"Well, what do you want from me?" A.Y. said. He motioned to the files and briefcase. "I've got to be in court in about fifteen minutes. We might want to talk about this later."

Stumpy edged a little closer to the desk. "I don't know that there's anything you can do to help, A.Y., unless you're willing to entertain a motion to let Bessie's choir sing. Other than that, I've just got to figure out what I'm going to do. And maybe who I'm going to do it to."

A.Y. frowned. "Be careful, Stumpy. Right now we don't have a client/attorney relationship, and anything you say to me could end up in court if something happens to somebody like Claymore Thomas."

Stumpy smiled, thinking of some things he'd like to do to Claymore. Then he shook his head. "I'm not going to do

any vigilante stuff," he said. "That is, unless I catch somebody around my house. But there may be other ways of doing things, ways that wouldn't land you or me in court. But
if I decide I need a lawyer, you'll be the first one on my list."

"Appreciate that," A.Y. said. "I'm sorry some idiot or idiots decided to state their opinions the way they did." He
put two more files in the briefcase and closed it. Come on.
I'll walk downstairs with you."

Stumpy waved at Gladys as they left, and they chatted
about the case A.Y. had in court. Two farmers were arguing
about the boundary line in a field, and one of them tried
to settle the argument by hitting the other one over the
head with a singletree. The metal-banded piece of wood
did enough damage to put the one who was hit in the hospital and get the other one charged with aggravated assault.
The funny thing, A.Y. said, was that the two farmers had
lived beside each other for nearly forty years, and they had
to wait until they were about seventy to get into a fight.

"People sure do pick some funny things to fight about,"
he said. "I guess it was just a fight whose time had come."

When they got to Main Street, A.Y. went to the left
toward the town hall and courtroom and Stumpy turned
right to go to his office. It wasn't until they separated that
Stumpy realized that A.Y. hadn't said anything about
whether he would allow a motion about Bessie's choir.
Stumpy believed A.Y. was sincerely sorry somebody messed
up his window, but he doubted that it would change A.Y.'s
mind about Bessie's choir and The Sing. The other thing
that stuck in Stumpy's mind was A.Y.'s comment about it
"being a fight whose time had come." The only problem was

that he didn't really want a fight. But then, he'd been raised to do the right thing, if he could just figure out what the right thing was. He thought about the next thing on his list — working on Woodall's corporate tax return — but he didn't feel like dealing with a bunch of numbers right now, so he turned around and walked to the other end of Main Street to the Singing Grove. When he got there, he sat down on one of the concrete benches and stared at the stage.

The River Falls Singing Convention had started in 1917 with just a few local groups standing on a makeshift stage in the middle of a grove of oak trees. By the middle of the 1920s, it had become important to the people who loved gospel music, and choirs, quartets, trios, duets, and soloists from all over eastern North Carolina came to compete. And thousands of people came to hear them. Little by little, the singing convention became more formal. A permanent stage was built at the back of the grove, seats were put in, and speakers were attached to the trees. Even people like Stumpy, who knew a lot more about bank notes than music notes, knew the annual singing convention was an important part of River Falls, even though it just happened one weekend a year.

As he sat there and stared at the stage, Stumpy realized that a lot of good things had come out of The Sing. It was, in fact, one of the few things that put River Falls on the map, that and the local bootlegger who got a write-up in the Saturday Evening Post. It had gotten some talented people some recognition. It gave the Boy Scouts a chance to direct traffic, something that Stumpy would always remember. And probably not the least, the people who came to listen left thousands of dollars in River Falls, mostly with the concessionaires who set up booths around the singing grove, with the drugstores and restaurants on Main Street, and with the gas stations. The Singing Convention was important to River Falls, and it continued to grow and bring gospel singers from further and further away.

Sitting on the concrete bench staring at the empty stage, Stumpy wondered if things weren't the way they were supposed to be. It's true that Bessie's choir couldn't sing there, but they were free to sing in other places. Nobody said they weren't good enough. It was just the way things were, and they seemed to work that way. Looking at the stage he could see the choirs and quartets and duets that had been there in all the years Stumpy had been coming to the Sing. They were good. They sang as if they loved it. And they were all white. And that included the choirs from several of the churches in River Falls.

Stumpy got up and walked around the grove, stopping occasionally to pick up a piece of paper or a drink bottle and put it in a nearby trash can. Up until now, he hadn't heard anybody complain about the Sing, and since somebody threw that weight through his picture window, he didn't think Bessie would complain any more. It seemed to Stumpy the reasonable and easy thing to do would be just to let things be. They were working. Nobody had to be upset. And maybe changes would come — when it was time for them.

Stumpy thought about the list that was lying on his

desk and decided it was time for him to get back to his office.

FROM THE RIVER FALLS CURRENT
Thursday, April 19, 1956

KIWANIS CLUB TO SPONSOR FAT STOCK JUDGES

The River Falls Kiwanis Club voted Thursday night to sponsor four 4-H Club members in the Fat Stock Judging Contest to be held in Raleigh in October. The contest is held each year at the State Fair by the North Carolina Department of Agriculture. It's open to any 4-H club members in North Carolina.

The four students representing River Falls in the contest are Arie Ellis, Charles Jennings, Billy Joe Clifford, and Junior Evans. Ellis was one of the finalists in the 1955 contest.

"We're proud to be a part of such a fine endeavor," Kiwanis Club President Al Jenkins said. "This is the fifth year that the club has sponsored the Fat Stock Judging team."

6

In River Falls, whatever happened or appeared to happen during the week was bound to be a topic of conversation at church on Sunday morning. At the Baptist Church, women in big hats whispered about what they heard had happened at the committee meeting on Tuesday night. Various versions included Stumpy Fowler demanding the Bethany A.M.E. Choir be allowed to sing, Callie Turlington fainting from the sight of Stumpy and A.Y. squaring off during the meeting, and even a unanimous vote of the committee to cancel the Sing rather than let the A.M.E. choir in. Outside the church, under the big oak trees, the men stood and smoked their cigarettes and voiced their opinions in two and three-word sentences. Almost all the sentences boiled down to "won't happen."

Up and down Church Street, the prevailing opinion was "this is not the time for a change like that." The only difference was the way it was said, and the conviction with which it was said. Several people were careful to add they had nothing against Negroes so long as they stayed in their place. They didn't say exactly what that place was, nor did they need to.

It was only at the River Falls Pentecostal Holiness Church that another opinion was heard. As the congregation was leaving at 12:30, a good half-hour after the Baptists and Methodists, Annie Mae Haller grasped Preacher McLamb's hand and said, "That was just a wonderful sermon."

"Thank you, Annie Mae. It's not hard to preach on the love of God. I trust you'll carry that with you in your walk this week."

"I certainly will, Preacher." She started to walk away but turned back, causing the line of worshippers leaving the church to bunch up behind her. "By the way, you didn't say anything about the Sing."

"I didn't know I was supposed to say anything about the Sing."

"Well, I just thought that—since you're the leader of this flock—you might have wanted to say something about the A.M.E. Church trying to get into the Singing Convention. You know that we've never had them before."

Preacher McLamb looked at Annie Mae Haller's fluttering hands and ruefully wondered why she hadn't been that excited when they had been talking about the love of God. His mind, full of the experience of more than fifty years of preaching and dealing with congregants, quickly weighed a variety of answers; then, based on the single fact that a 75-year-old man of God should speak what he thinks is the truth and not worry about consequences that he might not live to see anyway, he looked Annie Mae in the eye and said, "That's very Biblical, Annie Mae. That's probably exactly what they said when Paul tried to bring his uncircumcised friend into the church. And you know what would have happened if the people who said that had prevailed?"

"No, preacher, I don't know."

"You and I and the rest of us Gentiles would be going to hell. I don't know about you, but I'm very glad that some people based their decisions on God's will rather than just on what's always been done."

Simultaneously, Annie Mae's eyes and mouth opened wide, but then she shut her mouth. She just turned and walked quickly away. Preacher McLamb noticed that some people were grinning as they passed him, and some just muttered something and walked on. As he continued to shake their hands and nod his head, Preacher McLamb was wondering how, with all that was going on in the world, people had time to worry about what color a choir was at the Singing Convention.

* * *

The pastor of the Bethany A.M.E. Church, Reverend Amos Pickens, had already had a visit from Leola Campbell, a member of his congregation and president of the Women's Circle. She worked for the Pollards, and it seems that, according to Leola, A.Y. was very upset about the Bethany Choir wanting to be in the Singing Convention. Leola was about as skinny as a stick, and her face was pinched into a permanent picture of pious disapproval. There were very few things Leola liked, and she kept real quiet about those. However, she secretly felt some satisfaction in bringing the word to Pastor Pickens. What she knew was that Mr. Pollard had told her that what the church was doing would be bad for the community.

"He was standing right there in the kitchen drinking a glass of buttermilk," she told Pastor Pickens. "And you know he's as nice a white man as there is in River Falls. He said that if we kept trying to get our choir into their Singing Convention, it'd make a real mess."

"Uh huh." Pastor Pickens had already heard about the meeting. He had seen the signs on the telephone poles. And he had pretty much decided that if he just kept his head down, this whole thing would blow over without his having to be involved. Now, Leola was messing with his low profile.

"Did Mr. Pollard say anything else?" Pastor Pickens asked.

"Well, what he said was that," and her voice unconsciously slipped into an imitation of A.Y. Pollard's delivery, "this would certainly upset the fine relationship between the races in River Falls. That's what he said."

From some place in his memory that had been paved over for thirty years or more, Pastor Pickens felt a stirring. He was reacting to the idea of a "fine relationship between the races." It was fine if you were white. If you were black, you made do with it. But Pastor Pickens had a lot of experience in pushing feelings like that back down. Right now, he wanted to finish up with Leola.

"You know Mr. Pollard and the committee didn't even

consider letting our choir into the Singing Convention, don't you, Leola?"

"I know that. But I know that Mr. Pollard, he is mighty upset about it, and he says a lot of other white people are, too."

"Well, what do you think I should do?"

"You're the preacher; you know best what you should be doing. But if I was the preacher, I'd go see Bessie Williams and tell her that what she's doing ain't right, and it's going to cause a whole lot of problems."

"And you know Bessie had something to do with this?"

"Lord, Pastor Pickens, you mean that you think something like this happened all by itself." Leola almost smiled. "Bessie started the whole thing off. She talked to Mr. Fowler or Mrs. Fowler—I'm about sure it was Mrs. Fowler—and that's how it got brought up at the meeting. This didn't happen just because Mr. Fowler woke up one morning and decided colored folks ought to be in the Singing Convention."

"I suppose you're right," Pastor Pickens said. "I'll go see Bessie and Horace. We don't want to cause a stir."

And just because he had said that, he found himself at the front door of Bessie and Horace Williams' white frame house on Disciples Street in the middle of a Sunday afternoon. He started to knock on the door, but a picture of Daniel in the lion's den—a picture from one of his books—popped into his mind. He took a step back.

"God, you protected Daniel," he prayed. "Now, I ask you to protect me, because I'd really rather face that lion than Bessie." He stepped forward and knocked on the door.

Immediately, he heard footsteps in the house. Then the door opened, and Horace Williams filled the frame.

"Deacon Williams, I wonder if I might have a word with you and Sister Bessie. It's a matter of church business."

Horace Williams pushed the screen door open and stepped aside so that Pastor Pickens could come in.

"Just have a seat, Pastor. Bessie's out back. I'll go get her."

Pastor Pickens sat down in the big overstuffed chair. Everything in the room, he noticed, was big. The floral sofa. The dining table. The china cabinet. The upright piano that sat against the wall. Everything was big except the house itself. It was just like the rest of the houses on Disciples Street.

On the table beside the chair was a Bible with a half-dozen strips of paper sticking out of it.

Pastor Pickens heard the screen door open and close. Then Horace and Bessie came into the living room.

"Could I get you a glass of tea or something, Pastor?" Bessie said.

"No, thank you, Bessie."

From his sitting position, Pastor Pickens looked up at Horace and Bessie, and he thought about the reports that Joshua and the spies had brought back. "There are giants across the river." Everybody in town, black or white, knew that Horace Williams could take a hook, pull a 500-pound bale of cotton up on his back, and walk away with it. He was almost sixty years old, but he didn't show a sign of stooping, slowing down, or getting fat. At six foot one, Pastor Pickens was usually considered tall, but beside Horace, he wasn't tall at all.

Bessie, standing beside him, was about half a foot shorter, but she was every bit as wide, and — like Horace — she stood straight up, with no sign of bowing her head or bending her shoulders.

A thought bubbled its way up from that almost forgotten place in his memory. I ought to be standing with them instead of running an errand because Leola talked to A.Y. Pollard." But he pushed the thought back down as Bessie and Horace arranged themselves on the sofa.

"Bessie," he said, after a long, empty pause, "I need your help."

Bessie leaned forward, waiting for Pastor Pickens to continue. He looked at her, then he looked at the picture of Ruth gleaning in the Boaz's field that hung on the wall. Then he looked down at his shoes. Finally, he got it out.

"It's about the Singing Convention, Bessie. There are some rumors going around town."

Bessie smiled and nodded. "And what kind of rumors would those be, Pastor?"

"Well, I've been told—and I'm sure there's nothing to this—I've been told that you want our church choir to sing at the Singing Convention."

Bessie continued to smile and nod. "I'd say that's about true, pastor. We have the best choir around here. Shouldn't be any reason why we can't go up there and sing."

She sat back. She had quit nodding, but she was still smiling. But there was something about the smile that made Pastor Pickens want to consider what he was going to say very carefully.

"Do you think that's a good idea, Bessie? There's never been a Negro choir in the Singing Convention."

"I know. And I think it's about time that changed. We are a choir. We sing gospel music. And we ought to be able to sing it there."

"I agree, Bessie. And I think one day, we will be able to. But we have to keep in mind that we make progress one step at a time. Sometimes it's in small steps."

"Pastor, I don't mean to be disrespectful, but this don't have anything to do with progress. It has to do with singing. And our choir is as good as any choir in a hundred miles of here. And, Pastor, instead of sitting here in my chair trying to tell me why we shouldn't be in the Sing, you ought to be down at A.Y. Pollard's telling him why we should."

By the time she had finished talking, Bessie had moved to the edge of the sofa, looking as if she was about to launch herself right at Pastor Pickens. When she finished, she locked her eyes onto his face. It was clearly Pastor Pickens' turn. He looked at Bessie. Then he looked at Horace. Horace was sitting back with a small smile on his big face, watching the exchange like a proud parent.

Pastor Pickens took a deep breath. He knew this wasn't going well, but he also knew he couldn't quit now. "Bessie," he said, trying to make his voice conciliatory, "I understand how you feel. But there are bigger things than the Singing Convention that we have to worry about. And there are bigger things than the choir. And if we are going to keep moving forward, we're going to have to keep our eyes on the bigger things. We can't let things like this get in our way."

Bessie's face turned into a storm cloud. Her eyes squinted, her brow knitted, and her mouth clamped shut in a straight line. Pastor Pickens knew right then he had said the wrong thing, or maybe he had said the right thing in the wrong way.

Horace, who couldn't even see Bessie's face, evidently knew it, too. He hauled his big frame off the sofa and extended his hand to Pastor Pickens.

"I appreciate you coming by, Pastor. We'll sure think about what you said." And he stepped between Pastor Pickens and Bessie. Pastor Pickens got up, shook Horace's hand, and started to the door. He turned and looked at Bessie. She still looked like she was about to explode.

When Pastor Pickens was safely out the door, Horace sat down beside Bessie and put his hand on her shoulder. He could feel the rise and fall of shoulder as she tried to keep her breathing under control. He didn't say anything until the movement of her shoulder slowed, and he knew that she was breathing not a lot faster than she was supposed to.

"I thought you said you weren't going to have anything else to do with the Sing since somebody threw that weight through Mr. Stumpy's window. That would have made the Pastor a whole lot happier."

Bessie moved her shoulder out from under his hand. "I didn't say that. I didn't say that at all. What I said was that I wasn't going to ask Mr. Stumpy to do anything else. I don't want him or Miss Mae Beth or Li'l getting hurt. They're white folks and this ain't their fight. But Pastor Pickens ain't white folks — although I think he sometimes acts like he thinks he is. I'm not about to shut myself up just to make him feel better."

They both sat there on the sofa for a few minutes. Finally, Horace announced that he was going to get a glass of ice tea and went into the kitchen. He wasn't particularly worried, but he sure was curious about where all of this was going.

* * *

"And God, we know that you gave us special responsibilities, and one of those responsibilities that You're going to hold us accountable for is keeping the white race pure and keeping our society as You ordered it. With Your help, God, we'll do our duty and protect our families. We pray in the name of Your Son. Amen."

Even before the Kludd had finished his prayer, Otha Forster had opened his eyes, looking at the men gathered in the tobacco barn. Years ago, the Klan had seemed important. He had really believed that something had to be done to protect the white race. His daddy had told him that from the time he could walk. Now, he was beginning to wonder. No nigger had threatened him. In fact, the ones he worked in the field with didn't seem to be any better or any worse than the dozen people at this meeting. He was having a hard time thinking about them as anything but people.

When the Kludd—a sometime preacher and full-time

farmer named Otto Smith—finished his prayer, there was a restless rustle as the group settled down for the main part of the meeting. Otha leaned back against the flue, trying to get comfortable. He could count on Claymore going on for an hour, maybe two.

Claymore Thomas strutted to the middle of the small circle of men. He was the only man at the meeting wearing a coat and tie. It occurred to Otha that if Claymore had his way, they'd all be wearing their hoods and robes to the meetings. Most of the time it was too hot for them, and when they did wear them, Otha felt a little silly.

He watched Claymore pacing back and forth, working himself up for his usual speech.

"Well, I guess we showed them. We showed them the white race isn't going to just lie down and let somebody run all over them."

Otha noticed that some of the men were nodding their heads, although he was fairly sure none of them had any more idea of what Claymore was talking about than he did.

"They thought they could just go in there and pollute a fine institution like our gospel singing convention, but that ain't going to happen, and that race mixer, Stumpy Fowler, knows that it ain't going to happen. Now he knows that when he starts causing trouble and confusion like that, trouble for him ain't far behind."

Claymore stopped and looked at each of the men in the circle. When he got to Otha, Otha just held his gaze with no expression at all on his face.

"And we got out there, and we put up signs, and we let them know that the Knights of the Ku Klux Kan was watching them. It worked. Stumpy Fowler ain't going to cause any more trouble, and there won't be any niggers singing in our singing convention."

Some of the men muttered "That's right."

"We're not going to let them take anything that's ours. This country was founded by white Christians, and it's going to stay in the hands of white Christians. It's like the boys over in Oak Grove did. They put up a big billboard; it said, 'This is Klan Country.' And it is, by God, Klan Country. That means that there won't be no niggers in the Singing Convention. And there won't be no niggers chasing after our daughters."

Otha tried to find a more comfortable position against the metal of the tobacco flue. It was obvious that Claymore was just getting started, and it was going to be a long night. In his head, Otha began going through the names of people that he had to contact to help him with his tobacco this year.

* * *

As Stumpy Fowler got ready for bed that night, he was still congratulating himself that he had almost put Bessie's problem out of his mind. At the church that morning, two or three of the men in his Sunday School class had told him they were sorry about his window, but it seemed like there was something left unsaid each time, something like "you really shouldn't have stirred things up." He just muttered something like "'preciate that," and let it drop. He knew that some of the people were talking about the committee meeting because when he walked up to the group, everybody got real quiet. But Stumpy didn't worry a lot about it. They could talk if they wanted to; he was just going to get on with his life.

Mae Beth came into the bedroom to hang some clothes in the closet. She hadn't said anything more about the Singing Convention since they got the window fixed. At least not to him. Stumpy wondered what she and Bessie had said. All that he knew was that Bessie had said that she didn't want to cause him or his family any trouble. And he believed that.

Stumpy sat down on the edge of the bed and wound the alarm clock. Mae Beth came over and sat down beside him.

"You know," she said, "I feel sorry for Bessie."

He turned and looked at her, wondering why they had to start this conversation just as they were about to go to bed.

"What do you mean?"

"She feels so bad about what happened with the window. She thinks it's her fault."

"Well, tell her that I don't blame her. I blame some idiot with a cotton weight. She shouldn't worry about it. That's all over now."

They sat there a moment. Then Mae Beth said, almost under her breath, "But is it?"

"Is what?"

"Is it over? I can't help but wonder what's so bad about

what Bessie wanted, and why this town can't see that. We've known Bessie and those other people in the choir for years, some of them for all of our lives, and then, on this thing, we act like they're some kind of strangers."

"Mae Beth, strangers would have a better chance of getting into the Sing. All a stranger needs is $10 for the entrance fee. Bessie needs a lot more than that. That's the way it is."

Mae Beth nodded. "I know that's the way it is. I just wonder if it's right." She kissed Stumpy and went back to get some clothes to hang up.

He lay down on the bed staring at the ceiling. For all these years, he had used Mae Beth as a sort of moral compass. She was smart, and while she was as sentimental as most women, she didn't let it make her do things that were dumb. And she was better at reading people than Stumpy was. Stumpy knew he generally accepted everybody at face value; that made life easier, but sometimes Mae Beth looked beyond the obvious. It bothered him that Mae Beth was still thinking about Bessie and the Sing when he had pretty much put it out of his mind.

He looked at the ceiling and wondered if sometimes he wanted life to be too easy.

7

Stumpy sat at the kitchen table staring at his unfinished list. The first thing on it was to finish the corporate tax return for Gilbert's Dry Goods Store. He knew there was a second thing, and a third, and a fourth, but try as he might, he couldn't make his mind focus on them. He wondered if it was because he had dreamed all night. He couldn't remember the detail, but it seemed like they all had to do with unfinished business — tax returns not done, statements that didn't balance, all the things CPAs dread. He had gotten up this morning as tired as he was when he went to bed.

Then, he was thinking about Mae Beth and Bessie. It still bothered him that Mae Beth didn't think all of this was over. Bessie had already said that she didn't want to cause Stumpy any more trouble, and if he kept rocking the boat, there'd be no end of trouble. He looked at his list and hoped that Mae Beth would go on to something else. For some reason, he had written down:

2. See Horace Williams

Stumpy didn't remember writing it, and he really wasn't sure why he thought he should go see Horace, but he figured that it must be important since he put it on his list.

* * *

It had bothered Stumpy that his list only had two things on it, but the Gilbert's tax return had taken all morning, and he had run into Gerald Rainey at the Main Street Cafe, and they'd sat there for more than an hour laughing about some of the things they'd done in high school. Stumpy ended up having lunch at the Main Street Cafe with Gerald about once a week, and they always talked about the tricks they'd played on people in high school, sometimes telling the same stories they had told a week or two earlier. Every time, when lunch was over and Gerald had gone back to his insurance office and Stumpy was heading back to his CPA office, he was a little sad, partly because the time when they could play outrageous tricks on people without thinking about the consequences was over. Now, everything had consequences that could be anticipated, so you thought of a lot of things you didn't do. The other part of Stumpy's sadness was that Gerald, a man with a wife and two children, had never quite gotten beyond what they did in high school. He didn't play the tricks any more, but for anybody that knew him, that was his identity. Stumpy enjoyed recalling those days, but he liked to think he had moved on.

He stood in front of the Main Street Cafe. Gerald waved his hand and headed up the street. Stumpy started to go back to his office, but then he remembered the second thing on his list: See Horace Williams.

Because it was still spring, the cotton yard was nearly empty. A few bales of cotton, white fibers sticking out around the edges of the burlap cover, stood against the wall, left from last summer's picking. Against another wall, bags of fertilizer were stacked about head high. Stumpy saw Horace bringing more bags to the stack. Horace threw the bags on top of the stack, and when he turned he saw Stumpy.

"Mornin', Mr. Stumpy," Horace said. Then he glanced up at the sun. "Guess it must be afternoon."

"Just," said Stumpy. "You got a minute, Horace?"

"Sure. Not much to do around here this time of year. Just move some stuff from here to there, then move it somewhere else." Horace nodded with his head toward the narrow strip of shade next to the building, and the two men walked over there. "I heard about what happened at your house. I sure am sorry."

"Thanks, Horace. There's no accounting for how dumb some people can act."

"Bessie told me it was about you talking about the A.M.E. choir at the meeting. She was real upset that she had caused you and Miss Mae Beth so much trouble."

"We don't blame Bessie. It's all fixed now, anyway."

Stumpy noticed that Horace was glancing toward the flat bed of fertilizer that he'd been unloading. There must be more than a hundred fifty-pound bags left on the truck, and Horace evidently wanted to get back to them.

"Horace," Stumpy said. "I wonder if I could come by and speak with you and Bessie this evening."

Horace Williams face seldom showed any emotion beyond a calm amiability, but for an instant his eyes grew a little wider and his eyebrows went up just a bit.

"You'd always be welcome at our house," he said. "Could I ask you what it is you want to talk about?"

Stumpy shook his head. "I don't exactly know, Horace. I'm just trying to get some things straight in my mind, and I think maybe you and Bessie could help me. That's all."

"Well, this time of year we generally sit on the porch for a while after dinner and have a glass of tea. Maybe you could come sit with us for a bit."

"That'd be nice. What time do you finish dinner?"

"About seven o'clock. I'll tell Bessie that you're coming."

Stumpy nodded, and Horace turned and started walking back to the truck. Stumpy watched him. That afternoon Horace would probably make fifty or more trips across the cotton yard with a hundred pounds of fertilizer each trip, and it didn't seem to bother him.

* * *

After supper, Stumpy told Mae Beth that he was going for a walk. He didn't bother to tell Mae Beth where he was going or why. In truth, he wasn't sure why he was going to

Bessie and Horace's house. He had just felt like he needed to understand more about what they were thinking.

Stumpy walked along the sidewalk, occasionally looking at the white houses that he passed every day. It seemed that nothing changed along Main Street. After two blocks, he cut through the alley beside Dr. Benson's house, and then through another alley to get to Disciple Street. There were no sidewalks along Disciple Street, and the houses were smaller, some of them covered in fake brick sheeting. Stumpy stepped into the street to go around an old car parked in front of one of the houses, and noticed there weren't that many cars on Disciple Street.

He also noticed that most of the houses weren't set as far back from the road as they were on Parrish Drive, the street right behind it. Most of the front yards were tidy enough, although most of them didn't have grass. They had hydrangeas and other flowering bushes. Some of them showed signs of recent sweeping, and occasionally there was a picket fence across the front yard.

When he got to Bessie and Horace's house, he noticed that the fence was a little whiter than the other ones he'd seen, and the plants in the yard were well cared for. It was a neat little box of a house with a small front porch across the front and two rocking chairs sitting on the porch. Stumpy had been to Bessie's house any number of times, usually bringing her home in the car when the weather was bad, but this was the first time he had come here planning to enter the house. He wondered how the people who lived in this house and the other houses on Disciple Street were different from the ones who lived on Main Street.

His house was bigger than theirs, and he had a car that was in the garage set off in the back of the house, but that was mostly just a matter of money. Did they wake up in the morning and make a list of the things that they had to do that day? Did they worry about how their children were doing in school, and what they were doing with their friends? It occurred to Stumpy that he didn't know. He did know that Bessie's children had gone to college in Georgia and lived up north somewhere. Years ago, when they were small, the children would sometimes come to Stumpy's house with Bessie and play in the back yard. He had known them then, two well-mannered boys who played quietly and didn't interfere with Bessie's work. But he didn't know exactly what they did now. Mae Beth probably knew, but that wasn't something they talked about.

He stopped at the gate in front of Bessie's house. They weren't on the porch so maybe they hadn't finished supper. He wondered whether he should walk around a little more, just to make sure they weren't eating. As he stood there trying to make up his mind, Horace came out the front door, a tall glass of iced tea in his hand.

"Mr. Stumpy. It's good to see you."

Stumpy opened the gate and walked up to the porch. He started to shake hands with Horace; that's what he usually did when he got to somebody's house, but he stopped. He'd never shaken hands with a Negro, and he didn't know how Horace would feel about it. He just smiled, greeted Horace, and stood at the foot of the three steps leading up to the little porch.

Horace walked over to one of the chairs and motioned Stumpy to the other one.

"Come up and sit, Mr. Stumpy. Bessie, she'll be out in just a minute. She don't know how to leave a dirty plate in the kitchen, so she's just finishing washing the dishes. Could I get you a glass of tea?"

"No, thank you, Horace. I just had supper." he said. He walked up the three steps and sat down in the rocker beside Horace.

"You have a nice yard here, Horace," Stumpy said, not knowing anything else to say right then.

"Thank you. We like to sit out here in the evening and look at it sometimes. Some of the bushes just started blooming, and we'll have some more next month."

The conversation dribbled to a stop. Horace sat there sipping his tea, and Stumpy stared out at the yard, then beyond the yard. Across the street some children were playing tag, running from yard to yard, occasionally yelling at each other. An older couple walked slowly down the other side of the street. As they walked by, Stumpy noticed that the man had his arm around the woman's shoulder. That could be Mae Beth and me, he thought, in thirty years or so. Despite the sounds of the playing children, everything seemed to be quiet and peaceful on Disciple Street.

Behind him, the screen door opened. He turned and saw Bessie coming out. She saw Stumpy and stopped.

"Mr. Stumpy, I didn't know you were already here," She said. "Did Horace offer you some tea?"

Reflexively, Stumpy stood up.

"Hello, Bessie," he said. "Yes, he did, but I just finished

supper, so I didn't need any." Then he realized he was standing. For years Bessie had been coming into rooms where Stumpy was sitting, and he had never stood. He wondered why he was standing now.

"Why don't we all go in the house," she said, "where we can be more comfortable?"

Stumpy saw Horace start to say something, but he didn't. Then he saw Bessie holding the door open for him.

It was dim in the parlor of the little house, but by the light of the single lamp, Stumpy could see the big, well-worn chair, obviously the chair that Horace sat in, and he could make out a deeper depression in one end of the sofa. He figured that was Bessie's favorite spot. On the table between the chair and the sofa were a radio, a Bible, and a small vase. Stumpy saw a chair on the other side of the room. He sat down in it.

Stumpy saw that he was right in the seating plan. Horace settled down comfortably in his chair and stretched his legs out in front of him. Bessie took her corner of the sofa, sitting straight with both feet flat on the floor. If it hadn't been for the table between them, it could have been a portrait of a contented older couple, either colored or white in their most comfortable setting. Stumpy tried to find a comfortable position in the chair, but couldn't bring himself to just lean back.

"I appreciate you both letting me come over," he finally said.

Bessie smiled. "You know you'd always be welcome here, Mr. Stumpy, but I got to admit that I'm curious about why you wanted to come over now. Is it about the Singing

Convention? You know I'm real sorry about all the trouble that caused you."

"I know that, Bessie. As I told you, we don't blame you for any of that. I don't know exactly why I'm here. It's just that I'm trying to understand some things."

Bessie smiled and nodded. Horace said nothing.

"But to be truthful," he continued, "I'm glad that you decided not to push this anymore. I don't think what you wanted to do is wrong, but I wonder if this is the right time for it."

"And when might it be the right time, you think, Mr. Stumpy."

His first thought was "later," but that didn't make a lot of sense. What if things were the same later as they were right now. Finally he said, "I don't know, Bessie."

"I don't either," she said, "so I imagine this time might be as good as any. I didn't say that I wasn't going to ... what did you call it? ... push it anymore. What I said was that I was real sorry it had caused you and Miss Mae Beth so much trouble, and I didn't want to cause you anymore. That just means I don't want you to try to do any more about it."

She paused and looked at Horace. He hadn't said a word since they sat down, and as best Stumpy could tell, he hadn't changed the expression on his face. Stumpy wondered what he was thinking as Bessie seemed to be declaring war on the Singing Convention. Stumpy only had a moment to reflect on that, because Bessie started talking again.

"Not being in the Sing is our problem, and we'll deal with our own problems. I shouldn't have said anything to

Miss Mae Beth to begin with. I'm sorry I did, because every time I try to take the easy road on anything, it ends up in a mess. I suppose that God doesn't want anything that's good to be easy."

Bessie's voice was still soft, and she still had a pleasant expression on her face. She could have been telling Stumpy what they were going to have for dinner, but the words didn't match the expression or her tone of voice.

"I believe it's about time we did something that everybody says it's not time to do. It's not an important thing, like having colored children get a good education, but it's something we can do here." She leaned forward a little bit and looked straight at Stumpy. "And I aim to see it done, or maybe make a mess trying."

Stumpy didn't know what to say. Finally, he turned to Horace, "What do you think about that, Horace?"

"I do believe, Mr. Stumpy, that our church has a mighty fine choir, and I think it might do the white folks in River Falls some good just to hear it. I'm sorry that some folks don't like that, but maybe Bessie and the others can just help change their minds."

Stumpy felt even more uncomfortable. He had hoped Horace would help him talk Bessie out of trying to change the Singing Convention, but it was obvious the big quiet man was right beside his wife.

"You know that whatever you do is going to come right back at me, don't you, Bessie? After all, you've been with us for nearly twenty years. You're like part of the family, and this is going to hurt the family."

Bessie nodded. "It just might, I guess. So, if you want

me to, I'll quit right now. You can even tell Mr. Pollard that you fired me because I was causing so much trouble."

Stumpy knew that if he went home and told Mae Beth that Bessie had quit, he'd probably be sleeping on the sofa for the rest of his life. Worse than that, he couldn't imagine his household without Bessie any more than he could imagine it without Li'l. He shook his head.

"I wouldn't have you quit, Bessie. I'm not sure we would know what to do without you. And I don't really know that I want you to give up what you think is important just because it might cause me some trouble. I guess that's my problem. I just really don't know. I like things to be neat and orderly, like my columns of numbers, and this isn't. We've done things one way all my life, and now you're telling me it would be better if we did something another way. I think you might be right. But I don't know what to do about it. I need you to help me understand, I guess."

For an instant, the expression on Bessie's face changed. Just a little. Her eyes softened, and the small smile that he always saw on her face became a little sad.

"I wish I could help you understand, Mr. Stumpy, but I don't think you could ever know what it's like to be colored. You're a good man, and you've always treated me nice, but I don't think you can have any idea about how different where you live is from where we live. We know pretty good what it means to be white; we see that every day up close. In fact, we know what's going on in a lot of the white folk's houses because we wash your clothes and cook your meals and clean your houses. But when we leave in the evening, you don't know anything about what we go home to. It's real different."

Stumpy made a weak gesture to the living room.

"This doesn't look all that different from our house, Bessie. It's nice. It's clean. It looks like a good home."

She nodded. "All that's true, I suppose, and thank you for noticing I try to keep it clean. But you're looking at the wrong things. Like, did you ever wonder why, since I'm fifteen years older than you are, I call you Mr. Stumpy and you call me Bessie?"

Stumpy shook his head. He had never wondered, and he didn't know what she was driving at.

"It's a little thing, but it's important," she said. "Mister and Misses are important words. Too important to give to colored people. If one of ours goes off to college and gets a degree or gets two or three degrees, he's still not a mister to the white folks. He can be professor. If a girl goes to school and becomes a nurse, she's not a Miss or Misses, but she's 'Nurse Somebody.'" She nodded her head toward Horace. My husband is a good man. He goes to work every day, and he pays his bills. He's a deacon in our church, and he's helped out a lot of people, colored and white, when they needed it. But he's still not Mister Williams to you or to any other white man. He's Horace, or if it's somebody like that Claymore Thomas, he's 'boy.' You see, words like 'mister' or 'misses' mean respect, and we've learned that white people are real stingy with that."

When she quit talking, the silence hung in the air. Stumpy looked from Bessie to Horace and back to Bessie again.

"You can call me Stumpy, if you want to, Bessie. I don't care. Or I'll call you Mrs. Williams. I never meant to show you lack of respect."

"I know that, Mr. Stumpy. And I'll go on calling you Mr. Stumpy, and you'll go on calling me Bessie. We've done that all our lives. That's probably what we'll do the rest of our lives. But maybe that's not what your son and my sons will have to live with. Some time that has to change, that and a lot of other things. I won't be able to change that, but maybe I can change one little thing."

Stumpy took in a deep breath. He still didn't understand, but he knew this was important to Bessie. And he knew whatever she did, Horace was going to stand with her, not because he was afraid of losing his rights in bed or her chicken stew, but because he thought what she was doing needed doing. He let the breath out slowly. He stood up, and when he did, Bessie and Horace stood up.

"I appreciate you and Horace talking to me, Bessie," he said. "I didn't know when I came here exactly why I was coming, and I still don't. I guess I'm trying to figure out what I'm supposed to be doing."

"Like I said, Mr. Stumpy, this ain't your problem. You don't have to do anything, but we do appreciate you trying to understand what's right. I wish everybody, white and colored, would do that."

Stumpy nodded and turned to go. Then he turned around and stuck out his hand to Horace. Horace hesitated just an instant before he reached out and shook Stumpy's hand. Then Stumpy turned and left.

Bessie and Horace watched Stumpy walk down the

sidewalk and through the little gate at the edge of their yard. Horace looked at Bessie.

"And I thought all we were goin' to do is sit on the porch and drink our tea and talk," he said.

"I didn't think it would be a good idea to be seen sitting on the porch talking to Mr. Stumpy. With some of the people who go up and down this street, we might get a cotton weight through our window."

Horace nodded. "I guess you're right. All the crazy folks ain't white." And he went back to the porch to resume his rocking.

As Horace rocked, Stumpy Fowler was walking slowly up Disciple Street, trying to make sense of everything he had learned that evening. He wondered if he'd learned anything at all, except maybe that Bessie and Horace were more like him and Mae Beth than he'd ever considered, although he couldn't remember ever thinking about it one way or another. As he walked along focused inside his head, he felt an automobile slide up beside him. He looked down at the long hood of a Cadillac coasting to a stop only a few feet from him. The car stopped, and a very black man got out, walking around the front of the car to where Stumpy was.

"You be a long way from Main Street, ain't you, Mr. Fowler?"

Stumpy looked hard at the man. If he had ever seen him, he couldn't remember it. He couldn't have been more than about five four or five and was thin as a reed. He was wearing a green jacket with wide lapels and a darker green shirt. He leaned against the fender of the car, a broad smile on his face, a gold tooth glinting on one side.

"I'm sorry. I don't believe I know you," Stumpy said.

"I imagine that's right. I don't get over to Main Street much. They call me Rabbit, and there ain't much that goes on here that I don't know about. And I been wondering what you're doing stirring up such as mess as you are."

The smile never left Rabbit's face, but the more he talked, the more Stumpy wondered if that smile didn't hide some kind of evil, but then he wondered what a small man could do to hurt him on a deserted street.

"I don't know what kind of mess you're talking about," he said.

"I imagine you do," Rabbit said. "The mess with the coloreds and the whites getting together at the Sing. You know that ain't going to happen, and it's just going to upset a lot of people."

"You may be right. It probably won't happen, but if it did, I don't see why it would bother you."

Rabbit reached leisurely into his jacket pocket and slowly brought out a knife. Stumpy flinched a little when he heard the switchblade snap. Rabbit began cleaning his finger nails with the four-inch blade, appearing to think about what to say next. He looked up at Stumpy, the smile still in place and the gold tooth still shining.

"Well, you got folks over on Main Street who takes care of stuff on Main Street. And we got folks on Disciple Street who takes care of stuff over here. And that works right well. None of us folks who take care of stuff need that to change much." He waved the knife in the air. "Y'all got what you need over there, and we got what we need over here. That's the way I like it."

He folded the knife and dropped it back in his pocket.

"Nice talking to you, Mr. Fowler. But I wouldn't walk along here much. Ain't a good place for white folks to be walking. Some bad things could happen." He walked back around the Cadillac and got in. Stumpy stood there as the car drove away. He felt like he was shaking. He had just been scared by a black man about half his size, and it wasn't just because of the knife. Stumpy thought he had never seen anybody who radiated evil like Rabbit or whatever his name really was. At the first alley, Stumpy turned toward Main Street.

8

Stumpy sat at the kitchen table, a cup of coffee and his little notebook in front of him. He'd started making his list for the day, but he'd only gotten through items one and two. As he sat there sipping the coffee, it seemed that the biggest thing he had to do that day didn't really fit on the list. He was trying to decide what he had learned from his visit to Bessie's last night—if anything—and what he should do about it—if anything. He doodled along the edges of the almost uncluttered page and thought about Bessie calling him Mr. Stumpy. He'd never thought about it one way or another.

He had always thought that Bessie was one of the most even-tempered and probably the happiest person he knew. She always had a smile on her face, and most of the time, when she was sweeping or dusting or folding clothes, she was humming or singing one of her gospel hymns. Now there seemed to be another side to Bessie, one that he hadn't seen in all the years she had worked at their house. As he drank the last of his coffee, he wondered if, maybe, he had just seen the surface of it. Stumpy tried to force his mind back to his list so he would know how to get through the day.

* * *

Bessie had left home a little early. She had to stop at Patience Purewood's before she got to the Fowlers. On weekdays, Patience was the Ryals' help, but on Wednesday night and Sunday she was the anchor for the alto section of the Bethel A.M.E. Choir. A big woman, larger than Bessie, Patience was given to wearing bright flowered dresses on Sunday and every other day of the week. There was really nothing quiet about her, from her dresses to her voice, to her laugh. And Patience spent more time laughing than almost anybody Bessie knew. Sometimes Bessie wondered what Patience had to laugh about. She was married to one of the sorriest men Bessie had ever seen. If Purdy Purewood had liked to work as well as he liked to drink, he and Patience would be rich. Instead, he worked some in the fields in the summer and spent most of the winter sitting in their parlor with a glass of bootleg whiskey in his hand listening to the radio or talking to whoever would listen about how he could have been a fine musician if he could have ever gotten out of River Falls.

Bessie would give him his claim to being a fine musician. He could play the piano, guitar, and trumpet, and when they were all younger, he had played in small bands in the juke joints around River Falls. Bessie had tried to get

Purdie to come play at the church, but Purdy made excuses to Bessie and told Patience privately that he'd never set his foot in a church again. He didn't think God thought much of him, and he felt pretty much the same way about God.

When Bessie knocked lightly on Patience's front door, Patience opened it almost immediately. She looked at Bessie and laughed.

"Lordy, Bessie, you're out early this morning. Y'all run out of coffee or something?"

She stepped back and motioned Bessie into the house. Bessie shook her head.

"No, I just need a minute to talk to you about the choir."

"Yeah, I been hearing a lot about the choir these last couple of days. At dinner last night, that's about all the Ryals wanted to talk about — how come Mr. Fowler was trying to get the choir in the Singing Convention. You know, they kept calling it 'that colored choir' just like they didn't know that I sang in it every Sunday. And they didn't bother to ask me what I thought about it either." She laughed again. "Course, that didn't surprise me."

"Well, I want to ask you what you thought about it. Do you think that our choir ought to be at the Sing?"

Patience looked serious for a moment. "I do. But I don't imagine that what I think makes a whole lot of difference."

"If you thought we might make some difference, would you help me?"

"You know the Ryals ain't going to like it if I try to stir up a bunch of trouble." She stopped, and then grinned. "Course, I don't know what they would do about it if they didn't like it. Mrs. Ryals can't cook a lick, and Mr. Ryals is about the most finicky eater I've ever seen. Lordy, I guess if I wasn't there, Mr. Ryals would probably starve to death."

"Probably nobody going to be real happy if we do anything, but I think we've spent enough of our lives making all those folks happy. I think maybe we just ought to stir things up some."

It only took about two minutes for Bessie to lay out her plan. By the time she finished, Patience was laughing out loud and clapping her hands.

"Honey, you're right. Ain't nobody going to be real happy with us when we do this. But I bet they sure will pay attention. I'll be ready tomorrow night at choir practice."

Bessie gave Patience a hug and hurried out the door. She was going to have to walk faster this morning, but there was a spring in her step that helped her along. She felt like she'd been wrong to ask Mr. Stumpy to do something about this. It wasn't his problem; it was hers, hers and the rest of the choir's. So it ought to be up to them to do something about it. And they surely would.

By the time Bessie got to the Fowlers, her entire plan had unfolded in her head. The when, where and what, and she thought this was a statement River Falls couldn't ignore.

When she walked in, Mae Beth Fowler was already cleaning up the breakfast dishes, and Li'l was sitting at the table eating cereal and studying his driver's manual. Mae Beth turned when she heard Bessie close the door. Li'l looked up, waved, then went back to his manual.

"Morning, Bessie," she said. "You want a cup of coffee before we get started?"

"No, ma'am. When I get here I'm ready to go to work. Why don't you let me take care of these dishes?"

Mae Beth stepped back from the sink. "That's fine. I do want us to do the windows today. That new one is making all the other ones look dirty."

Bessie took her apron from the hook on the back of the pantry door and put it on. She started running the water in the sink. She knew Mae Beth had gone to the bedroom to start making the beds. She couldn't just leave things for Bessie to do. And Bessie knew when they washed the windows, Mrs. Fowler would be on one side and she'd be on the other. Sometimes she couldn't understand why the Fowlers kept her. She cooked most of the meals, but Mrs. Fowler was a fine cook, too, and could have cooked anything her family needed. And Bessie cleaned the house, but usually with Mrs. Fowler's help. It was different at the Pollard's where Leola worked, where Virginia Pollard almost never lifted a finger to do anything, or at the Ryals' where Patience worked. Mrs. Ryals couldn't cook and didn't even try any more. Patience had to fix Sunday dinner on Saturday so Mrs. Ryals could just heat up the vegetables.

As Mr. Stumpy left, Bessie heard Li'l ask him if they could go driving after school, and Mr. Stumpy said he'd see. Bessie shook her head. It hadn't been long since that long-legged boy had been in diapers and crawling around under foot. Now he was in high school and just aching to get his driver's license. She thought about her two boys and now her grandchildren. Seems like some things change real fast. And some things don't change at all.

By the time Stumpy and Li'l had left, Bessie and Mae

Beth had made the beds, swept the kitchen, taken out the trash, and gotten out the rags, soap powder, and buckets for washing the windows. Mae Beth bound her hair up in a red bandanna. They stood in front of the sink filling their buckets up.

"Mr. Stumpy came to see me last night," Bessie said.

Mae Beth looked at her. "Really? He didn't tell me where he was going. What did he want?"

Bessie shook her head. "I don't know for sure. He seemed sort of upset about us wanting to sing in the Singing Convention, but he wasn't mad or anything. He just seemed worried about it. I told him that he didn't need to do anything, and that I was sorry I brought so much trouble on you and him."

Mae Beth turned the water off and turned to face Bessie.

"Bessie, we've told you that nobody blames you for what they did to the window. You can't be responsible for every idiot out there. Besides, all that's in the past now."

"I don't know, Miss Mae Beth. I told Mr. Stumpy that he didn't have to do anything, but that don't mean that I don't have to do something. And, like he says, whatever I do could just wash back on you."

"What are you talking about, Bessie?"

"I really believe it's time for some changes, Miss Mae Beth. Some things I can't do nothing about, but one thing I think I can. I'm going to have my choir stand up there on that stage and sing to the glory of God and do it better than any of those white folks' choirs."

"I'm sure you could, Bessie. But Arthur's already brought

it up at the committee meeting, and he says A.Y. Pollard isn't going to make any changes for anybody. Maybe next year would be better."

Bessie shook her head. "You know I love you, Miss Mae Beth, and all your family, but we've been hearing 'later' since I was a little girl. And I ain't a little girl any more, and I'm still hearing 'later.' I've about decided that it's late enough, and I'm going to try to do something about it. Like I told Mr. Stumpy, if you want me to leave so it don't cause you trouble, I'll do that. There ain't nobody I'd rather work for, but this is something that it's time to do. I don't want to be waiting for 'later' when Jesus calls me home."

Mae Beth stood there, her lips pursed and her brow furrowed.

"We don't want you to leave, Bessie. We don't want any trouble, but we don't want you to leave."

They each lifted a pail of water out of the sink and went to wash the windows.

* * *

That afternoon when Li'l came out of school, Stumpy was waiting for him, sitting in the Oldsmobile in front of the school. Li'l had been asking Stumpy almost every day to take him out for a driving lesson. He kept a Mutual Insurance Company calendar in his room where he marked off the days until he turned sixteen and could get his learner's permit. Now there were just twenty-one days left, and he could legally learn to drive, but no boy and very few girls were willing to wait until they were actually sixteen before they started driving. The license examiner came to River Falls on Tuesdays, so the usual thing was to take the written test and get the learner's permit one Tuesday and then come back the next week for the road test and a real driver's license. The license examiner was supposed to be surprised that you could learn to drive so fast, but everybody knew that on the back roads all around River Falls fifteen-year olds were driving with a death grip on the steering wheel while some family member — usually a father or big brother — sat in the passenger seat, stomping on an imaginary brake pedal.

When Li'l and Stumpy went through town on their way to the dirt road out beyond Woodall's farm, Stumpy was always at the wheel. They didn't expect to meet a lot of traffic on that road since it only went to one house and a couple of tobacco barns. When they got to the dirt road, Stumpy pulled over to the side, and Li'l ran around the car to get behind the wheel.

"Don't grind the gears, Li'l." That was the first thing Stumpy always said when Li'l got behind the wheel, but the gears still ground as he pulled away from the side of the dirt road and shifted from first to second. Li'l saw Stumpy's lips moving and decided that he was praying the Oldsmobile would live through the lessons.

As Li'l slid the gearshift from second to third without complaint from the transmission, it looked like Stumpy was almost relaxed. His fists weren't clinched, and it didn't look like his feet were jammed into the floorboards.

"That's the way it should sound every time," he said. "You do that and pretty soon you can do all sorts of fun things, like take your mother to Grandma's."

Li'l didn't respond. He figured that he didn't have to tell his daddy that he had other things in mind when he got his driver's license.

"Turn to the right up there," Stumpy said, pointing to another dirt road. "We'll get some different scenery.

Li'l gingerly applied pressure to the brake, slowing the car almost to a crawl. He put his arm out the window and made a right turn signal, and then turned.

"What's down there?" he asked.

"I don't know. I just thought we might as well look at some different fields for a while."

As well as he could without taking his eyes off the road, Li'l looked at the fields passing the car. He decided they might be different, but they all looked the same. Half-grown corn. Tobacco. Occasional rows of truck: beans, peppers, peas. Although he was only four or five miles from River Falls, to Li'l this was a different world. Back from the road he saw small unpainted houses, usually with an old car or pickup sitting in the yard and an icebox or refriger-ator sitting on the front porch. Children were playing in front of the house, and one or two men sat on the edge of the porch or stood in the front yard talking. The men were almost always wearing overalls, their uniform for going to work in the fields during the week and sitting at home on Sunday. Their children came to school in flour-sack dress-es and sometimes barefooted. They farmed on halves with people like Mr. Pollard and other men in town who had either bought up farms over the years or had gotten them when the farmers couldn't pay back their planting money.

"I'd hate to live like that," he muttered as he drove by one of the houses. There were three small children playing around an old tire swing suspended from an oak tree.

"Me, too," Stumpy said. "But it won't be many years before they don't even have what they have now." Li'l drove along for a few minutes, being careful to keep his eyes on the road and his hands on the wheel.

Plowed fields with young crops slid by on either side of the car, interrupted occasionally by stands of oaks, maples, and pine. Stumpy pointed to a house sitting back from the road, and Li'l stole a quick glance before turning his eyes back to the road. But, in a glance, he had seen that the front door of the house was hanging open, and there were no signs of life anywhere. There was trash in the yard and a lone child's dress still hung on the clothesline.

"That's what I mean. They just don't need as many people to farm the land now. They have machines, tractors and such. I read the other day that they're testing a machine to harvest tobacco. It won't be long before these people won't have a place to be. Even this kind of place.

Li'l and Stumpy drove around for another half hour, up one dirt road and down another. Stumpy didn't have much to say except to start slowing down sooner at the stop signs and let the clutch a little further out before pressing the accelerator. Eventually they got back to the paved road, and without being told, Li'l pulled over to the side so that Stumpy could drive the rest of the way in. It wasn't likely that Earl Holland or either of the other two policemen in

River Falls would give Stumpy a ticket, but Li'l knew that Stumpy wouldn't want to put them on the spot.

"You've just about learned to drive," Stumpy said as they pulled back into their driveway. "You did very well, and I'm proud of you."

Li'l almost blushed. It was the first time he had ever been complimented on his driving, and it made him feel good, even if the compliment was from his father.

* * *

That night before he went to bed, Stumpy locked the front door, then the back door. He had already checked to make sure the window screens were hooked. He thought for a minute about closing and locking the windows, but fresh air blowing gently in the window still had a touch of the day's warmth, and it wasn't something he wanted to do without. Some people were putting in air conditioning units, but Stumpy thought the cold, dry air that came from the noisy boxes was worse than the hottest summer nights. He went back into the living room and looked out the new picture window. It was clean, and so far as anybody could tell, the crashing and flying shards of glass had never happened. But it had; so for the first time in his life, Stumpy was locking up his house every night.

Mae Beth was already in the bedroom, sitting on the edge of the bed leafing through *"Woman's Home Companion."*

"I hear you went to visit Bessie and Horace last night," she said, without looking up.

It didn't surprise Stumpy. In fact, he had been wondering if he should bring it up. Bessie would have mentioned it to Mae Beth, and it would seem like Stumpy was trying to hide something from her. But he didn't mention it, because he couldn't tell her why he had gone there. He still didn't know.

"Yeah. We talked."

"Bessie said you seemed upset."

"I guess you could say that. I haven't been in a fight or wanted to be in a fight since I was in grade school. Now, twice in two days, I'd have been happy to fight somebody. I'd have been glad to hurt them."

Mae Beth looked up from the magazine. "Twice? I figured you were pretty upset with whoever threw that thing through our window. Who else?"

"I ran into Claymore Thomas downtown. I don't like Claymore, never have, but I never really thought much about him either. He had something to say about the window, and I offered to knock him on his butt. I guess what makes me upset is that I'm not the kind of person that goes around looking for fights, or at least I wasn't until now."

"I think that's pretty normal," Mae Beth said. "This will all pass over. Although I don't think Bessie's ready to give up yet."

Stumpy shook his head. "She's not. And maybe the other thing that's upsetting me is that I'm not sure she should. I know it's just a singing competition, but I get the feeling it stands for a lot more than that to Bessie."

"Bessie says it's not our problem, and we shouldn't do any more about it. I think she's right."

Stumpy looked at her. She was the one who had said that Bessie was family and he shouldn't let anybody insult their family. And she was the one who always stood by what she thought was right. Then he understood. She was afraid. Somebody had assaulted their house, and she was afraid that he or Li'l would be next. He sat down on the bed beside her and put his arm around her shoulders. She dropped the magazine on the bed and hugged him, burying her face into his shoulder.

"I don't want you to get hurt," she said, her voice muffled against his shoulder.

He just pulled her tighter to him. He didn't want him to get hurt either, but he sat there wondering what would happen if they let people like Claymore Thomas make all the decisions in the world. They sat there for several minutes before he got up. She looked at him.

"What are you going to do?" she asked.

He shook his head. "I don't know. Probably nothing, just like Bessie said. But I wonder if I've been taking too much for granted. I always thought Bessie was one of the happiest people we knew. And I always thought we treated her just like we ought to. But off and on all day today I've been wondering why I called her "Bessie" and didn't think it was funny she called me Mr. Stumpy, or that she would sit down at the table with Li'l or even you, but when I come home for lunch, she doesn't sit down to eat with us. I sort of accepted it just like I accepted the fact that debits and credits had to match. That's just the way it is."

Stumpy sat there, looking at Mae Beth, gnawing a little on his lower lip, trying to think of how to explain his thoughts.

"There're some things that will always stay the same way. And they should. But I'm not sure how many of those things have to do with people. Do we keep things the same because they are right? Or do we keep them the same just so we're not bothered."

"Bessie says that it's up to them," Mae Beth said. Softly. Not arguing. Just reminding Stumpy that he didn't have to do anything.

"Yeah, I know," he said. "I'll probably have all of this out of my head tomorrow. I guess I don't deal with learning new things all that well." He walked over and kissed her gently. "Go on to bed. I'll be in as soon as I get my pajamas on."

He put on his pajamas, brushed his teeth, and slid into bed beside her. He felt her move closer to him and put her arm across his chest. Stumpy just lay there. He hadn't told her about Rabbit and how confusing it was that he had been warned off by a white man and a black man. He wondered just how many sides this puzzle had, and when he couldn't answer that, he finally went to sleep, wondering what his life would have been like if he had been born on Disciple Street.

9

The Bethel A.M.E. Church had been sitting on the same land just on the edge of River Falls at the end of Disciple Street since the beginning of the century. At first it had been a small, unpainted building, large enough for the thirty or so worshippers who came there every Sunday. As it absorbed the congregations of other Negro churches in the area, it outgrew the little building, and the congregation replaced it with a big white wooden rectangle, sizeable enough, but with no particular architectural distinction. The tall windows were not stained glass; they were purely functional, letting in the breeze during the hot summer months and making an ineffective effort to keep out the cold in the winter months. At one point the church had been heated with two coal stoves, one at the back and one at the front, but when some stray embers almost caused the building to burn down, the congregation raised the money to put in an oil-fired furnace that carried the heat all over the building. That and the hundred and fifty or so bodies there on Sunday morning kept the church sufficiently warm. Too warm, according to Pastor Pickens. It made it even harder for some of the older members to stay awake.

Their first pastor, Reverend Obadiah Ennis had been born a slave on a plantation near New Bern. After the war, his parents had moved inland to River Falls. Obadiah worked in the fields alongside his parents, but at night he taught himself to read and to do numbers. By the time he was twenty, he had gotten a job working a debit route for a northern insurance company. He went door to door every week collecting the quarters and half-dollars that paid the premium on tiny life insurance and burial policies. He liked to joke that he'd get their money as long as they lived, but he'd put them away in style. Before he was thirty, Obadiah not only had his own debit route, but was the district manager. He had people working in towns for thirty or forty miles around River Falls. He had married and had two daughters. For a Negro, Obadiah Ennis was living very well and dressed in suits as fine as most of the white men in the area.

But somewhere along the way, Obadiah developed a conscience. He had been at too many front doors to take quarters that were attached to falling down houses or where the children were half-dressed or less. He began to wonder if a life insurance policy or a good funeral was the best way these families could spend their money. So far as he knew, the insurance company always paid off; they always did exactly what the contract said that they would do, and the policyholders almost always paid their quarter or half-dollar, almost superstitiously. It was, as best Obadiah could tell, an equitable business arrangement, except that he still had the nagging feeling that he was taking money that could better be used in other ways.

His wife, Calena, was religious. She read the Bible regularly and had taught their daughters to read it. When she went down east to visit her parents in New Bern, she always went to church, a church that had been there since before the United States was a country. A few times Obadiah had gone with her, but going didn't seem to make much difference to him. He liked the service, the solemn singing and the preaching, but when he left it didn't make much difference in his life. But he did start reading the Bible with Calena, and the more he read and the more he looked at the people whose money he took, the more he was convinced that something was wrong with his life. He decided he was looking for something, but it wasn't the solemn worship of the church his wife grew up in, a worship that was nice on Sunday, but not very helpful on other days of the week. He went to a tent meeting that was being held by a traveling evangelist and heard a different kind of music, louder and more joyful. In addition to the piano that Obadiah was used to, the tent meeting had a band, including a trumpet, guitar, drums, and a fiddle. Instead of feeling the music washing over him like he did in his wife's church, Obadiah could feel it boring inside him, lifting him up. There was, he decided, something wonderful about the music there.

But he couldn't say the same thing about the evangelist. Obadiah went to the tent meeting four nights in a row, and for four nights the preacher told him that if he didn't repent and come to Jesus, he wouldn't go to Heaven. He would, in fact, go to Hell and burn forever. Obadiah looked around at the people, poorly dressed, mothers with two children on her laps and one on either side. Men already bent in their thirties. He wondered if the hereafter was all that they could hope for. What they had here was barely endurable. And he was ashamed. They had so little and for years he had been taking their money, mostly so they could be sent to the hereafter in some kind of style.

On the fifth night, he stood outside the tent. He listened to the music, and he heard the preacher tell them that they would go to Hell. He heard some of the people crying, and at the end of the service, before any of the worshippers left the tent, he turned and walked away. Obadiah walked miles down the dirt road leading away from the tent, then down into the woods and through some plowed fields. He didn't know where he was going or what he was looking for. Finally, he crossed another field and entered the woods again. He stopped at a fallen tree and fell on his knees and cried. For more than thirty years he had lived right on the crust of his life and had never looked beneath it. On that night, he peered deep into it, and he prayed.

"God, I don't know much about Heaven. I do believe that you sent your Son down here, and He healed the sick and all that. He didn't say that we just had to wait 'til we died.' I believe you want me to do something about the here and now and let you take care of the hereafter. I'm ready to do it, if you are ready for me."

When he got back home the next morning after being on his knees in the woods all night, Calena fell on him, weeping.

"I just knew you were dead," she said. "I just knew some of them white folks had taken you."

Obadiah held her and caressed her shoulder until she quit crying.

"I been out praying. And thinking. And I think God wants me to do something."

It took some convincing to make Carlena agree to his quitting his job and using their savings to buy a piece of land for a church. He and a few others threw up the wooden building, and Obadiah started preaching every Sunday. His message was that God loved them now, and he wanted them to be happy and to prosper. True, he would love them even better in Heaven where there would be no pain and where they'd have everything anybody, even white folks, had. But if they worked hard and loved each other, they could have a better life here. Carlena used the little wooden building to teach the children to read and write. They studied the Bible. Obadiah went to all the people he had been taking money from and told them that his church would bury them in its cemetery when the time came, and they could save their quarters for what their family needed.

Whenever somebody needed something, a new roof or a well, Obadiah would bring some men from his congregation, and they would mend the roof or dig the well. Obadiah kept telling his people that doing good works didn't save them, but if they were saved and didn't do good works, they were being stingy with God's gifts. By the time Obadiah died thirty years later, the church, now the Bethel A.M.E. Church, had more than a hundred members.

The second preacher was from the north, from a little town in Massachusetts. He'd been sent down by the denomination after Obadiah died, and when he arrived he wasn't sure what he was doing there. He had graduated from the seminary, and he had never stepped off the sidewalk for anybody, white or Negro. Calvin Elijah Conley was a big man, well over six feet tall, but he dressed fancier than any of the people in his church was used to. His hands, when they shook hands with him, were soft. They'd never dug in the dirt or held the reins of a mule team. When he came to River Falls, his congregation accepted him because he did seem to love the Lord, he preached a good sermon, and he was faithful to visit the sick. But they didn't really expect him to be around very long. Besides, he wasn't married.

But the entire community learned what appeared to be softness in Calvin Elijah Conley was only skin deep. One night when he was walking back to his little house after praying over Ornin Fletcher, two men in hoods and white robes stepped from the trees beside the road. One of the men was carrying a horse whip. Pastor Conley stopped, not sure what to make of them.

"So you're the Yankee nigger," the one with the whip said, walking slowly toward Conley.

"I'm Calvin Conley, pastor of the Bethel A.M.E. church," Conley said.

The second one moved up behind the first one. "An educated nigger," he said, "the worst kind."

The hooded man with the horsewhip just laughed. "Ain't no such thing. Give 'em all the education you can, and he's still a nigger."

The two men stopped about three feet away from Conley. "On your knees, nigger, or you're going to get the beating of your life."

"No. I don't bow to anybody but my God. If you and your friend want to kneel here with me, I'll be glad to pray with you."

With a roar, the man raised the horsewhip, but before he could bring it down, Conley took two steps forward and smashed his fist into the hooded face. Before the man had hit the ground, Conley had snatched the horsewhip from his hand and turned to the second man. The man turned and ran back into the trees, stumbling as his brogans got caught up in the long white robe. Conley bent over and removed the hood from the downed man. It was stained with the blood that was pouring from his nose. Conley made sure that he was breathing and moved him over to the side of the road so that he wouldn't be run over before morning. Then, carrying the hood and the whip, he walked on home.

There was a lot of conversation among the Negroes and the whites about why the Klan didn't come after Pastor Conley, and the explanations ranged from supernatural intervention, where the Lord sent an army of angels to protect him, to a more likely explanation that even the Klan didn't want to get involved with somebody with connections in the north who could bring the government down on them. Whatever the reason, when Calvin Elijah Conley left River Falls ten years later to take a pastorate in Richmond, he left with the respect of his congregation and most of the white community, and the only Klan hood most of the congregation had ever seen that closely. He had continued Obadiah Ennis' works, holding that the congregation, while anticipating the hereafter, had to help their fellowmen now. The church had continued to grow, with about a hundred and fifty congregants on any Sunday.

This was the church Pastor Amos Pickens came to. Because Bethel had grown larger, the A.M.E. committee that assigned pastors had not sent a newly minted seminary graduate as they had with Pastor Conley. Pastor Pickens had already been at two churches, one about as large as Bethel. He had been born and raised in the county, had gone North to college and seminary, and had asked to return to the south. He thought he could do some good.

In the beginning, Pastor Pickens followed in the footsteps of his predecessors. He and his wife Agnes visited the sick, interceded with the law when one of the congregants got into trouble and found food and clothes when they were needed. But in the nearly twenty years Pastor Pickens had been at Bethel, times had changed. Not many of his congregation needed help in getting food and clothing. The children were going to school, growing up, and—in many cases—leaving River Falls for better jobs in Chicago or Philadelphia or Pittsburgh. They were a stable community, and for most of them, what they had here was not so bad. At the same time, the administration of the church took more and more of Pastor Pickens' time. Just keeping up with the maintenance, planning the services, and making sure he didn't slight one of the ladies' circle meetings by not putting in an appearance kept him busy. The congregation had built a parsonage on the grounds next to the church, complete with electricity and indoor plumbing. In all, Pastor Pickens had gotten comfortable.

As he stood at the back of the church watching Bessie

conduct choir practice, he thought about what she had said when he visited her and Horace. He had told himself the greater good was keeping the good will of the white community while they clawed small gains in education and health care. He had gotten the county to hire two Negro nurses to call on pregnant women and to hold baby clinics around the county. That was a big step forward. He and two other Negro pastors had gotten the county to buy new books for the colored schools, at least part of the time, instead of passing down broken and torn textbooks that were no longer useful in the white schools. He had almost convinced himself that these accomplishments were far greater than whether this choir sang in a competition that had always been entirely white.

On this Wednesday night, there were only about thirty people in the church. Levon Lassiter sat at the upright piano, staring at Sister Bessie. About twenty choir members, most of them still dressed in work clothes sat in the choir, also staring at her. A half-dozen people sat scattered around the sanctuary, waiting for their spouses to finish so they could go home. Pastor Pickens saw Bessie take a deep breath and made three small gestures with her left hand. On the fourth one, Levon crashed into the piece with notes flying in every which direction. The choir members began to softly clap their hands to the rhythm. Sister Bessie gave Levon two full choruses just to get everybody warmed up, then she held her arms up, and the choir stood up.

"My God is a rock!"

It was a proclamation from twenty voices.

"In a weary land."

The choir's clapping got a little louder as they absorbed the energy of the song. Sister Bessie motioned for the sopranos to sing louder and smiled when they responded. She couldn't help but feel when her choir praised the Lord, He had to feel good about it. When they finished the first chorus, Elbert Stevens, with his booming bass sounding for all the world like the voice of God, sang the solo. Elbert had no problem being heard over the other nineteen singers. When they came back in on the chorus, every member of the choir was swaying, their faces shining. Elbert sang another verse, then the choir, raising their voices as they carried the children of Israel out of Egypt and into the Promised Land.

Pastor Pickens stood there, smiling. They were a fine choir, and if the white people of River Falls didn't get to hear them, it was the white people's loss. Pastor Pickens went out the front door and walked across the churchyard to the parsonage, humming the old spiritual.

If Pastor Pickens had stayed for another half hour he would have heard a noise that was not nearly so joyful. Everybody seemed to be talking at the same time, until Violet Kinner's soprano, much more shrill than usual, cut through the general hubbub.

"We ain't ever done anything like that. It's just going to cause a bunch of trouble."

Bessie looked at her and tried to smile. She knew this was going to take some persuading.

"I can't see why it's going to cause so much trouble, Violet. All I'm asking you to do is go downtown with me Saturday and sing some of our songs on the corner at the bank."

Patience stood up. "I don't know why we're having so much of this talking. I think we ought to be proud to praise the Lord on Main Street just like we do here at the church. I'm going to be there, and I'm going to sing to the glory of the Lord just like I do right here."

There were several nods and a couple of "amens," and it looked to Bessie like she had most of the people on her side.

Pearlie Hudson sat on the back row of the choir loft, just listening. Pearlie sang bass, shoed horses and mules, and didn't usually have much to say about anything. Bessie had often thought that Pearlie and Horace would make a good pair, just sitting around and not talking to each other. In a gap in the general hubbub that was going on he said, "This is because of the Singing Convention, ain't it?"

Bessie turned to him. "And what if it is, Pearlie?"

He shrugged his shoulders. "If I gotta go down and sing in the middle of a bunch of white folks, I just wanted to know why I was doing it. Some of them probably ain't going to be too happy."

Several of the men laughed. "You got that right," one of them said.

Finally, Bessie asked for a show of hands of all those who would be there at three o'clock. About half of the choir immediately raised their hands, followed by most of the rest, some slower than others. Violet sat in the soprano section, her hands in her lap and a frown on her face. Finally, eighteen of the twenty choir members sat in the choir loft with one hand raised. Bessie looked at the Violet and Minnie Sanders. She knew why Violet wasn't going, but she was surprised that Minnie, a young wife and mother and a pretty good alto, wasn't.

"Minnie, you not going to be with us?"

Minnie looked down at her hands. "I'd truly like to, Bessie, but my little boy's birthday party is Saturday. He's been looking forward to it all week. I can't make him miss that."

"No, you surely can't, Minnie. You just be with us in spirit."

* * *

Roscoe Allen Tart was used to people listening to what he had to say. When he made speeches, a hundred or more pairs of eyes were fixed on him and the same number of ears heard his every word. He hadn't driven nearly sixty miles from Durham to this two-bit town to have somebody like Claymore Thomas argue with him. Roscoe and Claymore stood in Claymore's yard under the tree. When Roscoe had shown up an hour earlier, Claymore had pushed out the door and led him into the yard instead of inviting him in. That didn't bother Roscoe so much, since he had already met Ruby and wasn't particularly interested in meeting her again. What did bother him was that Claymore didn't seem to be listening.

"I'm telling you, Roscoe, it's already been taken care of. There ain't anything else to do."

"Let me go through this one more time," Roscoe said

slowly, as if he were talking to a dim wit. "You got a nigger choir who wants to get into a white singing convention. And you're telling me there ain't anything else to do."

"They're not going to get in. The committee has seen to that."

Roscoe threw up his hands. "The committee. Whatever happened to the Klan? If you sit around and depend on a bunch of committees to do your job, we'll all be working for niggers before you die." He started pacing up and down in front of Claymore. I hear somebody threw a cotton scale weight through that nigger lover's window. Who did that?"

Claymore wanted to say that he had, but he figured Roscoe wouldn't have asked the question if he didn't already know the answer. "I don't know. I thought it might have been one of my boys, but they say it wasn't."

Roscoe stopped pacing. "So let's see. The committee stopped the nigger choir, and somebody we don't know sent a message to the nigger lover that started this mess, and you did exactly what?" he said with elaborate sarcasm. "Can you give me one good reason I shouldn't just boot your ass out of this klavern and out of the Klan and find somebody who'll deal with the niggers like they're supposed to? You don't seem to understand the Ku Klux Klan is all that's stood between us and the niggers since the Yankees took over down here. And if you're what we've come down to in River Falls, I don't hold much hope for the future."

Claymore took the pack of Chesterfields from his pocket and shook one out. He struck a match and lit it with a shaky hand.

"You've got no need to talk to me like that, Roscoe. I've

held this bunch together since Ferd died, and the reason we ain't done much lately is that we don't have to. Our niggers behave themselves. So Bessie caused a little stir, but it didn't go nowhere, and we won't hear no more about it. We didn't have to do nothing to Stumpy Fowler, because somebody else did. And I don't doubt that whoever did it did it because they knew about us. Maybe we'll find another member there. If anything else happens, I'll take care of it."

Roscoe shook his head. Claymore just wouldn't listen, but he didn't know who else he would get if he chased Claymore off. He was having enough trouble just trying to keep the Klan alive in these parts. People didn't want to do their duty like they used to, and you'd think that with that bunch of black-robed nigger lovers in Washington saying their white children had to go to school with niggers, every white man in North Carolina would be signing up. He'd had a visit from the Grand Dragon two weeks ago, telling him he had to do something about membership and dues. It wouldn't do him any good to chase Claymore off now. It would help if he could just put a little fear of god into him.

"Okay, Claymore. Let's say you're right. If you are, then I did talk a little rough." He took a step closer to Claymore. "But if you're not, and if we have any nigger trouble in River Falls, you won't ever see the inside of a Klan meeting again, and everybody in North Carolina will know just what a screw-up you are. You understand that?"

Claymore nodded his head. Roscoe turned on his heel and stalked to his car, not waiting for any more conversation from Claymore. Claymore stood there and watched the car's taillights diminish until they disappeared as the car turned onto the dirt road. Claymore squatted beside the big tree, staring at where the taillights had been. He looked at the window in the house. Somewhere in there, Ruby was busy doing something. She was always busy. Roscoe didn't think he was paying enough attention to Klan business. Ruby thought he was paying too much. He didn't know who was right, if either one of them was. He did know he had to make sure there were no nigger problems around there, or Roscoe would make good on his threat. What kind of man would he be if he got kicked out of the Klan, especially after all the work he'd done on it?

As he squatted beside the big tree and smoked, Claymore started thinking about what he could do if he had Roscoe's job. He imagined himself riding around a dozen counties throwing the fear of God into men who had quit doing their duty. Not like Claymore, of course. He was doing his duty. But there were others who weren't. He'd make them shake. He'd make them get on the stick and do something. Then he came back to himself. He had to do something. He just had to figure out what that was.

* * *

Stumpy and Mae Beth had just gotten into bed. He lay there with his head propped on his arm, staring at the ceiling.

"Bessie have anything to say today about the Sing?" he asked.

"Not really. It was just the usual day around here. I did get a call from Ida Ryals, wanting to know if it was true that you were going to make A.Y. open up the Singing Convention to what she called that 'colored music.' I told her that you were the treasurer, and you probably couldn't make A.Y. do anything. Then I asked her if she didn't think Patience should have a chance to sing in the Singing Convention, and she said certainly not. I asked her why not, and she stammered a minute and hung up on me."

Stumpy turned toward her. "I thought you were going to just leave this to Bessie," he said. "You know Ida's going to tell everybody in town that you're leading some sort of crusade to integrate the Singing Convention. First me, then you."

"I don't guess I thought about it. Ida's sanctimonious nature just sets something off in me. Patience has worked for the Ryals almost as long as Bessie's worked here, and sometimes she just acts like Patience doesn't exist. I know for a fact that Ida couldn't cook worth a flip when she and Roy got married and still can't. Patience may be the only thing that keeps Roy at home."

Stumpy smiled. "You're beautiful when you're riled."

She leaned over and kissed him, then laid her head on his shoulder. "I don't want any trouble. I truly don't. But it bothers me that we treat Bessie one way at our house — she's pretty much like family here — and then treat her like she's gone to a different country when she goes back to Disciple Street, like she wasn't even a citizen here."

"You ever been in her house?"

"Yes. I took her soup when she had the flu. And I took a load of old clothes for her church clothes drive. Maybe another time or two."

"I'd never been in her house until Monday night. I don't know what I thought it was going to look like. It's smaller than ours, and maybe the furniture's a little more worn, but it's a lot like our house."

"What were you expecting, African masks and a cooking fire in the living room?"

"I don't know what I was expecting. You know my granddaddy never said Negro. He didn't even just say nigger. It was always "lazy nigger" or "dirty nigger" or something like that. I guess that even though I know Bessie isn't lazy or dirty, and Horace sure isn't lazy, I just figured that on Disciple Street, I'd find something different. It's just something I'm bred with."

"Considering how Bessie keeps our house, it never occurred to me that she'd keep hers any different," Mae Beth said. "I learned a long time ago that a speck of dirt is a mortal enemy to that woman."

Stumpy sat up and looked at Mae Beth. "How'd you feel if Bessie or somebody like her moved next door?"

Mae Beth started to answer, then stopped. She looked down at her hands, then back at Stumpy. "I started to say that I wouldn't mind it, and I hope I wouldn't, but I don't know. I never thought about any Negro living next door to me. It's just not something I thought about. Just like I never thought of Arthur dating a Negro girl. I don't think he would, but if he did, I don't know how I'd deal with it."

Stumpy put his arm around Mae Beth and pulled her closer to him. "I know what you mean. We were raised a certain way, and I suppose that's the way we expect things to be. They've been that way for about a hundred years, and until this week, I just assumed they would be that way for another hundred. Now I don't know."

They sat there not talking for a while. Then Mae Beth pulled away, turned off the lamp, and pulled Stumpy down to her.

* * *

FROM THE FALL RIVER CURRENT
Thursday, April 26, 1956

Local Man Drowns in Irrigation Pond

Amos Phillips of Route 2, River Falls died Monday when his tractor fell into the irrigation pond. According to witnesses, the tractor sank immediately, carrying Phillips with it.

Although nobody could say why Phillips apparently drove the International tractor into the water, it is not believed that alcohol was involved. According to his wife, Edna Mae Phillips, the deceased man hadn't had a drink in more than five years.

Friends pulled Phillips and the tractor from the pond, but too late to save him. Services were held at the Broadway Prim-

itive Baptist Church on Wednesday with Elder Poppy Prince presiding.

10

For a Saturday morning, Mae Beth was dressed up. She wore a pale blue skirt with a starched white blouse. Her hair was done up and her makeup carefully applied. Stumpy, sitting at the breakfast table, couldn't help but wonder if just going shopping with a bunch of women in Raleigh was worth the trouble, but then, he didn't think any kind of shopping was worth any kind of trouble.

"You boys'll be on your own for lunch," Mae Beth said.

"We'll probably get a hamburger at the cafe. I promised Li'l I'd take him out for a driving lesson this morning. Then I think I'm going to work a while this afternoon. We'll be fine."

Mae Beth smiled at him. "We should be back by three or four. Really depends on how many shoes Alene has to try on before she makes up her mind."

"What are you shopping for?"

"Nothing, really. I'm just going along for the ride. Maybe catch up on the gossip. I can't think of a thing I need right now."

"You ladies be careful. Lots of crazy folks on the road between here and Raleigh."

Mae Beth kissed him on the cheek and went out the back door. In a minute, Stumpy heard the neighbor's car start and back down the dirt driveway to the street.

Stumpy took out his pad. He didn't usually make a list on Saturday, but since he planned to work in the afternoon, he needed to know what he was going to work on.

It was only a few minutes later when Li'l came in, dressed and ready to drive. Stumpy tore the page off his pad and put it in his pocket, and they went out to the car.

"You think you're ready to drive on a paved road?" Stumpy asked. He already knew the answer. Li'l and most of his friends felt like they had been born ready to drive anything anywhere. The biggest thing Stumpy was trying to teach Li'l was to have some respect for the difficulty of driving safely, especially when so many other people didn't.

Li'l grinned and headed for the driver's side of the car.

"But not until we get out of town," Stumpy said.

The grin faded a bit, and Li'l got in on the passenger's side. Li'l turned on the radio as Stumpy backed out of the driveway and tuned it to the rock and roll station in Raleigh. Soon they were driving down Main Street, accompanied by Fats Domino.

"Do you like music, Dad?"

"I guess. I don't know much about any kind of music. That guy sounds about as good as any. I guess some people grow up with a love of music and some others grow up with a love of other things, like machines or numbers or fishing. I think I like numbers best."

"I like some kinds of music. Like Bill Haley and Fats Domino. Some grownups don't like them."

"Some grownups don't like much of anything. I don't see anything wrong with that music. I don't think it'll turn you into a criminal or anything."

They rode along without speaking, listening to the radio. When they were several miles out of River Falls, Stumpy pulled to the side of the road.

"Okay. Your turn," he said, getting out and walking around the car.

Li'l slid over behind the wheel, carefully adjusted the mirror, and pushed the seat back. "Where are we going?" he asked.

"Let's go out to the Crossroads. I want to drive by Claymore Thomas'"

"You want to see if he has a picture window?"

Stumpy laughed. "Not really. I've just been wondering about people like Claymore lately, and I want to drive by his house. See if I see anything that'll help me understand better."

"If he's like Petey, he's just mean and dumb," Li'l said.

Stumpy looked at his son. Maybe life is easier when you're fifteen and don't try to look too deep into anything. He knew that life was becoming more complicated for Li'l every year. He'd heard Li'l talking to Billy Royce on the phone last night, and from Li'l's end of the conversation, Stumpy could tell that Billy Royce wasn't going to be available tonight because he had a date. He wondered how long it would be before Li'l would be going with one girl, and he and Mae Beth would be worrying about what they were doing and whether they'd get through school.

Stumpy noticed that Li'l was keeping the car in his

lane, both hands on the wheel, and checking his rear-view mirror frequently. So far, so good. They got to the Crossroads, and Stumpy told Li'l where to turn. In a minute, they were in front of the overgrown driveway that led down to Claymore Thomas' house.

"This used to be a big farm," Stumpy said. "Still is bigger than most of the farms around here, but Claymore and Ruby've had to sell off a good bit of it. I thought about buying a piece last time they were selling it, but I didn't like the idea of having anything next to Claymore."

"What would you have done with it? You don't want to be a farmer, do you?"

"I'd have rented it out. Like we do the land down at Allen's Creek. That had a little bit of a tobacco allotment, so I could get more for it."

"Why do you think they hate Negroes so much?"

Stumpy didn't answer right away. He sat in the passenger's seat watching the fields slide by. It was a good question, and probably didn't have a simple answer. Stumpy looked at Li'l, sitting tall, keeping both hands on the wheel and his eyes on the road. He wondered what kind of world Li'l would have to live in because there were so many questions that didn't have easy answers.

"I don't know," he said, finally. "I guess everybody wants to have somebody to look down on, especially if things aren't going too good for them, and for some people, the only way they can have somebody to look down on is because of the color of their skin. When I was in the navy there was a fellow from North Dakota who couldn't understand why the people in the south treated Negroes like they did. But he couldn't stand Indians. I guess he needed somebody to look down on and since they don't have any Negroes in North Dakota, the Indians had to serve."

"Who do you look down on, dad?"

Stumpy squirmed a little in his seat. The driving lesson was getting deeper into philosophy than Stumpy was used to.

"I don't guess I look down on anybody. At least I hope I don't. My mama—your grandmother—had one thing she said over and over. She said for me not to look down on anybody and to be sure I didn't let anybody look down on me. I guess she told me that enough that I believed it. I hope maybe I've passed that along to you."

They drove through the country for another half hour before Stumpy told Li'l to head back to River Falls. With gas near a quarter a gallon, they didn't want to run the whole tank out.

It was after eleven when they got back to River Falls, and with Stumpy driving, they fell into a slow-going line of traffic going into downtown. Pickups. Cars ranging in age from nearly new to prewar. An occasional slat-sided truck with children in the back. It was Saturday, and everybody had come to town.

"Let's leave the car at home and walk downtown," Stumpy said. "I'll buy you a hamburger."

* * *

A little over an hour later when Stumpy and Li'l walked out of the Main Street Cafe, the weekly population explosion had about reached its peak. Almost everybody who was coming to town was there, and the sidewalks in front of the stores had people from wall to curb.

At the corner, they stopped for a minute to listen to Tat Stynchcomb. Tat was a small man, one who seemed to be shrinking inside the too-large shirt collar and too-big coat. His long black hair was slicked back, and his shoes were shined to a high gloss. Every Saturday, Tat put on his suit and tie and took his place on the corner of Main Street. He could have been mistaken for a small, meek man until he opened his mouth, and in a voice much larger than his body, proceeded to tell everybody who would listen that they were going to hell, the reasons varying according to what was going on at the time. The people walking down Main Street would stop for a minute to hear what he was screaming about, then they would walk on, evidently not particularly concerned about an imminent journey.

Stumpy and Li'l leaned back against a window ledge, watching the people and Tat. Today Tat seemed to be particularly concerned about what race mixing in the Singing Convention would do to River Fall's collective afterlife.

"I guess Tat didn't get the message that there still aren't any Negro choirs in the Singing Convention," Stumpy said.

"God set a plan," Tat screamed, waving a tattered Bible over his head. "God set a plan, and He put everything in its place. The fish in the water. The horse in the pasture. And as long as everything stays in its place, God's plan works perfect. God's plan is for the whites to stay in their place and the negra to stay in their place. If God had wanted the whites and the negras to mix, he would have made them all the same color. And he would have made the negras as smart as whites."

He stopped to catch his breath, glaring at the people who walked by him.

"When we change the plan of Almighty God, we condemn ourselves to burn forever in the fires of Hell, and there ain't no relief from the burnin'."

"Is he another one that feels like he has to look down on Negroes?" Li'l asked.

Stumpy hesitated so that Tat could finish this section with a crescendo. In the brief silence that followed, he said, "Not like Claymore and his boys. Fact is, I don't think Tat has anything against Negroes or anybody else. In fact, about the only time I see Tat is when he's trying to raise money to help some family, and about half the time, it's a Negro family. He was in the cafe last week trying to raise enough to pay medical bills and buy food for one of Enoch Wilson's sharecroppers. He just told us that the husband had been hurt in an accident. I knew who it was because I had already heard about the accident from Mr. Wilson. I think Mr. Wilson's a good man, but it was Tat that took the time to get help for the family, and I know he had enough to do in his own field."

"Then why does he talk like he does?

"I think Tat actually believes that you have to have things separate. I guess he'd say separate but equal, like with the schools. I really believe Tat thinks that about everybody has the same chance of going to hell, but I would be a bit surprised if he doesn't think that there'll be signs over the doors saying 'white' and 'colored.'"

Li'l watched Tat as he started another verse. "I don't think there's any such thing as separate but equal."

Stumpy smiled. "Anybody who's seen the school the Negro children go to would have to think that way. It's separate, but it's nowhere equal to the white schools. For the most part we've been lying to ourselves for a long time."

Tat Stynchcomb was finally getting to the point. He was asking the singing committee to repent of their plan to let the A.M.E. choir into the Singing Convention and to fall on their knees and ask forgiveness for trying to change God's plan.

Stumpy shook his head. "I don't doubt that God talks to Tat, but I do wish he'd keep him a little more current."

They joined the crowd streaming down the sidewalk, bumping shoulders with farmers in overalls and trying not to trip over knee-high children hanging on to their mother's skirts.

"What are you up to this afternoon?" Stumpy asked.

"I don't know. I'm probably going to go by Billy Royce's and see if he wants to do something. He has a date for the picture show tonight with Jean Dale."

"You thought about dating yet?"

"I've thought about it. I just haven't done much about it. I asked Zona Faye to go to the show with me, but she hadn't said she would."

"You have a good afternoon," Stumpy said. "I'm going to work a while and I should be home by the time your mother gets back."

Li'l nodded and flipped him a small wave. Then he cut across the street to head to the Pollard house. Stumpy just watched the people as he strolled back to his office.

11

Stumpy made it all the way to his office without thinking of much of anything until he saw a knot of people down the street on the bank building corner. A bunch of people standing there wasn't necessarily good news or bad. It might be somebody selling something on the sidewalk, like the man who came through town selling Indian Tonic every year. He'd draw a crowd by juggling things, and when he got enough people gathered around, he'd tell them how Indian Tonic could cure everything that was wrong with them. But usually he didn't have that many people. It might be that somebody had passed out on the sidewalk or maybe dropped dead. That didn't happen often, but when it did, there was usually a pretty good crowd. Stumpy decided to wander down and see what was going on.

As he came closer to the crowd on the corner, Stumpy could see a cluster of blue overalls and some dresses of different faded colors, and in the middle of it, brighter than anything around it, a bright flash of gold and maroon. It didn't take many more steps for him to see that the gold and maroon was the Bethel A.M.E. choir, and the surrounding subdued colors was a very curious crowd, staring at the choir and murmuring to each other.

When he got to the edge of the crowd, Stumpy saw Bessie, wearing her gold choir robe with the dark red stole, surrounded by nearly twenty others, all wearing the same thing. Bessie was moving one person in one direction, then another in another direction, ignoring the growing crowd that surrounded her. She didn't look at anybody but the choir. Finally, she seemed to be satisfied with the way they were standing, and she stepped back, raised her hand, hummed a note, and dropped her hand.

The sound that came from the choir was of a single piece, a chord that pushed the closest listeners back and overcame the murmuring of the crowd like a cinder block dropped on an ant hill. The chord had a deep rich bottom, swelled in the middle, and was held within the reach of human ear by the sopranos on top.

Precious...

The *shuuuu* seemed to hang in the air forever, until, with a quick hiss, the choir moved to the next word.

Lord!

The choir members, focused intently on Bessie, pushed the sound from the bottom of their bellies and through their rounded mouths, making it wash over the people.

Take my hand.

The slow cadence of the last three words rolled out into the crowd, wrapping them in the spiritual's plea. Then the sound was punctuated with a crack. Bessie had clapped her hands, then the choir followed her, clapping and swaying as they sang the verse.

Lead me on, let me stand
I'm tired, I'm weak, I'm lone
Through the storm, through the night
Lead me on to the light
Take my hand precious Lord, lead me home. Take my hand.

Standing on the edge of the crowd, Stumpy turned his attention away from Bessie and the choir and began watching the crowd. Most of them were nodding in rhythm to the singing. A few were swaying. Four or five were standing dead still, scowling. Stumpy spotted Claymore Thomas on the other side of the crowd, his round mouth pursed into a very small "o," and his arms crossed in front of him. Claymore was looking around the crowd, too, trying to judge the response of the white people to the Negro choir.

Bessie and the choir sang another verse, clapping and swaying, then, when they got to the third verse, they stood still, no longer clapping, and the sound became a plea.

Precious Lord, take my hand
Lead me on, let me stand
I'm tired, I'm weak, I'm lone
Through the storm, through the night
Lead me on to the light
Take my hand precious Lord, lead me home.

The words seemed to reach out to the farmers and their wives, some of whom had been up since long before daybreak, feeding stock, milking, doing all the things that had to be done every day whether they felt like it or not. It reached out to people who were worried about making it another year, paying back their planting loans, and keeping the children fed and clothed. Stumpy saw the connection between many of the listeners and the golden robed choir that was singing. The choir was singing softly, drawing the crowd closer to them, and when they finished, very quietly, on the last words, Stumpy heard an old man next to him say quietly, "Amen."

The people started shuffling around, and Stumpy noticed that several men on the back edge of the crowd were huddled together. There was an urgency in their attitude that made them look different from the rest. They'd talk for a moment, stop and look at Bessie and the choir, then talk some more. From where Stumpy was standing, it didn't look like they were enjoying the music.

Then Bessie's clear, rich alto stopped them again.

If you want to go to heaven, come along,

And the choir sang: "*Come along.*"

Bessie repeated the invitation, calling out and the choir responding. They started clapping again, swaying in time to the music. Stumpy noticed that a few people in the crowd were clapping along with the choir. One old farmer, one strap of his overalls pinned up and the sleeves of his blue chambray work shirt rolled up to his elbows, looked to Stumpy like he was ready to take Bessie up on her invitation. Stumpy was enjoying watching the reaction of the crowd when he felt a touch on his arm.

"You know what's going on here?"

Stumpy turned and saw Earl Holland standing beside him, his policeman's cap pushed back on his red hair. Stumpy shook his head.

"Don't have the slightest idea. They breaking any kind of law?"

Earl stood there listening to the choir and looking at the crowd.

"I imagine they are. Probably need a permit to sing on a public street like this, but I ain't about to break up a church choir singing gospel music. So I'm just going to stand here and listen."

"I'm guessing Bessie is making a statement about the Sing, but she didn't tell me anything about it," Stumpy said.

"Fat chance of that. But if she wants to try, good luck to her. Long as they don't break any serious laws, I'm not going to try to stop her."

Stumpy nodded in the direction of Claymore Thomas. "Claymore'll probably take care of that."

Bessie and her choir were finishing the song, joyfully shouting out the chorus.

Did you hear my Jesus when He call you?
Did you hear my Jesus when He call you?
Did you hear my Jesus when He call you?

Stumpy saw two of the men in the back row suddenly jerk their heads down, then he saw a gooey, yellow spot begin growing on the wall of the bank building behind them. It took a minute to register that it was an egg and that it had been thrown at the choir. Just as Stumpy started to try to see where it came from, a second one hit Bessie in the back, the yellow just a shade darker than the gold robe she wore. She turned, looking to see where it came from. Then she turned back to the choir and they sang:

For to try on your long white robe

Stumpy saw Earl Holland moving to the outer edge of the crowd, trying to see where the eggs had come from. He started around the edge on the other side, but all he saw were people looking at each other, wondering what was going on. They began to wander off. As the crowd thinned, Stumpy saw Claymore and a couple of his friends walking toward the choir. Earl Holland came up beside him.

"Uh-oh," Earl said. "I think Claymore wants to talk to Bessie. Maybe I better go listen in."

He and Stumpy began walking toward Bessie. They managed to get there in time to meet Claymore before he said a word.

"Enjoy the music?" Stumpy said. He was enjoying what was evidently a bad time for Claymore.

Claymore's brows were furrowed, and his mouth was still scrunched into a little "o." He looked at Stumpy, then at Earl, then at Bessie, then back at Earl.

"You're the chief of police. Why didn't you do something about this?"

"I am. I am trying to find out who threw those eggs. Hitting people with things is assault."

"I mean about those niggers. They can't just stand around and sing anywhere they please. Arrest them or something."

Earl shook his head.

"No. Don't think I can do that. This is the Bethel A.M.E. Church choir, and as best I can tell, they didn't start a riot or damage public property or beat up on anybody. In fact, I thought they sang right good." He turned to Stumpy. "Didn't you think they sang good, Stumpy."

"I did," Stumpy said, grinning. He was enjoying Claymore's anger. For a minute, Claymore's round face was scrunched up like he was going to cry. Finally, he just turned and walked off, his two friends trailing along behind him. After a couple of steps, he turned around.

"Next time it might be something more than a couple of fresh eggs." He walked off.

"You think they'd do something to Bessie over something like this?"

"Well, they put that weight through your window just because there was a rumor that something had happened. What do you think they might do if something really did happen?"

It hadn't really hit Stumpy that they might try to do something to Bessie. He'd thought that the weight through the window was the work of just one more crazy, but the more he thought about it, the more likely it seemed that somebody like Claymore Thomas would try something serious, like maybe burn Bessie and Horace out. The Klan had been known to do that in the past.

"Is there anything you can do to stop it?" he asked Earl.

"Uh-uh. One of the problems with the law is that you can't arrest somebody because you think they might do something. Thinking don't get anybody arrested around here, not that there's that much thinking going on."

"Could you sort of keep an eye on Bessie's house?"

"We've been doing that since you went and got your window broke. I figured if they'd break yours, they might try to do something to Bessie's."

With a little two-finger salute Earl wandered away.

Stumpy walked over to where Bessie and the choir were standing. Bessie was looking over her shoulder at the gooey yellow stain while one of the choir members was trying to wipe it off. From her expression, Stumpy couldn't tell whether she was mad, concerned, or not particularly interested.

"You okay, Bessie?" he asked.

"I'm alright, Mr. Stumpy. I wished they hadn't thrown the eggs, though. These robes ain't washable. They have to be dry cleaned, and there's no way I can get it cleaned before service tomorrow."

"Your choir sounded good."

"Thank you. I just wanted to give the folks here just a little taste of what they were missing. I think some of them liked it."

"I know they did." He stood there for a minute, wanting to say something else and not knowing what that should be. Finally, he just said, "I'm sorry they threw the eggs, Bessie. There was no need for that."

"That's the truth, Mr. Stumpy. But there's no need for most of the meanness in this world."

* * *

It took Horace Williams two or three minutes to rouse himself from a sound sleep to something that resembled wakefulness and look at the round clock beside the bed. It was just after midnight. He lay there and listened. What had awakened him was the sound of muffled voices just outside the house. Then he heard a scraping, some sort of tool.

Horace slipped out of bed, being careful not to wake Bessie, pulled on his pants and walked very softly to the living room window. He crouched in the dark at the corner of the window, trying to get a clear view of the front yard. He saw them, right in front of the fence near the gate, three figures in white robes and pointed hoods. They were struggling with a cross that looked to be about eight feet high. Its contours were softened because it was wrapped in something. Horace knew it must be burlap; that was what the Klan usually did when they burned a cross.

One of the men seemed to be trying to dig a hole, and the other two were holding the cross up. They put the cross in the hole, but as soon as they turned it loose, it started to tip over, so the two men pulled the cross out of the hole again. Horace watched this for a minute. He thought that maybe he would have been more scared if the men had looked like they knew what they were doing, and he was tempted to just crouch there and see if they ever got the cross in the hole. As he was thinking about it, they tried again. This time the cross stood up, not quite straight, but it didn't fall. It just looked like it was wilting. Horace decided he better do something.

Staying away from the window, he crossed to the front door, stood up as tall as he could, and flung it open.

"What in the hell do you fools think you're doing?" he roared.

One of the robed figures was standing there with a can, and the other was trying to light a torch. They looked at Horace as he started walking down the steps. The man with the can threw the contents in the general direction of the cross, and the man trying to light the torch forgot the torch and threw the match at the cross. The gasoline that had hit the cross burst into a bright flame. About the same time, the gasoline that had hit one of the Klansmen did the same. Two of them were running back to a pickup that was parked down the street and the other was trying to get out of his burning robe, screaming at his friends to help him. Horace stepped up and slammed the burning Klansman to the ground, and rolled him over several times until the fire was out. He grabbed him by the nape of the white robe and yanked him up.

"Get away from my house," he said, giving the Klansman a couple of quick kicks in the rear of his smoldering sheet. "If you come back, I'll see you're sorry."

The Klansman ran after the other two, still trying to get out of his robe. Horace turned his attention to the cross. The place where the gasoline had hit was still smoldering, but the rest of the cross had never caught. Horace reached up under the crossbars and pulled it out of the ground. Then he dragged it around to the back of the house. He figured the wood might be useful for something. He stopped by the faucet behind the house and washed his hands, then went back in.

As he came in, Bessie was standing at the door, still trying to get the sleep out of her eyes.

"What was that all about?" she asked.

"Not much. Just go back to sleep," he said. She nodded, and headed back to the bedroom. He was glad. He didn't want to tell her that some dumb white folks had tried to burn a cross outside their house because her choir wanted to sing in their Singing Convention. He still didn't understand why that was so important to Bessie, but, then, there were a lot of things he didn't understand about Bessie, and that had been fine for a lot of years. It wasn't long before Horace drifted off to sleep.

12

That Sunday Reverend Amos Pickens got up at his usual hour, read the Bible, and knelt and prayed. He got dressed, found the folder that held his sermon notes, and went to church. It was a Sunday like most of the other Sundays in spring in River Falls, except as he did all the usual things, Reverend Pickens didn't feel as he usually did. He was not approaching the Lord's house with the expectation of blessing. He was approaching it with a rock of sorrow weighing on his heart. He could not get the image out of his mind: Bessie turning to the crowd and singing the last line of that old gospel song with the yellow egg yolk running down the back of her gold colored robe. He had stood in the crowd and watched the choir sing, at first a little sorry they were going to make a spectacle right there on Main Street and wondering what kind of trouble it was going to cause. Then he felt a good deal of pride in the way the choir sang, but when Bessie had been hit with the egg and had still finished the song, he felt like Paul at the stoning of Stephen. Bessie was showing courage while he was standing on the edge of the crowd holding their coats.

He took his seat behind the pulpit. Sister Bessie had the

chair next to him. This morning she had on a purple frock instead of her usual gold robe. He imagined that it still had egg on it. He nodded to her as she sat down. She nodded back, no sign of worry in her face. Obviously, Bessie was coming to worship in a more tranquil mood than he was. She got up and led the congregation in singing "Nearer My God to Thee." Bessie's clear voice, and the mixed voices of the congregation filled the sanctuary, rising through the ceiling and going straight to God. This is the way man should worship, he thought, not whipped into it by being afraid of Hell or lured into it by the thought of Heaven, but just because we know that God is God.

When the hymn was finished, Reverend Pickens stood up and prayed, but he had one prayer in his mind and another one on his lips. Then he sat back down while Bessie led the choir. This morning they sang "My God is a Rock," and they did it with joy. From his chair, the Reverend could see Bessie's ample body bouncing up and down as she pulled chorus after chorus from the choir. The congregation was clapping and rejoicing, all caught up in the spirit of the music. Then it was over, and it was time for Reverend Pickens to preach. He waited a minute for the congregation to get its breath, and got up and walked slowly to the pulpit, pulling his handkerchief from his pocket as he walked. When he got there, he stared at the people before him. They lifted their faces expectantly.

"Sometimes a man is not true to himself, and if he is not true to himself, he cannot be true to his God." The faces in the congregation were puzzled. They had not gotten his point yet, he thought. So, he would make it clearer.

"I have not been true to myself. And I have not been true to my God." Around the room, he could see the mouths dropping open. He certainly had their attention. He walked out from behind the pulpit. The pulpit wasn't where he needed to make his confession.

He walked down to the floor in front of the pulpit. "I have learned to love comfort more than I love truth. I have learned to love peace more than I love truth. And I have learned to turn my head away from those who try to tell me the truth... because it might take away my comfort and my peace. But I tell you now, in the name of the Lord, that comfort will not set you free. Peace will not set you free. Only truth will set you free."

There were cries of "Amen" and "That's right" around the congregation.

"A few weeks ago, I tried to tell Sister Bessie that she ought to be quiet, that she ought not to cause a disturbance. Not because what she was trying to do was wrong, but because I wanted to keep my comfort and my peace. But Sister Bessie loves the Lord, and she has faith. She told me this choir sings to the glory of God, and it ought to be able to sing anywhere any other choir sings."

The shouts had suddenly stopped. Now everybody knew what the Reverend was talking about. They just didn't know what he was going to say.

"I tried to convince myself and God that I was doing this for the good of the community. But this community isn't helped when we sit on the sidelines. It's helped when we praise God and do his work. Yesterday, while Sister Bessie and our choir were praising God and doing his work, I stood on the sidelines. I stood there, doing nothing while Sister Bessie and the choir called people to Jesus. I stood there and did nothing…" He stopped for a moment, a catch in his voice, and continued softly and sadly, "while Sister Bessie and the choir were attacked by some people who didn't think we should be praising Jesus on Main Street on a Saturday afternoon."

"This morning I'm not going to preach a long sermon. I've got some praying to do. I've got some confessing to do. And while I'm doing that, I want every one of you to pray your own prayer. How are you going to help this community by serving God?"

Reverend Pickens looked around at the congregation. They sat there, some with their mouths hanging open, all silent. He saw Leola Campbell sitting in the third pew, her dark face pulled into a scowl under her purple wide-brimmed that. That would be another conversation he'd have to have, he thought, but he could deal with it. He felt like God had reached down and pulled a big rock off his heart.

"There's one other thing. From this time on, when any of you are doing the work of the Lord and somebody wants to throw something, or even do something worse, I'll be there with you. They will have to strike me down before they can strike you."

With that, Reverend Amos Pickens went to his knees in front of the pulpit, bowed his head and began to cry. He heard other members of the congregation coming up beside him and kneeling, murmuring prayers, and occasionally saying, "Please, Lord" and "Yes, Jesus." He felt a hand on his shoulder. He opened his eyes and saw that it was Sister Bessie, kneeling beside him with Horace beside her. He closed his eyes and continued to pray.

* * *

A.Y. Pollard couldn't decide whether to stay home, go for a walk, or go down to the office. He had already suggested to Virginia that they take a ride, but she said she didn't want to. Then he went into the living room to read the paper, and she roamed around the house, picking things up and putting them back down, then moving to another room. He wondered if it wouldn't just be kinder if he left the house for a while. Virginia was fidgeting; she was trying hard not to pull out one of the bottles of vodka while he was there, afraid he would see her. People said that you couldn't smell vodka, but too often he had come home and smelled the sour smell on her breath when he kissed her on the cheek.

A.Y. wondered if Virginia knew or acknowledged to herself that he knew she drank. He even knew the bootlegger that brought it to the house, and if he told the bootlegger to cut Virginia off, A.Y. had no doubt the deliveries would stop. He'd thought about doing that, just as he had thought about confronting her and demanding that she quit or that she check into the hospital in Raleigh where they said they could cure alcoholics. But he hadn't done any of that. Because he always came back to the thought that if being married to him caused that much pain, it would be cruel to deny her the one thing that gave her some peace.

It wasn't that she couldn't function. Sometimes, when Billy Royce and Zona Faye had been home all day, her movements became jerky and her voice brittle, but she still did the things she was supposed to around the house and sometimes at the church. But she only functioned. There had been no joy in her eyes for years, and the gaiety that had set her apart from all the others in college was replaced by what seemed to be a dull desire simply to get through another day, the way the ashes replace the flame. A.Y. Pollard heard her go up the stairs, then back down the stairs and into the kitchen. He folded the newspaper, put it in the magazine rack, and walked to the front door.

"I'm going to the office for about an hour," he called. An hour should be long enough.

"Okay," she answered. He tried to determine whether he heard any relief in her voice, but he couldn't tell.

As he walked down the street, he wondered how he could help Virginia. He would do anything or pay any amount of money to bring back the woman he married, but he knew that she was buried under ten years or more of grief and vodka. His question was not how he could bring back young Virginia, but how he could make this Virginia's life bearable. By the time he got to the bank building, he still had no answers. As he turned the corner to go up to his office, he noticed the dried egg yolk clinging to the stone on the side of the building. It had run down in streams almost to the ground before it dried. Somebody would have to wash that off tomorrow. That would be just one of the minor problems connected to Bessie Williams and her wanting to get into the Singing Convention.

* * *

It was just about dusk when Stumpy and Mae Beth started walking over to Disciple Street. They would have been earlier, but there had been a long discussion about whether they should go to Bessie and Horace's house without either an invitation or letting them know. Since Bessie didn't have a phone, they couldn't call and ask if it was a convenient time. Stumpy thought they should just wait and speak to Bessie when she came to work tomorrow, that Bessie and Horace probably wouldn't appreciate somebody, even Bessie's employers, just showing up unannounced. But Mae Beth had been worried about Bessie ever since she heard about somebody throwing an egg at her on Main Street.

Stumpy knew that Mae Beth was worried about Bessie being hurt, but the more she talked, the less he knew about what Mae Beth thought they should do. At one point in the discussion, he thought she wanted them to stand beside Bessie no matter what she was going to do to get the choir into the Sing. Then, five minutes later, it sounded like she was not only afraid of Bessie being hurt, but of them losing their friends and Stumpy losing clients. It hadn't really occurred to Stumpy that whatever happened would affect his business, but when Mae Beth mentioned it, he thought about the clients who might decide to find a new CPA just because they didn't agree with what he did, beginning with A.Y. Pollard. A.Y. could afford to hire a big CPA firm from Raleigh. In fact, he already did some business with one, but the work he gave Stumpy was enough to make him Stumpy's biggest client. Because they had been friends all their lives, Stumpy hated to think that something like this would make A.Y. take his business somewhere else. But maybe the time had passed for the kind of friendly business they had always done.

Worse than that, Stumpy thought he heard some fear in Mae Beth's voice, this woman who had never seemed to be afraid of anything. She had gone through the long illness of her father without flinching, saving her tears for late at night when she was at home and her mother couldn't see her. She had gone through the pregnancy with Li'l, accepting without a word the doctor's pronouncement that it would be a difficult pregnancy and a difficult birth. He had offered, in order to protect her health, to end the pregnancy. She was, he said, liable to have much more than the normal problems that accompanied pregnancy. Stumpy had been willing to do anything to protect Mae Beth, but she wouldn't hear of it. She had spent a large part of the pregnancy in bed, but in the end, had delivered a large, well-formed baby. The doctor had told her she should never have another one, and they hadn't tried.

But there was something in the venom of what had happened on Main Street and what had happened to their window as well as the comments of Mae Beth's friends that seemed to make her see the danger of this to be different from anything she had faced before. Stumpy wondered if the greatest danger in her mind was their losing their position in the town they'd lived in all their lives.

When they got to the little white house and knocked on the door, Bessie opened it. Three expressions flashed across her face in an instant. The first was eye-widened surprise at seeing Stumpy and Mae Beth standing on her front porch. That was replaced by a look of chagrin which might have been because she had company and hadn't fixed refreshments or perhaps because she really didn't want to have company. Then all of that was replaced with a smile as she opened the screen door and invited them in.

As they came into the living room, Bessie turned and called to another part of the house. "Horace, we have company. Mr. Stumpy and Miss Mae Beth."

Remembering where Horace and Bessie had set the other time he was in their home, Stumpy guided Mae Beth to the other end of the old sofa. He went to the chair he had occupied before. Horace came into the room. Stumpy noticed that he walked to Bessie's side, but didn't say anything. Stumpy stepped over to him and held out his hand.

"Evening, Horace. I'm sorry just to barge in on you, but Mae Beth and I were concerned about Bessie."

Horace shook Stumpy's hand and seemed to relax. Stumpy wondered if Horace had thought they had come to fire Bessie. There was just too much confusion here, and Stumpy felt a real need just to leave and go back to his house or his office where he knew how things were supposed to be, but when Horace motioned for him to sit down, he sank into the chair.

Mae Beth was the first to speak. "I'm sorry about what

happened yesterday, Bessie. I'm sorry that somebody could do that to you.

Bessie nodded. "Yes, ma'am. It seemed like a real mean thing to do, but I suppose that some people think we hadn't ought to have been there. That's their way of saying it."

"I can't imagine what you must think of white people who'd do something like that, Bessie," Stumpy said. As soon as it came out of his mouth, he wondered why he'd said, "white people."

Bessie smiled. "It ain't exactly a white people thing, Mr. Stumpy. We know a lot of good white people, like you and Miss Mae Beth. And we know a lot of mean coloreds. Take Patience's husband, for instance. He's bad to drink, and when he gets in his drinking, there's no telling what he'd do. When he's not drinking, he's just no account, but most of the time he's drinking."

She looked at Horace for confirmation. He just nodded.

"And there's the Jenkins boy down the block here. He's been sent off to the county farm for stealing at least three times, already got babies by two women, and him not yet thirty years old."

Stumpy looked from Bessie to Horace. Bessie looked disgusted enough to spit at the idea of the Jenkins boy's stealing and making girls pregnant. Horace's expression didn't change. Stumpy wondered how long it had taken Horace to learn to keep all his emotions inside him like that, not showing hate nor pain nor fear, just keeping that placidly pleasant expression. His thoughts were interrupted by Bessie as she continued her list of Negroes who didn't do what they were supposed to.

"Do you think these people will try to do something more than throw eggs, Bessie?" Mae Beth asked.

"Already did." It was Horace, the first thing they'd said since they sat down. "Tried to burn a cross in our front yard last night. Didn't do a very good job of it. Nearly burned one of their own up."

Bessie whipped her head around toward Horace. "You never told me about that."

"Wasn't a whole lot of need. If you want to see it, it's around back of the house. I plan to cut it up for firewood."

Stumpy put his head in his hands, rubbing his temples.

"What did they think they'd accomplish by burning a cross outside your house, Horace? I've never understood that."

Horace smiled just a little bit. "Supposed to scare us. It's a warning that if the colored folks didn't quit doing whatever it was the Kluxers didn't like, the next thing they'd do is pull them out of their house and beat 'em. Or worse."

"Do you think they'd do that to you or Bessie?"

"I don't know. Claymore Thomas is probably too much a coward to try, but they's a lot of other Kluxers around, and some of them might want to."

Stumpy looked at Mae Beth. She was staring at Bessie. Her hands were knotted in her lap. She looked like she might cry. Bessie just sat there, apparently comfortable in her corner of the old sofa, next to Horace. He wondered what the real difference was between the Negro couple sitting beside each other across the small living room from them and him and Mae Beth. They were a few years older. They hadn't been to college, but they had put their boys through college. They went to work and came home. They obviously loved each other. Stumpy was surprised that he really seemed to want to find something different, something that would justify what had happened on Main Street and in their front yard. He pushed his attention back to the conversation. Mae Beth was talking.

"Do you really think you ought to keep going with this, Bessie? We're afraid you might really get hurt."

Stumpy nodded. "I can't do anything with A.Y. right now, Bessie, but he won't be chairman after this year. We might be able to get something done with a new chairman. I promise I'll help you."

Bessie looked at Horace, the expression on her face just like the one she had when she was sweeping or cooking or washing dishes at their house. Stumpy had always thought that it was a pleasant expression, showing that Bessie was happy to be there. Now, seeing it return to her face so quickly, he realized it was her "white folks" expression and didn't show anything behind it.

"I understand what you're saying, Mr. Stumpy, and I surely do appreciate you being willing to help us make this happen sometime. But I have this strong feeling that I've just run out of sometimes. I've been some timing for over fifty years, and I hope the Lord God'll forgive me if I've gotten impatient. There are some things I want to see before I die, and this is just a little one. I don't think those crazy people will hurt me or Horace, not any more than they have for all these years, but I'm just not wanting to wait around anymore."

She looked at Stumpy, then at Mae Beth, and her white

folks expression dissolved from her face and she looked at them with a real sympathy.

"I know that this has already cost you something," she said softly. "And I don't want it to cost you anymore. Like I told you, you can tell folks you fired me because I wouldn't stop raising such a ruckus. That'll keep the other white folks from blaming you. We understand. We really do understand."

Stumpy saw the tears welling up in Bessie's eyes. He turned to Mae Beth. The tears were already streaming down her cheeks. He looked at Horace. But Horace's expression hadn't changed. Then he looked down at his hands, knotted on his knees with the knuckles showing white as he clasped them harder and harder. When he looked up, Mae Beth was staring at him. She moved down the sofa and took Bessie's hand, still looking directly at Stumpy. He recognized the look, the old Mae Beth who never flinched. He wondered if he was as strong as she was, but he knew he'd have to try.

"No, Bessie. We won't tell anybody anything like that. I'll do whatever I can do to help you. On one condition."

"What's that, Mr. Stumpy?"

"You don't do anything else like what you did Saturday. If everything calms down, I just might be able to get a vote through the Sing committee, and once the committee approves it, there's nothing anybody else can do."

"But you already brought it up to the committee," Mae Beth said.

"I brought it up, but that's all. I think there might be something else I can do. At least I can try."

"I don't know that I like you having to do our fighting for us, Mr. Stumpy." It was Horace's deep voice. Stumpy hadn't thought of it so much as a fight as a campaign. He wasn't sure what he'd do if it turned into a real fight, but then he thought how much he'd like to have knocked Claymore Thomas on his ass on Main Street, and he thought maybe a fight wouldn't be a bad thing. So long as Mae Beth and Li'l didn't get hurt.

"If I thought it was going to be a real fight, Horace, I think you'd do a whole lot better than I would. But I'm thinking more of a political fight, and since I'm on the Sing committee, it seems like I may be the one to do it. Of course, then it might turn into a real fight, and I'd be happy to have you involved."

For the first time since they got there, Horace's smile broadened beyond the genial expression he always put toward the world.

"There's surely a few folks I wouldn't mind having just a few minutes with. Not that it's something I'd do real often, but just once or twice would be alright."

Stumpy wondered just how often the big black man had had to use all his energy resisting spending "just a few minutes" with some farmer who was ordering him around.

"Could I see that cross, Horace," he said.

As Horace and Stumpy went to the back door, Stumpy saw that Mae Beth was still sitting beside Bessie, her hand on Bessie's arm and both women had tears on their cheeks.

The cross that lay on the woodpile behind Horace's house didn't look particularly scary. It was misshapened, with one arm noticeably longer than the other. The burlap was charred near the bottom of the post, but not a lot. According to Horace's account, the Klansman who caught on fire was probably charred as bad as the post.

As they stood there, staring at it, Stumpy said, "I met a man named Rabbit the other night."

Horace looked around at him, a look of pure disgust on his face. "Where did you meet him?"

"When I was walking home from your house. He didn't seem to think I ought to be walking on Disciple Street."

Horace nodded his head. "He might be right about that, though Rabbit ain't right about much. He thinks he's the big 'un on Disciple Street, and if you want some whiskey or maybe to gamble, he probably is. Those of us who try to do right and tend to our own business don't have nothing to do with him."

"Is he as bad as he looks like he is?" Stumpy asked.

"I expect he is. He's killed four or five folks who crossed him."

"Then, why isn't he in jail."

"The folks he killed were coloreds. That don't get a lot of attention, even from somebody like Chief Holland." Horace stood quietly, still staring at the remains of the cross on the woodpile. "I think I'll walk up a ways with you and Miss Mae Beth tonight."

They stood there and stared at it for a few minutes, then they went back into the house.

When they got home that night, Mae Beth took his arm and pulled it close to her.

"I'm proud of what you said back there," she said. "You're a good and honorable man."

Stumpy held her close to him. He didn't want to tell her that he didn't have any idea what he was going to do or how he was going to do it.

13

Stumpy had no better idea about what he was going to do on Monday than he had had on Sunday night. He had thought about it. He had even tried to make a list of things he needed to do, but the list just had an ending; it had no beginning and nothing in the middle. Stumpy sat at his desk staring at a file, but not seeing it. He wanted everything to be orderly, but what he was trying to do would unleash a flood of disorder. He tapped his fingers on the file and thought. He shuffled the file around and thought. But none of his thinking seemed to produce any kind of action. All he knew at this point was that it had to do with the Sing committee, and it had to overcome A.Y.'s resistance.

When he went to lunch at the Main Street Cafe, he found that he was looking at the regulars differently. Which ones of them would avoid him once he started his campaign, whatever it might be? Which ones might walk by and congratulate him, but in a voice so low no one else could hear it? Which ones would put on a sheet and try to burn a cross in his yard? He ordered the meat loaf special, just as he usually did on Monday, but he didn't taste it. He absentmindedly stuck it in his mouth while he watched the people around him. Several of them stopped at the table and spoke to him. None of them said anything about Bessie.

After lunch, he walked down to the Singing Grove again. It hadn't changed. It didn't look much like a battleground, but Stumpy knew that looks were deceiving. He walked around to the edge of the stage and looked for a particular board on top of the cinderblock foundation. Up next to the stage floor he could run his fingers along the letters MB + AF. He had carved it there one night many years before when he and Mae Beth had walked through the grove and hid themselves in the shadow of the stage. He had never had kisses so sweet as Mae Beth's, and he wanted to make something permanent to remember them. She had stood silently by while he carved their initials into the board. Then they had walked home holding hands.

Stumpy stood there, rubbing his fingers over the old board, feeling the years of grit embedded into the knife cuts. Right then he wished he could just kiss Mae Beth and get the same joy from it as he once had before his love had been burdened with responsibilities. Then the eminently responsible Stumpy Fowler wiped the dust away from the initials and mentally kicked himself in the rear for being ungrateful for all that came with those responsibilities, with being a grown-up. He took one more look at the carving, wiped his fingers on his handkerchief, and started back to the office.

It wasn't until Thursday that he decided he had to do something. He decided he would call A.Y and try to reason with him. He dialed A.Y.'s number and told Gladys that he needed to speak to A.Y.

It was only about a minute before A.Y. picked up the phone.

"What's on your mind, Stumpy?" A.Y. said.

"I've been thinking about this thing with Bessie and the choir, A.Y."

"Yeah, you and everybody else in town. You have any idea how many people have stopped me on the street to talk about that. Then, I think about half of the old ladies in town have called me. I keep telling them that nothing's happened, but most of them act like they don't believe it."

"Maybe something should happen."

There was a silence, just a few seconds of silence, but when A.Y. finally spoke, his voice was guarded, what Stumpy identified as his lawyer voice.

"Exactly what do you mean, Stumpy?"

"I mean I think we should let Bessie's choir sing in the Singing Convention. We let anybody else who's got the entrance fee in without question..."

"As long as they're white."

"Right. As long as they're white, but we don't let one of our local choirs sing, one that we know most of the people in, and the only reason is — they're not white."

"That's enough reason for a lot of folks, Stumpy." His voice changed back to the plain old A.Y. voice. "Look. I don't know whether we ought to let Bessie's choir sing or not. What I do know is that it'll cause a big fuss, and it might wreck a tradition that's put River Falls on the map. I wish you'd talk Bessie into just biding her time. There'll probably be a time when it won't matter if you're colored or white in something like the Singing Convention, but I think that's a long time off. Just ask Bessie to bide her time a bit."

"I already did."

"And what did she say."

"She said she's tired of waiting. That she's been waiting a long time, and it's about time something happened. I don't think those were her exact words, but that's about the gist of it. I think she's planning to do some more stuff like singing on Main Street last Saturday, things that'll keep this stirred up right through the Sing. And it wouldn't surprise me if Bessie and her choir didn't show up across the street from the grove if we don't let them on the stage. That'd be a mess if all those newspaper and television people were here, and we had something going on like that."

"It's not going to happen, Stumpy." A.Y.'s lawyer voice was back. Stumpy might as well have been a jury on the other end of a telephone. "It will not happen. There are laws that must be upheld. There are traditions we have to keep. And while I'm chairman, we will not destroy those traditions. And we will not let anybody break those laws."

"What kind of laws are you talking about, A.Y.? I don't know of anything on the books that says that colored choirs can't sing in a singing convention."

"But there are laws against unlawful assembly and inciting to riot. If they cause a lot of confusion at the Sing, it will likely cause a riot."

Stumpy could no more believe that the taciturn Horace or Bessie would even be in a riot, much less incite one. He could believe that mules would talk like Balaam's ass if that happened, and he started to say so, but A.Y. broke in.

"Stumpy, this is not going to happen. I'll see to it that it doesn't, and you don't want to tangle with me on this." Then he hung up.

Stumpy sat there, the dead phone in his hand. He had never been hung up on before, and in forty-something years of talking to each other, A.Y. had never talked to him like that.

He sat at the desk for a long time, hardly thinking any new thoughts, just the same ones over and over. Several times he reached for the phone to call A.Y. back, but he didn't know what he would say if he talked to him. Once or twice, he picked up a file, thinking it would be better to do some work than sit there with the tape of the telephone call playing in his head, making him madder by the minute. Each time, he shoved the file away and stared at the wall. The next time he looked at his watch, it was five-thirty, a half-hour after he usually left the office. He looked at his desk. All day he had accomplished nothing, not one thing had been checked off his list, and when he had tried to talk to A.Y. to find a reasonable solution for this mess, A.Y. had hung up on him. But only after threatening him. As he thought about it, Stumpy felt his chest get full, like his lungs couldn't get all the air they needed. He opened his mouth and tried to breathe deeply. He wondered if this was the beginning of a heart attack, but he didn't feel any pain in his chest. He sat back in the chair taking deep breaths and realized he was angry and had damn good reason to be. Whether what he was doing was right or not — and he was convinced that it was right — A.Y. had no reason to threaten him or slam down the phone. That's not what friends did when they disagreed, and that's not what they were going to do now.

Stumpy got up from behind the desk, cut off the lights, and walked quickly out the front door. About two steps down the street, he stopped, remembering that he hadn't locked the door. He went back, locked it, and headed toward A.Y. Pollard's office. He hoped that A.Y. was still there, because the conversation he wanted to have with him wasn't one that should be shared with Virginia, or Billy Royce, or Zona Faye. They were at least going to talk about this like grown men, and grown men who had been friends for forty years with no hang ups and no threats, or Stumpy was going to find out exactly why.

The sidewalk was nearly deserted, a few of the store owners closing up. Most of them spoke to Stumpy; he just nodded back to them, not even turning his head. He felt his feet hit the sidewalk in tempo with the pounding in his temple. He noticed his fingers were clinched, and with an effort, he turned his fists back into hands. By the time he got to the bank building and turned the corner to go up the steps, he had the first two or three things he was going to say already in his head. Where it would go from there, he didn't know.

He opened the wide double doors and took the stairs to A.Y.'s office two at the time. The door was closed, but when he turned the knob, it opened. Gladys' desk was neatly cleared, and she wasn't behind it. Stumpy took several quick steps across her office and opened the door to A.Y.'s office. It took him a minute to figure out what he was seeing.

As the door opened, two faces turned to him, almost cheek-to-cheek. The face on the taller body was A.Y.'s. Just a couple of inches below that was the face that belonged to Emil Barnes. Stumpy noticed that Emil didn't have his coat on. Then he noticed that the two men had their arms around each other, like they were holding each other up. Finally, the instant before they turned toward him registered in his mind. They had been kissing. Then they had turned their faces toward him. Finally, they dropped their arms, and A.Y. stepped backward, dropping heavily into his leather chair. Emil just stood there, staring at Stumpy. Stumpy couldn't think of anything to say.

"Why don't you go on, Emil," A.Y. finally said. "I think Stumpy and I have some things to talk about."

Emil reached down, picked his coat up from the floor, and walked quickly by Stumpy, shoving his shirttail back in his pants.

A.Y motioned to a chair, and Stumpy sat down.

A. Y. looked straight at Stumpy. If his eyes hadn't been so tired, it would have been a look of defiance.

"So, I guess you're going to use this," he said softly. "Don't know that I'd blame you. You're doing what you think is right, I guess."

Stumpy shook his head. "I think so. I actually think there's a right way to do this and a wrong way, and we've been doing it the wrong way for a long time."

"We've been doing it the way it's always been done. That's been good enough for me."

"Was for me, too. But about me using it, I'm not going to do that. I wished I hadn't come in here, because this is something I really didn't need to know about. It's sure something that everybody else doesn't need to know about. I'm going to try to forget I ever barged in here."

A.Y. leaned back in his chair, staring at his hands. "I don't know that it'd make all that much difference," he said. "I don't think Virginia cares who I have sex with. As long as it's not her."

Stumpy started to say something about the difference between catching him with another woman and catching him with Emil Barnes, but he decided it didn't really need saying. He got up and started out the open door. Then he stopped and turned.

"Nobody's ever going to hear anything about this from me. Tell Emil that I said that. You and I have been friends a long time. I guess we still will be. That's what I came over to talk to you about. But I also was going to tell you that I think it's time to make a change, and if I can't convince you, we'll still be friends, but we'll be in a fight."

A.Y. nodded his head slowly. "I guess we'll be in a fight. But I won't forget we're friends."

As Stumpy walked slowly down the stairs, he was surprised that his anger, that unfamiliar feeling, had drained out of him. He tried to determine exactly what he felt, but his emotional vocabulary was very small, and it was difficult for him to make fine distinctions. He decided that one thing he felt was sadness, maybe because he had found a friend in the arms of another man. He couldn't think of A.Y. Pollard as queer. Emil had always been a little prissy, but he hadn't thought anything about that. A.Y. was just the opposite, as manly as anybody he knew. They had played football together.

When he got to the street, he turned left instead of right. He'd walk up Church Street and then back over to his house instead of straight up Main Street. He didn't want to run into anybody right now. As he walked, he noticed that his step was lighter than it had been going to A.Y.'s. He couldn't understand why he felt better knowing that A.Y. wasn't going to help him, except that he didn't have to wonder about it anymore. Whatever he did would have to be done on his own.

14

By Monday morning, Stumpy had formulated the skeleton of a plan, had worked out the numbers, made his list, and was ready to begin his campaign. He didn't tell either Mae Beth or Bessie about it. There was no point in either getting their hopes up or getting a lot of advice that would just complicate his thinking. He knew what he had to do: get a majority vote on a motion at the Singing Convention committee meeting.

There were nine people on the Sing committee, and of the nine, one of them never came. Alton Jeffries was eighty-three years old, hard of hearing, and was only on the committee because he had always been on the committee. Nobody really had nerve enough to tell him that he wasn't on the committee any longer.

Of the eight remaining, Stumpy could be sure of one vote. His own. And A.Y. could only vote if there was a tie. So, Stumpy thought when he scratched the figures on a note pad, he needed to find three more votes. That would make it four to three, enough to get the motion passed, and one of those would have to have enough nerve to actually second the motion. That person's name would go down in the minutes, and for all Stumpy knew, in infamy. But any blame anybody else got would be pale beside what was going to fall on Stumpy for bringing it up in the first place. He had already decided he was willing to deal with that. Now all he had to do was decide which three members of the committee he was going to have to convince, and how he was going to convince them.

Callie Turlington was out. He could probably convince her to vote with him, but as soon as he said anything to Callie, it would be all over town, and there was no telling how much pressure would be put on A.Y. to stop him. Somebody might even get him kicked off the committee. Kenneth Adams wouldn't do either. Kenneth had held a grudge for thirty years, and he wasn't about to stop now. It looked like it was down to Gerald Raney, Pete Jennings, and Al Jenkins. It was going to take some selling to get those three votes.

He decided to start with Gerald Raney. Gerald had always been partial to practical jokes, and Stumpy and Gerald had been partners in crime on several occasions, including the time they had climbed the town water tank and painted an improbable suggestion for Principal Morgan. They were disappointed when somebody alerted the city and their artwork had been painted over before many people had a chance to see it, but it had given Stumpy and Gerald a bond that Stumpy felt he could leverage.

Some people say dogs and their masters start looking alike after a while. The same thing was true of Gerald and his insurance office. Gerald had always had some problems with neatness. Even as a teenager, he tended toward fat, and his shirt tail kept coming out of his pants, and his shirts looked either too big or too small since his parents had thought that as fast as Gerald was growing there was no point in buying something that fit him. In fact, it had seemed to Stumpy that all of Gerald's clothes had fit for about fifteen minutes between being too large and too small. Now, Gerald had achieved fat and his belt buckle kept sliding under his belly, and his chins came down over his shirt collar and almost hid the knot of his tie. His office consisted of a front where Gerald's wife, Inez, worked when she came in once a week to file everything and a back where Gerald sat in a worn brown swivel chair behind a desk that showed a clear space about six-inches square. He kept pushing things out of that clear space so that he would have room to sign policies or write checks. Only the fact that Gerald was the only real insurance agent in River Falls (since you couldn't count Fleet Minor who ran the debit route over on Disciple Street) and was the most dependable one in the county if you ran into a problem with the insurance company, kept him in business. If you had a question, Gerald could find your policy, but it took a while.

When Stumpy got to Gerald's office, he could tell it wasn't Inez's day to work. Her desk was covered with manila files of insurance policies, stacks of renewal notices, and other stacks of claims forms. Stumpy walked on to the back to where Gerald was sitting, talking on the telephone.

"I'm sorry, Jerry, but these people have got some rules, and one of them is that they are not going to insure a sixteen-year-old who drives a Thunderbird. That's just the way they are. I can keep you on the policy you got and put Bruce on an assigned risk policy if you'll sign a statement saying he won't drive your car."

Gerald waved at Stumpy and went on listening to Jerry.

"I understand that, Jerry. Bruce ain't ever going to want to drive your Buick if he's got a brand-new Thunderbird, but you still have to sign the form. I'll drop it by your house on my way home tonight, and I'll write up an assigned risk policy for Bruce. When he gets to be twenty-one, he can get off it if he doesn't have any accidents or speeding tickets."

Gerald listened some more.

"That's fine. I'll be by tonight." He hung up, shaking his head and making his second and third chins wobble. "Some people don't have the brains God gave a gnat. Jerry ups and gives his son a brand-new Thunderbird, and the boy just got his driver's license last week. Now he's wondering why Mutual doesn't want to carry the boy's insurance. Because he's an accident waiting to happen, that's why."

He leaned back in his chair and grinned. "Now, what can I do for you, Stumpy?"

Stumpy took a stack of insurance folders off the chair and sat down. "You remember how upset A.Y. got at the last Sing meeting?"

"Yeah, I thought he was going to blow his stack. You really stuck it to him."

That's the reaction he wanted from Gerald. Gerald either didn't understand what he had been trying to do or didn't care. What he remembered is that A.Y. almost exploded over it. After the two men had laughed at the mental image of A.Y. changing colors and about blowing up, Stumpy said, "I've got an idea that will really cause him to bust a gut. If you think he turned purple last time, this'll make him turn twice as purple." Gerald leaned forward and put his elbows in the six inches of clear space on his desk, waiting for Stumpy to go on.

"In the last meeting when I brought it up, I didn't make a motion, so A.Y. just threw a fit, and it didn't go any further," Stumpy said. "Then I got to thinking what he would do if I made it a motion, and he had to take it to a vote. The man would wet his pants."

Gerald had a grin that stretched across his face and faded into a jowl on either side. He was thinking about the pain that this would cause A.Y. and enjoying it. Then the smile faded. "You're talking about making a motion for Bessie's choir to sing in the Singing Convention, aren't you?"

Stumpy nodded. "It'd sure get to old A.Y."

Gerald leaned back in his chair and made a tent of his fingers under his third chin. "I don't know that you ought to do that. It would upset a lot of people. It's just never been done at the Singing Convention." He started swiveling back and forth in his chair, a sure sign that he was getting nervous.

"It'll only upset people if it passes, and it won't pass if just you and me vote for it," Stumpy said. "But it'll never get to a vote if I don't have a second. I make the motion, you second it, and vote for it. We go down in flames and A.Y. has a cow trying to make sure it doesn't pass. It's sort of like the time we put the wagon together up on old man Pinter's front porch and they had to take it apart to get it off. That didn't do anything, but we had a lot of fun watching them get over it."

Gerald chuckled. "Or the time we dammed the creek and let it overflow into Mr. Brown's watermelon patch," he said. Then he caught himself. "That wasn't a good example. All the watermelons rotted. But I know what you mean."

He sat there, swiveling back and forth for a minute. "You sure this thing won't go through," he said, finally.

"You're kidding. Who would vote for it? Besides you and me, I mean."

"Yeah. I guess." He looked very serious for about thirty seconds, then the grin came back. "Okay, count me in."

"Good. This'll be fun."

"I'm just glad A.Y. don't have a heart condition."

Stumpy left the insurance office mentally chalking up one vote. It crossed his mind that, unfortunately, this was the easiest one. Gerald had always been ready to do almost anything to anybody that didn't really hurt them and just hurt their pride or dignity. He drew the line at anything that caused real property damage. Even as a teenager, he must have had some insurance agent in him.

Back out on the street, Stumpy was trying to decide whether he would make his next stop Pete Jenning's service station or Al Jenkin's hardware store. The hardware store was closer, but Stumpy figured that Pete was going to be an easier target than Al, so he would start there and work up. He walked the two blocks to the service station. When he got there, Pete was pumping gas for Mrs. Blackmon's Cadillac. Stumpy walked inside and pulled an RC Cola out of the drink cooler. He opened it and waited for Pete to come back inside. Since it was Mrs. Blackmon that he was waiting on, Stumpy knew it would be a while. Mrs. Blackmon didn't get out much, but when she did, she made the most of it.

It took Pete a good five minutes to fill up Mrs. Blackmon's car, check the oil and the tires, and wash the windshield to her satisfaction. When he came back in, smoothing out three one-dollar bills, he greeted Stumpy. "You know Mrs. Blackmon has a boyfriend," he said.

"Nope. Haven't been keeping up with Mrs. Blackmon's love life."

"She's off to meet him for dinner now."

Stumpy looked at his watch. "Sort of early. Just three-thirty."

Pete put the money in the cash drawer. "Yeah. I guess dating is kind of hard when you're too old to drive at night. I noticed you walked here. Your car somewhere I need to go get it?"

In addition to running the service station, Pete also had the only towing service in town. He probably knew more about the love life of River Falls's teenagers than anybody else because of the times he had had to go jump start their cars after they had been parked for two or three hours with the radio on. But Pete wasn't likely to tell.

"No. I just need to talk with you about something."

"Okay." Pete plopped his long body down in the rocker he kept in the station office. "So talk."

"You remember when you and Frances were having

trouble a couple of years ago," Stumpy said. From the cloud that passed over Pete's face Stumpy knew he was remembering getting kicked out of the house because his wife thought that when he was going out on towing calls at night he was really meeting Hazel McQuorqendale, a waitress at the truck stop on the highway. No amount of denying it could change Frances' mind, and one night he came back from towing a tourist's car into the station to find all of his clothes out in the front yard. He loaded his clothes up into his tow truck and drove to Stumpy's house. Stumpy had let him sleep in the spare bedroom for several nights, even though Mae Beth raised Cain because she thought he was taking up for somebody who was running around on his wife. Frances had finally calmed down, especially when Pete showed her the towing bills for the nights she thought he was out with Hazel. Then he moved back home. Just to be safe, he usually took Frances with him on the towing calls at night.

"Yeah, I remember. I'll never forget."

"I think I helped you out a little during that. You agree?"

"You must want something real bad to bring that up. You know I owe you."

"Okay. But this isn't going to be easy. And if you say you can't do it, I'll understand. But my life at home will still be hell." Stumpy figured that Pete could understand a ruptured home life easier than he could purely a question of right and wrong. It wouldn't hurt Mae Beth to have part of the blame for this, so far as Pete was concerned.

"What's going on with you and Mae Beth?" Pete asked. "I thought y'all always got along better than anybody I knew."

"We do... or we did. She wants me to do something, and if I don't get it done, I don't know what she'll do." Stumpy didn't have any problem looking appropriately worried. "She wants me to get Bessie Williams' choir into the Singing Convention. She says that if I don't, Bessie'll probably quit, and I don't know what Mae Beth will do after that."

Pete pulled a tire gauge out of his pocket and started pulling the stick out and pushing it back in.

"I wondered what that was about when you brought it up at the last meeting, but you didn't seem real concerned about it."

"That was before I told Mae Beth that I hadn't gotten it through. I thought if I made a pass at it she and Bessie would figure I'd done my best and let it go. Seems like Bessie isn't letting it go; so Mae Beth isn't." Stumpy took a big breath and let his next sentence come out as one long string of words. "I'm going to make a motion at the next meeting that we let the A.M.E. choir compete in the Singing Convention, and I need you to vote with me on it."

It took Pete a minute to separate the sentence into individual words and process them. "You know if I vote for this it could cost me a bunch of business, don't you?"

"I imagine it might cost you some for a little while, but you have the only tow truck in the area. I don't think anybody's going to stay stuck somewhere just because you voted to let the negra's sing at the Convention. Besides, I think I can get this voted on with a secret ballot. Nobody has to know how anybody voted."

"How you going to do that?"

"A couple of years ago, Callie, Emil, and I were appointed to review the organizational constitution and by-laws and make sure there wasn't anything that could get us in trouble with the IRS. We went over it line by line, and we only made a couple of changes. But one of the things I remember is that anybody can request a secret ballot on anything. I don't think anybody ever has, but I'll ask for it on this."

"You really want Bessie's choir to sing? You know that'll cause an awful fuss."

"I really don't care if Bessie's choir sings or not. Doesn't bother me, but I wouldn't go through all this for it. What does bother me is that Mae Beth is treating me like something that grows between her toes, and the looks that Bessie gives me would chill the ice tea. I want my home back and if I have to lean on people to get it, I will." It amazed Stumpy how easy it was for him to lie to Pete. He was just having to make sure he didn't lay it on too thick.

Pete held up his hand. "You don't have to get all excited with me. I owe you, and I'll do it. But I do hope you can get it made with a secret ballot. You don't know how easy it is for people to complain to somebody who's pumping their gas."

Stumpy put his RC bottle in the crate. "I appreciate that, Pete. I hated to ask you, but—like I said—I'm desperate. Now if I can just get Al to vote with us."

"You think Al Jenkins is going to vote to let the negras sing? You're kidding. Or did his wife throw him out of the house, too?"

"No, I'll just have to come up with some logical way to persuade him."

"Good luck on that."

* * *

"You'd do what!"

Al Jenkins, owner of River Falls Hardware, was a deacon in the Baptist Church and president of the Kiwanis Club. It was in the latter capacity that he and Stumpy went to Atlanta to a convention, and they had explored some of the nightlife. Right now, Al's hands shook so much that the bolts he was pouring into the hardware bin started falling on the floor. Stumpy bent over to help him pick them up. As they were putting the bolts in the bin, Stumpy slowly shook his head, a mournful expression on his face.

"I've been carrying this burden around a long time, and I guess, in my discomfort, I might start rambling. I might even talk about that lady from the..." Stumpy stopped and scratched his head. "What was the name of that place again? You know, the one where you got so friendly with the hired help."

Al just sat there, his face getting redder and redder, pressing his lips tighter and tighter together.

Stumpy got up and walked over to a rack where the wrenches were displayed. "Oh, yeah. It was called the Zebra Lounge and the lady's name was Celeste."

"You were there, too. How you going to explain that?"

"Yeah, like you, I wandered into the place by mistake. I thought it was some sort of cultural thing. But when I left,

I went back to the hotel, by myself. Who knows where you went with that Celeste lady."

"You know, I didn't go anywhere with her. I didn't do anything. You know that."

Stumpy leaned it back against the counter. "I know that. But you think anybody in this town would believe that, especially as slow as the gossip's been lately. By the time Hattie Mae Langdon gets hold of it, she'll have you and old Celeste building a love nest in Phenix City, Alabama and producing a whole brood of love children."

Slowly, Al let the breath escape through his compressed lips, like he was a tire going down. His shoulders sagged. He looked at Stumpy.

"But we've been friends. How can you do that to me? We were in the first grade together."

"I know. I don't want to. But Mae Belle's been giving me hell for a month now, and she's going to go on doing that until I get this done. So I'm going to get it done. I'll try to make sure you don't get any of the blame. I'll try to get it on a secret ballot." Stumpy figured that Al was another one who could understand the need for marital harmony better than he could questions about right and wrong. He wondered if this wouldn't have been easier if Mae Beth had just continued to be mad, cold, and distant. It was considerably more incentive than questions of morality.

Al nodded. "Yeah, get it on a secret ballot."

Stumpy started to leave, and Al stood up and leaned over the counter. "I want you to know something. I really don't care if Bessie's choir sings. I've known Bessie and Horace a long time, and I think that if anybody means it when they sing gospel music, it's Bessie. It's just not something I'd want to cause a fuss about. I don't want to cause a fuss about much of anything."

That night Stumpy lay on his back on the bed, watching Mae Beth brushing her hair. They hadn't said very much to each other since he had gotten home; each one of them had been caught up in their separate thoughts. Li'l had tried to start a conversation at dinner, but after a while he gave up, too, and retreated to his own thoughts. As Stumpy lay on the bed, waiting for Mae Beth to finish brushing her hair, he wondered why it was so hard for anybody to do anything just because it was the right thing. It was easy enough for him to convince Pete and Al that he was leaning on them because Mae Beth had cut him off. They understood that. But he probably would have never convinced them to go out on a limb because it wasn't right to keep Bessie's choir out of the Singing Convention. They had been a part of River Falls since long before a lot of the people who did sing there. At first, he'd done what he'd done not because it was right, but because of Mae Beth. And Mae Beth had done what she had done because she didn't want to lose Bessie. He shrugged in his mind; who knew why Bessie had done what she'd done.

"I had an interesting day today," he said to Mae Beth's back. She didn't answer.

"I lied to one friend. I called in a big favor from another one. And I blackmailed another one."

Mae Beth quit brushing her hair and looked at him.

"I got the votes to get Bessie into the Singing Convention — if everybody does what they say they're going to and I can get A.Y. to let us vote on it."

Mae Beth put the brush down and walked over to the bed.

"I got the votes, but I don't think my friends are really going to think the same way about me, now."

Mae Beth sat down on the edge of the bed. "Was it that hard?"

"It was every bit that hard. But you know what, I learned some things. One of them is that Bessie is probably right. But folks probably don't do much just because it was right. I think maybe I did, but I know I started this because I love you."

Tears welled up in Mae Beth's eyes, and one made a shiny trail down her cheek. She wiped it off. "I love you, too," she said. Then she lay down beside Stumpy and pulled him to her, burying her head into his shoulder. "I'm sorry it was so hard."

FROM THE RIVER FALLS CURRENT
Thursday, May 10, 1956

CONGRESSMAN TYLER PREDICTS RECORD TOBACCO
PRICES

Congressman Richard Tyler predicted record tobacco prices for 1956 in a speech to the Oak Grove Farmer's Cooperative. Noting that flue-cured tobacco was essential for making fine cigarettes, he said that he had been involved in writing laws to prevent tobacco imports from the Middle East.

Tyler also noted that stabilization prices are being held at 1955 levels despite efforts by urban congressmen to lower them.

Henderson's Barbecue catered the meeting, and Congressman Tyler pronounced it to be among the best he'd ever eaten.

15

So far as Stumpy could tell, the rest of the week had gone by without anything unusual happening. Whenever he ran into Emil downtown, Emil spoke, but he wouldn't look Stumpy in the eye. Stumpy couldn't really blame him. Uninvited thoughts had invaded Stumpy's nighttime hours wondering what A.Y. and Emil were about to do or had done before. He told the thoughts that things like that were none of his business, but they came back anyway. Stumpy couldn't understand it and really didn't want to.

When he had gone to church that morning, most of the talk was about the new preacher the Methodists were getting and whether any of the Methodists would get upset enough to come down to the Baptist Church. Stumpy just stood on the edge of the knot of men gathered in front of the church and listened. He wondered what they would be saying if they had known what he was about to do.

Stumpy wandered away from the men toward the front of the church. He was trying to think if there was anything in all the sermons he'd heard that would help him know if he should do what he had decided to do.

* * *

At the Bethel A.M.E. church the choir had sung, and the Reverend Alonzo Pickens had just about wound up his sermon. Some of his congregants were sweating from Amening and yes, Jesusing so hard. His sermon had been on faith and its uses.

"If you go into a fight you're supposed to win, that isn't faith. Goliath didn't need any faith to fight David. Goliath was bigger. Goliath was stronger. Goliath carried a spear that was taller than David. For him to go out on the battle-field and face that boy didn't take faith. It was just common sense that he was going to win."

There was a small chorus of Amens and That's Rights. Mostly the congregation just sat there, waiting for Reverend Pickens to go on.

"But, not so with David. He was just a boy. He couldn't even carry the armor that you needed to go into that kind of fight. He didn't have a sword. He didn't have a spear. What he did have was...faith." The congregation was with him now, nodding and affirming. He went on.

"It doesn't show our faith when all we do is what we know we can do. It shows our faith when we step out onto the battlefield against the giant and his huge weapons with nothing more than a few smooth stones and a belief that

God is on our side. Then we testify." He turned and looked at Bessie, sitting quietly in her seat in her clean choir robe. "Then we testify we are people of God who know the power of God. This week I charge you to go out and live in faith, doing what you're supposed to do, whether it is the possible or not. Remember, through God all things are possible.

"And what I'm going to do, to show my faith, is very simple. This Tuesday night, the Singing Convention Committee will hold its last meeting before this year's Convention. It will be the last time this year that they will have an opportunity to consider Sister Bessie's request that the Bethel A.M.E. church choir compete. I plan to be at that meeting. I don't know what good it will do. I don't have a vote. I don't have any way to influence those men who do have a vote. But I believe God has something in store for us if we're there to take it. And I plan to be there. If any of you would like to be there with me, you'd be welcome."

He looked around at Bessie again, and she smiled and nodded. Then she got up to lead the congregation in the invitation hymn.

16

Stumpy Fowler was tying his tie and planning his day. Now that he had told Mae Beth he had the votes to get Bessie's choir into the Singing Convention, he had to make sure he delivered. As much as Mae Beth had appreciated what he had done already, he wasn't sure she would really understand if it didn't work. But, he thought as he straightened the knot in his tie, the next part should be simple. Callie Turlington would be a lot easier to deal with than Gerald, Pete, and Al. He started planning his lie even as he put on his coat, kissed Beth good-bye, and left the house. Since the library didn't open until ten o'clock, he had time to go by the office and get some work done.

At ten o'clock sharp, Stumpy got up from his desk, put on his coat, and walked around the corner to the River Falls Town Library. The library was upstairs over the police station and firehouse in the red brick building that served as the City Hall. The rest of the upstairs space was used once a week for Recorder's Court. Stumpy opened the door of the library and saw Callie sitting behind her desk, stamping books. Stumpy had always thought that if any woman was born to be a librarian, it had to be Callie. She had been a bookworm in high school and an English major in college until she'd had to quit to take care of her mother. Except for her clothes — a skirt and sweater — she could have been a librarian in the twenties instead of the fifties.

Callie had heard the door and looked up from her work.

"Hello, Stumpy," she said. "You decide to take up reading?"

It was an old joke. Callie knew that since high school the only thing that Stumpy Fowler read was the newspaper, IRS memos, and an occasional magazine.

"No, I just need to borrow something."

Callie got up from behind her desk and put some books on the shelf. "Well, you've come to the right place. This is a lending library."

"I need a copy of the constitution and bylaws for the Singing Convention." He caught her sharp glance at him, and added, "I just saw something in an IRS circular that might cause a problem with our tax-exempt status. I thought I better check it before the meeting tomorrow night."

Callie nodded, and from her nod, Stumpy couldn't tell whether she had bought his lie or not. But she didn't question it. She just went back to her desk and pulled out a file folder and handed it to him. "Please make sure I get this back, Stumpy. I don't think there are but two copies, and I don't know who has the other one now."

"I'll have it back to you by this afternoon."

Callie nodded and began stamping the books again.

For the rest of the morning, Stumpy stayed in his office reading the constitution and by-laws. They had been written by a lawyer nearly thirty years earlier and suffered from both legal language and what the lawyer evidently considered eloquence. Finally, he found the passage that said — when translated into plain English — everything would be decided by a voice vote, unless a written ballot was requested by any member of the committee. Stumpy had been on the committee for nearly six years, and he could never remember anything ever requiring a written ballot. But, he thought, tomorrow night is going to change that.

* * *

In late May, when the days are growing longer and the nights are still cool, there are people alone or in couples strolling down the sidewalks of River Falls on nearly every street. On Disciple Street, where they didn't have sidewalks, the people strolled along the edge of the dirt street. It was a calming-down time of the day for most of them. But for one figure slowly walking along Main Street with his hands behind his back, nothing was very calm.

When A.Y. Pollard had gotten home from the store that evening he had, as usual, pecked his wife on the cheek, picked up the afternoon newspaper, and gone into the living room to read the paper and watch the six o'clock news on television. Virginia knew that she shouldn't have supper until six-thirty. But on this evening, he never made it to his big brown chair.

"Leola says that Reverend Pickens is going to the committee meeting tomorrow night," she said as he was walking out of the kitchen.

He turned and stared at her for a moment, not sure he had heard what he knew he had heard.

"Did she say why he was going to do that?"

"It's about Bessie Williams and the choir. Leola was really upset. She's afraid it's going to cause you trouble."

"She's right about that. I thought we were done with this thing about the negra choir."

He walked back into the kitchen and leaned against the counter. He rubbed his hand over his face.

"I told Leola that you wouldn't be upset, that you had a lot of respect for Reverend Pickens."

"I do. He's a good man. I just don't see why he has to mix into this. It's going to cause problems."

He looked at Virginia, hoping to see understanding in her face, but what he saw was confusion. "I don't understand why this is such a problem," she said. "When Charley Townsend died, we went to see his family at his house, and we went to the A.M.E. church for the funeral."

"Charley worked for me. He'd worked for me for ten years or more, and I owed it to his family to pay my respects. This is different. This is a public function."

"Yes, it is. But I remember the A.M.E. choir that sang at that funeral sang beautifully. It might be a good thing if a lot of white people could hear them."

"Virginia, I'm chairman of the Sing Committee. It's my

job to make sure the Sing is orderly and successful, and orderly means doing things like we've been doing them, not making a bunch of changes. If somebody else wants to take a lot of chances and make a lot of changes, they can when they are chairman, but I have to do my job."

And he turned and walked into the living room, wondering why Leola, who was black and not married to him, seemed to understand his problem so much better than Virginia who was not black and was married to him.

17

Stumpy Fowler was over a block from the bank when he noticed that something was going on. There was a crowd of people standing on the sidewalk waiting to get in. Up near the door, Reverend Amos Pickens was talking to Reverend Grant McLamb of the Pentecostal Holiness Church. Around them stood a knot of Negroes, all dressed as if they were ready for church. Scattered around on the sidewalk were probably two dozen more people. At the edge of the crowd, A.Y. Pollard was deep in conversation with Gerald Raney and Pete Jennings. Stumpy walked over to where they were.

"I don't see why we can't just go on up to your office and just leave them all standing on the sidewalk," Pete was saying. "It's your office."

A.Y. shook his head. "But it's a public meeting. Always has been. I don't like the idea of locking them out of a public meeting."

"What's going on?" Stumpy asked.

A.Y. looked at him. "You tell me. I figured you had something to do with this."

Stumpy shook his head. "Not me. I was just expecting our regular bunch. Why are all these people here?

"All I know is Reverend Pickens told everybody in church Sunday that he was coming to the meeting tonight to see why his choir can't be in the Singing Convention. Best I can make out, Reverend McLamb came down to help Reverend Pickens, and all the negras are here because Reverend Pickens invited them. I guess the other people just came to watch the fun." The expression on A.Y.s face made it clear he didn't consider it fun.

"We sure can't get all these people in your office," Stumpy said.

"I don't want to hold it down in the store. There's no place to sit down, and who knows what kind of merchandise would walk off when the meeting's over."

The four men stood there, looking at the crowd that seemed to be getting bigger. Stumpy saw Claymore Thomas walk up, his face looking like a thunderstorm about to happen. Claymore stood away from Reverend Pickens and his congregation.

"Why don't we take this over to the courtroom," Stumpy said. "There's plenty of room there."

A.Y. considered the idea. "Isn't it locked up?"

"Only the downstairs door. And Callie has a key to that. They don't lock the courtroom because there's nothing in there to steal."

"I guess that's as good an idea as any," A.Y. said. He turned to the crowd. "Folks, we're going to have our meeting over at the courtroom as soon as Callie gets here to unlock the door." Before he had even finished saying it, Callie Turlington came rushing up with a key in her hand.

As everyone crossed the street and went down Hargett Street to the city hall/fire station/library/courthouse, Stumpy was trying to decide what all these people would do to his plans. Part of his argument with Gerald had been that nobody else would be voting to let the A.M.E. choir in. If he thought that somebody else would, he probably wouldn't. To Gerald it wasn't a practical joke if something big actually happened. It could be that Reverend Pickens and his people might scare Al and Pete off, too. He had his plans all laid out, but they were based on a nice, quiet committee meeting without a lot of spectators. There was nothing he could do about it now. Just go and hope that Mae Beth and Bessie would give him some points for trying.

When they got to the door going up the steps to the courthouse, Callie unlocked it, and Stumpy held it open for the people to enter. Most of them spoke to him pleasantly, with the negroes generally saying, "Evening, Mr. Stumpy." As they passed, Stumpy calculated that almost half the group were Negroes, including Reverend Pickens and Bessie and Horace Williams. When Bessie passed, she just looked at Stumpy, nodded and smiled. Obviously, Mae Beth had told her that Stumpy had the vote in the bag. Stumpy let out a long breath; he just wished it was so.

By the time Stumpy got upstairs, the people had already found their seats. The room was, for a courtroom, almost makeshift. Although the elevated Judge's bench at the front of the room was stained a dark brown and tried hard to impersonate mahogany, it was obviously put together out of plywood. The two tables in front of the judge's bench were just light-colored wooden tables brought over from the library and the seats that the spectators were in were second-hand church pews. It was a big room because on Monday mornings there were a lot of traffic cases to try from the weekend before. A.Y. had climbed up behind the Judge's bench; the committee was sitting around the prosecution and defense tables, and most of the other people were sitting in the pews. The Reverends Pickens and McLamb had taken the relative comfort of the padded chairs in the jury box. From his place above the crowd on the Judge's bench, A.Y. was looking around uneasily. He tried to smile.

"I don't know why we suddenly got so popular," he said. "Everybody knows these committee meetings are pretty boring. Most of the time we have a hard time just getting the members of the committee here." He chuckled, but nobody joined him. He swallowed hard. "Callie, would you read the minutes of the last meeting?"

Stumpy raised his hand. "I move we dispense with the reading of the minutes. I've been on this committee for six years, and we've never changed the minutes yet."

"Second," said Gerald Raney.

"I don't know if we can do that or not," A.Y. said. "We always read the minutes."

Kenneth Adams was already wondering how long this meeting would last; there was a program on television that he wanted to see at nine-thirty. Anything that would save some time was a good idea to him. He raised his hand.

"A.Y., seems like you got a motion and a second on the floor. All you need to do is see whether there's any discussion and take a vote."

"But don't our by-laws say we have to read the minutes."

Stumpy raised his hand. "Nope, all they say is we have to record the minutes, and Callie does that every time."

"Okay, is there any discussion?" The members of the committee just sat there. "All in favor of dispensing with the reading of the minutes for this meeting say 'Aye.'" There was a chorus of "Ayes." "All opposed, say 'No.'" Silence. "Well, I guess we won't read the minutes tonight."

He looked at his notes. "The next thing on the agenda is the concessions. Malcolm Haller from Oak Grove wants to bring his hot dog wagon again this year and is willing to pay the same thing he paid last year. Anybody got any problem with that?" He looked at the committee at the prosecution table and the defense table. They were all shaking their head. "This year the Baptist Church wants to put a tent on the corner of the Singing Grove and give away lemonade. They don't think they ought to have to pay anything since they are not charging for it."

Emil Barnes raised his hand. "Do we have anybody else who wants that corner who is willing to pay for it?" Emil was a Methodist and wasn't willing to give the Baptists an unfair advantage.

"I don't think so. About everybody who has contacted me wanted their same place from last year. We put the First Aid tent on the back corner where we had it. Then we have the people who sell the Singing Convention souvenirs across the street, along with Mrs. Myrtle who always sells sandwiches. On the other corner, there's the barbecue wagon, and that's about it."

"I don't know," Emil said. "That's a prime spot, and I don't think we ought to give it away for nothing."

"Doesn't seem to be anybody who wants to pay for it," Gerald Raney said. He was a Baptist. In fact, he was head of the church committee to make the lemonade for the Sing.

"But we don't know that. It's nearly a month until the Singing Convention," Emil said, his voice getting a little prissy as it often did when he got mad.

Stumpy looked at the spectators. Some of them were fascinated with this battle between the Baptists and the Methodists. Some of them were bored, and a few of them were squirming in their seats, obviously waiting for something more exciting. He decided it was time to get off this subject.

"I make a motion that we tell the Baptists they can have that corner for their free lemonade unless we get a commercial offer before the Sing. If somebody makes us a better offer, we just move the Baptists across the street in front of the dress shop."

"Second," said Kenneth Adams. He looked at his watch. It was already a quarter 'til eight.

A.Y. went through the rest of his agenda without argument. As he droned on about entry fee receipts and new entries, Stumpy watched Reverend Pickens. He sat there, occasionally saying something to Reverend McLamb or chuckling at something Reverend McLamb said to him, but appearing to be the soul of patience. Stumpy wished he could have talked to the Reverend before the meeting; everything had been worked out, and it would have been over with. Now he just had to see what happened. The change in A.Y.'s voice interrupted his thoughts. "So, if there's no new business, I'll hear a motion to adjourn."

Stumpy started to stand up, but Reverend Perkins, still sitting, said, "Mr. Pollard, I would like to ask you and your committee a question?" There was a stirring among the spectators; they were finally getting to what they had come to see. A.Y. looked at Reverend Pickens, then he looked at the members of the committee, hoping somebody would say something that would let them avoid a scene with the Reverend. The members of the committee just sat there. Finally, A.Y. sighed, looked at his watch, and said, "Certainly, Reverend Perkins, but could we make it quick. We usually try to adjourn by eight-thirty."

Reverend Pickens nodded. "Yes, sir. I only want to ask one question. Shouldn't take a minute."

Stumpy looked from Reverend Pickens to A.Y. and then at the committee members sitting at the defense table. Everything seemed to be stopped in time. The Reverend was still sitting, looking perfectly relaxed, a small smile on his dark face. A.Y. was leaning forward as if bracing himself. Two of the three committee members at the defense table were leaning back, Kenneth Adams staring at a blank spot on the table, and Emil Barnes making a steeple of his fingers under his chin. Only Callie Turlington was leaning forward, her fountain pen poised above her legal pad, ready to take down the Reverend's question.

"You know my church has been a part of River Falls

for more than sixty years. And I believe this is the twenty-ninth Annual Singing convention," Reverend Pickens said.

"That's all true, Reverend. What is your question?"

Stumpy was amazed that A.Y.'s voice was so controlled. He was wound up so tight that he looked like he was about to bounce from behind the Judge's bench like a frog.

"Just this, Mr. Pollard. In the twenty-nine years the Bethany A.M.E. Church has shared this community with the Annual Singing Convention, why have we not been a part of it even one time? But more important, why can't we right this situation this year?" There was a murmur of "Yes, sir," and "That's right" from the Negroes in the crowd.

Stumpy noted that Callie was writing furiously, evidently taking the Reverend's remarks down word for word. He also noted the fleeting changes of expression on A.Y.'s face. Stumpy thought that if you could project the inside of the chairman's head onto the wall you'd see a bunch of little wheels turning furiously. Stumpy turned his attention back to Reverend Pickens. He just sat there, very calm, waiting for an answer. Reverend McLamb sat beside him, contentedly, like a man digesting a good dinner. From where he sat, it looked to Stumpy that the Negro preacher and the white preacher were more alike than they were different. They both sat there like they knew they were on the side of the angels. In fact, they were the calmest people in the room.

"All I can tell you, Reverend, is that the rules for the Singing Convention were written into our constitution and by-laws years ago, and we've never changed them. Changing them might cause us problems with the IRS."

That's pretty weak, Stumpy thought. He'd been on the committee to review and change the by-laws just three years earlier. He started to mention that, but he decided to wait and see what the preacher would say.

Reverend Pickens nodded his head. "I see," he said, "and your rules say that Negroes can't be in your Singing Convention?"

"We do have rules about who can compete. Yes."

"Could you tell me just what those requirements are, Mr. Pollard."

For all the urgency, anger, and emotion in his voice, the preacher might have said, "Would you please pass the buttermilk, Mr. Pollard?" Stumpy thought about "Come into my parlor said the spider to the fly." Just based on the tones of their voices, it sounded like A.Y. might not be a match for Reverend Pickens, but as chairman, it was his job.

"I wish I could, Reverend, but since we didn't know you were going to ask that question, we didn't bring a copy of the constitution and by-laws with us tonight. I'll be glad to look it up and let you know."

Stumpy had to admit that A.Y. had scored one there. If he could put the question off to the next meeting, the Sing would be over, and the committee would have a year to figure out how to keep the A.M.E. choir out of the convention. But Stumpy couldn't let that happen.

"Uh, A.Y., I have a copy of the constitution and by-laws right here. You want me to look up what it says about who can compete?"

A.Y. Pollard whipped around. The purple color was rising from his collar, a sure sign that A.Y. was about to pop.

He glared at Stumpy. Stumpy just smiled and held up the stack of papers.

"Thank you, Mr. Fowler. I'd like to know what it says," Reverend Pickens said, and Stumpy started flipping through the pages. A.Y. sat up on the judge's bench watching the exchange, but essentially left out.

"Here it is," Stumpy said. "Basically, it says they have to sing Christian music, and they have to pay the entry fees. That's five dollars for solos, quartets, and other small groups, and ten dollars for choirs. That's about all it says."

Reverend Pickens nodded again. "Well, we do sing Christian music. In fact, we sing it mighty fine." There were some "amens" from the spectators. "And we can pay the entry fee. So does that mean the Bethany A.M.E. choir can sing in the Singing Convention?"

Stumpy turned to look at the spectators. The Negroes, sitting in one corner of the room, waited expectantly. The whites were beginning to squirm. Suddenly Claymore Thomas stood up. "No, it don't," he said, and everybody turned to look at him. He was a good twenty feet from Reverend Pickens, but he stared at him like he was trying to pin him to the wall. Maybe Claymore had used that look to intimidate Negroes before, but it was obvious that Reverend Pickens had stood up to more than a Klansman's anger. Stumpy waited for A.Y. to call Claymore down, but he looked like he'd been left behind somewhere. The group of Negroes in the corner seemed to sink back in their seats. One or two of the whites began to smile, either because they thought that somebody was going to take their side or just because they liked to see a good fight. The committee members sitting at the table up front might as well have been cast in concrete; they didn't move, and they didn't say a word. Everybody just looked from Claymore Thomas to the Reverend and back again.

"I didn't know you were a member of the committee, Mr. Thomas, but perhaps you can tell us why we can't sing if we pay the entry fee."

"Because it ain't done. Because it's never been done, and because it ain't ever going to be done. Niggers are in one place, and white people are in another place. And you, preacher, ought to know that. It's in the Bible."

Reverend Pickens started to say something, but Reverend McLamb put his hand on his arm. Slowly, using the arm of the chair for support, Reverend McLamb got to his feet. It was like watching a wall unfold. When he was finally at full height, he turned toward Claymore Thomas and smiled.

"Mr. Thomas, I'm seventy-five years old, and ever since I can remember there's been somebody saying the Negro should stay in his place. And every single time those same people wanted to say what the Negroes' place was. And more times than not they said something about the Bible to prove their point. I believe I've read the Bible as much as most folks, and I have never seen anything in it that says Negroes can't sing in the Singing Convention. Or for that matter, that Negroes can't eat in restaurants with whites or even that Negroes shouldn't go to school with whites."

Two white men among the spectators got up and left the room. Stumpy supposed their disagreement with what Reverend McLamb was saying, especially as a white man, had overcome their curiosity and their desire to watch the contest. It was just like the Saturday baseball games he used to play. It was all right for the Negroes and the whites to be in the same game as long as they weren't on the same side. Reverend McLamb had just shown himself to be on the other side, and those two men couldn't deal with that.

"The Bible says that they will be 'hewers of wood and drawers of water.'"

"I do like to discuss the Bible, Mr. Thomas, but sometimes people just take a piece of something and don't take the rest. Like this one. You're talking about Joshua nine and twenty-three. It's one of my favorite stories, because it shows what happens when people try to deceive the Lord. These people were Gibeonites, Mr. Thomas, but I don't believe they stand for Negroes or whites or even Jews for that matter. I think they stand for anybody who thinks he can deceive God. You might want to think about that."

Stumpy looked at A.Y., wondering when or if he was going to try to get his meeting back under control. Obviously A.Y. was uncomfortable calling down a preacher, but if he didn't, Claymore and Reverend McLamb could be at it all night. Finally, Stumpy raised his hand, and A.Y., looking like he had been startled from a deep sleep, broke into the debate. "Excuse me, Reverend McLamb, but we need to get on to the business of the committee." He turned to Stumpy. "You got something to say, Stumpy."

Reverend McLamb lowered his bulk into the chair, and Claymore Thomas sat down. Now that he had the floor, Stumpy had to figure out something to say.

"Well, Mr. Chairman, it seems like Reverend Pickens

has brought up a good point. There's nothing in the Singing Convention constitution and by-laws that says that the Negro choir can't sing."

There was a mummer from the spectators, but Kenneth Adams voice overrode it. "But that doesn't mean they can," he said, loudly enough to be heard by everybody in the room. "The constitution and by-laws also say that all entries have to be accepted by a vote of the committee. We haven't voted on it." He looked at his watch again.

"So... let's vote on it," Stumpy said, trying to sound a whole lot more casual than he felt. The original idea had been to do this by a vote. The only difference was there were more people watching, and what he had hoped would be a typically boring committee meeting had turned into a spectacular.

"We don't have a motion to vote on," Kenneth said. "You have to have a motion before you can have a vote."

The physical possibility of two men squaring off from a sitting position is slight, but Stumpy and Kenneth managed to do it. It was the adult version of the school yard "go ahead, hit me." Stumpy, still trying to sound like it wasn't a big deal, raised his hand and said, "Mr. Chairman, I move that we approve the verbal application of the Bethany A.M.E. choir to sing in the 1956 Singing Convention."

There was loud applause from the Negroes sitting in the corner of the courtroom. There was equally loud booing from a small group of whites. For the most part, the white spectators were just sitting there waiting to see what was going to happen next.

A.Y. was looking at Stumpy as if Stumpy was something that A.Y. had just stepped in. Then he looked at each of the other committee members, evidently hoping that one of them would come up with a miracle that would get him out of this mess. Nobody said a word.

"We have a motion to accept the application of the Bethany A.M.E. Church. Is there a second?"

Stumpy looked at Gerald, willing him to second the motion. Gerald shook his head and scribbled a note on the yellow pad in front of him. He pushed it over to Stumpy.

"I can't do this. It's not a joke anymore."

That about sank it anyway. Without Gerald, Stumpy only had three votes. It didn't really matter whether he got a second or not, he would lose. The silence lengthened, and A.Y. was getting noticeably brighter.

Stumpy looked at Pete and Al. They were both studying the top of the tables in front of them.

"Is there a second? If there's no second..."

"I second the motion."

Stumpy didn't even have to look up to see who had seconded it. There was only one female on the committee, and the voice that made the second was female. When he looked, Callie Turlington was noting her second in the minutes of the meeting.

A.Y. squirmed in his chair. "We have a motion and a second. Is there any discussion?" He hesitated a moment, then added, "From members of the committee?"

"I think we all know what we're talking about here, A.Y.," Kenneth Adams said. "Let's get on with it."

Stumpy stood up. "I have another motion."

"We already have a motion we haven't voted on," A.Y. said.

"This one has to do with how we vote on the other one. I move that we vote by paper ballot rather than voice vote."

"What do you mean? We've always voted by voice vote."

"This is a waste of time," Kenneth said.

"I second the motion." It was Callie again.

"Why do you want to do this, Stumpy," A.Y. asked. "Yeas and nays have been good enough for everything else we've done."

"Doesn't matter," Stumpy said. He held up the copy of the constitution again. "The constitution says that any committee member can request the vote be taken by paper ballot on any motion. I've made a motion; we have a second. All we need now is a vote."

The courtroom was hushed. It was like Dragnet, with Joe Friday toe-to-toe with the bad guys, although there would have been severe disagreement among the spectators about which were good guys and which were bad guys. A.Y. didn't move. Stumpy just stood there. And nobody else said anything. Finally, A.Y. said, "Okay, we'll vote on whether the vote on the motion will be by voice vote or paper." Then he looked at Stumpy. "Unless you want to make a motion that this vote has to be done on paper, too."

Stumpy just shook his head and sat down. This vote should be safe enough. At least three members of the committee wanted it, maybe four. And one wouldn't care one way or another. "Voice vote will be fine," he said.

"Okay, I want to get this straight," A.Y. said. "This vote is on whether we're going to vote on Stumpy's motion like we usually do or whether we're going to use paper ballots. All those in favor of paper ballots say 'Aye'"

There was a chorus of "Ayes." As best Stumpy could make out there were at least four and maybe five.

"All opposed, signify by saying 'No'."

Kenneth Adams voted "No," loudly, but it was obvious that the motion carried.

"Okay, now we can get on to voting on the motion that we started to vote on ten minutes ago," A.Y. said. He pulled a sheet from his yellow pad and began tearing it into pieces. "Callie, will you give each member of the committee one of these to vote on."

Callie got up and approached the bench and distributed the yellow ballots to each member of the committee. Each one took the piece of paper, and Callie kept one and went back to her seat.

"Okay, y'all can just write down yes or no. The motion is that we let the Bethany A.M.E. choir sing in this year's singing convention."

Each of the members of the committee bent over the little pieces of paper and wrote a word. Callie got up, collected the ballots and took them back to the Judge's bench.

"You want to count these, A.Y., or do you want me to?" she asked.

"You count them, Callie. You're the secretary."

She took the votes back to her seat and began to open the folded papers, reading the votes as she opened them.

"No... Yes... No... Yes... Yes... Yes... Yes... the vote is five to two in favor of the motion."

From the back corner of the room, there came a loud,

clear "Hallelujah," and the Negroes in the courtroom began clapping. Most of the white people just sat there. Everybody looked at A.Y. He looked very sad.

"The motion is carried, and when we get the entry fee from the Bethany A.M.E. Church, their choir will be entered in the competition."

Reverend Pickens pulled his wallet from his pocket. "Mr. Pollard, I have the entry fee right here."

As they walked back home after the committee meeting, Bessie and Horace Williams were lost in their separate thoughts. Bessie was humming "Amazing Grace" as she thought about the songs her choir would sing and how many practices they would have before the singing convention. Horace was thinking darker thoughts. He had seen Claymore Thomas clustered with a group of white men after the meeting. Claymore was waving his hands, and the men were nodding their heads energetically. Horace knew this wasn't over; it was just beginning. And, like a lot of big men, Horace hated a fight, but if it came to that, he thought, he'd be willing to fight. He put his arm around Bessie's rounded shoulders, and they walked up Disciples Street.

If A.Y. Pollard had known what Horace Williams was thinking, he might have wondered at just how much they did have in common. A.Y. liked and respected Reverend Pickens, but he didn't like what the Negro preacher had pushed him into at the meeting. There was a way things were done, and all A.Y. wanted to do at this time in his life was keep things going. He thought about Annie, the Negro woman who had worked for his mother. She had cooked and cleaned for the Pollard family for more than thirty years, and when A.Y.'s father died, she came to the funeral home and found him standing on the porch. She had touched him on the arm.

"Can I go in?" she asked. "I'd like to see Mr. Pollard a last time."

A.Y. had taken her by the arm and guided her through all the people who had come to pay their respects to his father. It had never occurred to him that she shouldn't be there. Now he was wondering how different what Bessie wanted to do was from that and why she and her choir shouldn't be there. But he kept coming back to the same answer. It's never been done. So, it shouldn't be done.

Reverend Amos Pickens and Reverend Grant Mc-Lamb had stood on the sidewalk outside City Hall talking for a few minutes after the meeting, two tall men, one large and a little stooped and the other thin and straight, one white and one black. Reverend Pickens thanked Reverend McLamb for standing up for them. Reverend McLamb just smiled, and said, "People who love the Lord need to look out for each other." Reverend Pickens said, "Amen." Then they talked about their churches for a minute and walked off in different directions.

Stumpy was one of the last people to leave the court-room. He sat there at the defense table trying to put the votes with the voters. He knew Gerald had voted "no." And he figured Kenneth Adams had voted "no." Anything Stumpy was for, Kenneth was automatically against. That meant everybody else who voted had voted "yes." He expected Al and Pete to vote "yes;" they had made a deal.

And he figured Callie had, since she had seconded both motions. That meant Emil Barnes had also voted to let the Negro choir sing. That surprised Stumpy. He hadn't even considered talking to Emil, especially after seeing him with A.Y. He didn't think he had to have the vote, and if he had asked for it, Emil would have thought he was blackmailing him, although Stumpy couldn't quite make the fine distinction between blackmailing Emil and blackmailing Al. Maybe it was the fact that Emil's problem was a real one, and Al's was just something Stumpy had made up. He looked at the yellow scraps of paper on the prosecution table, five in one little bunch and two in another. He got up and scooped both piles into his hand. There was no need to leave them there for somebody to try to figure out the handwriting.

Just as he was about to leave, he heard a noise behind him. He looked around and saw Callie standing beside the light switch.

"Thank you for helping me out, Callie," he said.

"I was glad to do it. You know, even if you don't read much, sometimes you do the right thing. I think you did the right thing tonight." She looked up at him, her eyes big behind the glasses. "You know, I picked you out when we were in high school. It just didn't work out, probably because you and Mae Beth were just made for each other. I'm just glad to know I had such good taste back then."

She reached up and kissed him on the cheek, and before he could say or do anything, she walked over to the light switch and turned the lights off. She and Stumpy walked down the steps together, not needing to say a word.

Stumpy remembered wondering if anybody did any-thing just because it was the right thing. Callie did. Some-how that made him feel better. He walked out the door and Callie cut off the lights behind them.

18

The day after the committee meeting, it was as if someone had punched River Falls in the stomach, knocking all the air from its body, rendering it unable to move. Nothing was said in school about the committee meetings; for the most part, the students were more concerned with getting ready for their finals at school and helping their parents get the plants in the ground at home. Bessie Williams went about her work at the Fowler house singing under her breath and rejoicing that Mr. Fowler — or was it Reverend Pickens — had caused the committee to see the light. It didn't matter who did it. What mattered was that it was done.

* * *

Claymore Thomas was pacing back and forth in front of the big Oak tree in his back yard. Ruby had told him at supper that if he couldn't be still to go outside because it made her nervous for him to be so twitchy. So, as soon as he had finished eating, he went out back, thinking he would get in his truck and go somewhere where he could think in peace, but when he got outside he couldn't think of anywhere to go. He just paced up and down, smoking and occasionally having to step around Rascal, the dog that kept trying to run between his legs. Claymore pulled hard on the last puff of the Chesterfield and threw the butt on the ground.

He had called a meeting of the Klavern, but that wouldn't happen until tomorrow night. In the meantime, everything he had seen at that committee meeting the night before was festering inside him, threatening to erupt like a ripe boil. He tried to talk to Ruby about it, but she couldn't see how important it was. Now a bunch of white men had voted to let a nigger choir sing in the Singing Convention, and although Claymore couldn't say exactly what was wrong with that, he knew it was race mixing, and race mixing was wrong anyways. The only question in his mind was what he was going to do about it.

It'd been a while — a good while before Claymore had gotten involved — that the Klan in River Falls had pulled somebody out of their house and beaten them. But that was something they could do. The problem was, who would they beat? The committee that voted to let them sing? Sister Bessie, the leader of the choir? The whole choir or maybe just enough of them to make the point. A beating would put them back in their place. But, thought Claymore Thomas as he pulled the smoke from the Ches-

terfield deep into his lungs, did he have anybody in his
Klavern who had the balls to really beat somebody up. He
couldn't do it by himself, especially if they tried to pull Bessie from her house. Horace Williams wasn't somebody any
of them would want to fight.

When he was just a little boy, Claymore had seen a picture of a Klan meeting on a big stone mountain in Georgia.
There was a huge flaming cross and the grand dragon was
standing in front of a crowd that must have been nearly a
thousand robed Klansmen, his arms raised up. That was
what the Klan was supposed to be like, not a little knot of
people scared to do anything. If ever there was a time the
white man needed the Klan, this was it, and Claymore was
going to see that the Klan did its job.

He pulled on the Chesterfield again and stared at Ruby,
still washing supper dishes.

* * *

That night, after the eleven o'clock news had gone off,
Stumpy and Mae Beth were getting ready for bed. Li'l was
still in his room, studying for finals. Mae Beth was brushing her hair.

"Bessie told me what happened at the meeting," she
said. "Why didn't you tell me about it last night?"

"I don't know." Stumpy continued to button his pajama
shirt. He did know. He hadn't told Mae Beth about the
vote because he still wasn't sure how he felt about it. He'd

CHUCK HOLMES

set out to do something, and he had done it. He should have felt a swell of success, but what he felt was confusion. He really did want Bessie's choir to sing at the Convention; there was no good reason why one of the best choirs in that part of the country shouldn't compete. But he felt sorry for A.Y. All A.Y. wanted to do was finish his last year as chairman and be remembered as having a successful Singing Convention. Al and Pete would probably never think of him the same way. They'd been friends since the first grade, and he liked to think that he'd never really done anything to make their lives more difficult. There were a lot of people who didn't think the A.M.E. Choir should sing. In fact, he'd had two telephone calls about it today, loud angry calls by people who didn't tell him who was calling. One was a man. One was a woman. And they were both very mad.

The telephone calls didn't really bother Stumpy as much as the fact that the smooth surface of the town's existence had been disturbed. He could understand A.Y. wanting everything to stay calm and just continue on. It made life a lot easier.

Mae Beth put her hairbrush down and walked over to him. He realized now that he had sacrificed the peace of the town, and right or wrong, River Falls wouldn't ever be the same place again. He wanted to feel good about doing what he knew to be the right thing, but right now, he couldn't. He didn't want to face Bessie or Mae Beth or even tomorrow morning. He felt like something important had been lost. He kissed Mae Beth on the cheek and got into bed. He closed his eyes and pretended to be asleep.

THE SING

* * *

FROM THE RIVER FALLS CURRENT
Thursday, May 24, 1956

Editorial

*The vote to allow the Bethany A.M.E. to participate in the
1956 Annual Singing Convention was a milestone of some sort
for River Falls. Although the basis for the vote was cut and
dried—there is nothing in the governing documents of the
Singing Convention that prevents a choir from a negro church
from participating—the fact that the committee responsible for
approving each application for participation voted to approve,
it departed from a tradition in place for the entire twenty-nine
years of the Singing Convention's history. That was unusual
in itself; we do not easily move away from our traditions, no
matter what the cause.*

*What happened last night was not, however, the import-
ant part of this story. The important part is what happens now,
and it involves not just the members of the Singing Convention, but all the citizens of our community, Negro and white.
The question is whether this will be accepted as a part of a natural change that's been underway in our region for some years,
or whether it is an assault on our way of life and is to be fought
tooth and nail. Or, as one participant put it last night after the
meeting, "it ain't a big thing. It's just the Sing."*

*In the scheme of things, it's not a big thing. It is not the
Emancipation Proclamation, nor is it Brown versus the Board*

of Education, each of which were official and far reaching. It was, however, one community taking one step to include all its citizens, and for that reason the Current congratulates the members of the Singing Convention committee.

19

Saturday came, and as usual, the farmers and their families came to town to get their week's supplies. The stores were full, and little knots of people stood talking on the sidewalk. To most people, it was a typical May Saturday in a typical farm town. But for those who looked closely, some things were not exactly the same. On this Saturday, for instance, there were more people than usual downtown. Word of the Singing Committee's vote had spread throughout the county, drawing people who were concerned, some who were alarmed, and some who were just plain curious. A lot of the conversation that day started off with an opinion about what had happened to the Singing Convention.

About a block off Main Street, behind the mule stable, Claymore Thomas was deep in conversation with Otha Forster. Aaron Smelt was leaning in trying to hear what the two men were saying.

"You know you're talking about breaking the law, don't you," Otha was saying. "We could get a lot of jail time for something like this."

"It's not like we're killing somebody. We're just going to

get her and keep her for a few days. Not any harm in that, especially if nobody knows who did it."

Otha studied the ground around his feet. "I don't know," he said. "To me it ain't worth going to jail."

"You mean you'd just as soon stand there and let the niggers in the Singing Convention? You'd let them win."

"I don't even go to the Singing Convention. Haven't been since my mama made me go when I was little. It don't mean much to me. Staying out of jail and being able to take care of my family does."

Claymore threw his hands up, nearly hitting Aaron in the face. "I tell you, it's not just the Singing Convention. It's race mixing. We let them do this, and they'll be sitting at the dinner table with us. They'll be taking your little girl out. It ain't right, and we've got to stop it."

Otha turned around and walked over to the gate. Claymore sounded just like his daddy, and when his daddy had told him that twenty years ago, he had believed it. He wondered if the fact he didn't like Claymore was making him think different. There was such a thing as right and wrong, and who said it didn't matter.

"You say nobody'll get hurt?"

Claymore nodded his head. "I don't want to hurt Bessie. I just want to keep her out of the way, so her bunch won't sing. If we do it on Thursday, we can let her go on Monday. She's as good as she ever was, and we've solved the problem."

"You know if we try to take credit for this, they'll come get us."

"We'll just have to keep our mouths closed. But we'll

know that we did it. We upheld the rights of the white race."

"All right. I'll do it. If I don't, some of the people you'll get will probably screw it up and somebody'll get hurt."

"I keep telling you, Otha, nobody is going to get hurt."

* * *

It was about six o'clock, and the air was full of a promise of the heat that June would bring. Four members of the Sing committee, the four that didn't have retail stores to worry about, were gathered in A.Y. Pollard's back yard, sipping very sweet ice tea. Stumpy Fowler and Gerald Rainey were wearing Bermuda shorts and had on knee length socks. The first five minutes of the gathering was given to making jokes about Stumpy and Gerald's legs. Now, settled into lawn chairs with large sweating tea glasses in their hands, they were getting down to business.

A.Y. gestured with his glass at Stumpy. "You got us into this, Stumpy. I guess it's up to you to get us out of it. Bessie's choir's going to sing. That don't bother me a whole lot — although I think we'd been a whole lot better off if we'd left that can of worms closed. But what are we going to do about the other Negro choirs. It won't be long before white people won't participate because of so many Negroes."

Gerald Raney and Kenneth Adams nodded their heads in agreement. All three of the men looked at Stumpy.

This was something Stumpy hadn't considered. He'd done what he said he would do. Mae Beth had told him how much she appreciated it. Bessie had fixed a big pot of chicken stew, even though it was May and already too hot for chicken stew. He had hoped this was all over, and he could get back to business. He only had two more years to serve on the Sing committee, and he figured he could do that without causing himself or anybody else any problems.

"There aren't any more Negro choirs in River Falls that want to compete, A.Y. I don't see where that's a problem."

"I'm not worried about Negro choirs in River Falls. What about the A.M.E. choir over in Oak Grove? And Lord knows how many Negro choirs they have in Raleigh and Rocky Mount. Those are the ones I'm worrying about."

Stumpy looked at Gerald and Pete. Both of them were examining their tea glasses. They hadn't said a word on the subject. It was obvious to Stumpy the three of them had decided, as A.Y. had said, that Stumpy had gotten them into this mess, and it was up to him to figure a way out of it. Stumpy joined the others in examining their tea glasses. A.Y. waited. It was true that there were other Negro choirs around, some of them from big churches. It was also true that the Singing Convention could become a Negro event if there were four or five Negro choirs. It was also true that nobody on the committee would want to be part of the Singing Convention committee that killed a twenty-nine-year-old tradition that generated thousands of dollars in trade for the city and gave it publicity as far east as the coast and as far west as Charlotte. River Falls wasn't known for much, but it was known for the Singing Convention.

"All we did was abide by the constitution and by-laws," Stumpy said. Even as he said it, he knew it sounded weak and shallow. While the constitution and by-laws didn't say anything about Negroes being in the Singing Convention, everybody knew that was only because the Singing Convention was for whites, and no Negroes would want to participate. At least until Bessie decided she did.

"I guess we could vote on a change to the Constitution. Best I remember, it only takes a three-quarters vote to change it. We could probably get that." A germ of an idea was rolling around inside Stumpy's head. He knew they couldn't say that only White choirs and singers could be in the Singing Convention. Since they had already voted to let a Negro choir in, that would just be another fight. But what if they could limit it to the Negro choir that they had already agreed to accept? That would solve the problem, and Stumpy could go back home and tend to the things he needed to.

Gerald Rainey slapped his leg. "Damn mosquitoes. They're out early this year."

"No earlier than usual. They just like you," Pete Jennings said.

Stumpy sat up and took a long sip of his tea. "What if," he said, "we amend the constitution to say that only contestants who are invited can participate? We'll just invite any white groups that apply and not invite any Negro groups."

Gerald peered at Stumpy over the top of his glass. "Don't you think that's a little obvious, Stumpy?"

"More obvious than twenty-nine years of nothing but white singers in the Singing Convention?"

"Yeah, but we didn't write that into the constitution. Besides, if we do that we're going to have to go through this mess with Bessie's choir every year. You think she's just going to go away?"

Stumpy knew that Bessie Williams wasn't going to go away. Nothing would take her away short of chariots of fire. Suddenly Stumpy felt very tired. He had tried to please Mae Beth and Bessie and to do what seemed to be the right thing. He had tried not to hurt his friends. So far as Stumpy could tell, everything he had tried to do was right, or at least as right as it could be under the circumstances. Now he was sitting here with three men he had known all his life staring at him like they didn't know him at all. He looked down, noticing there were almost no hairs growing just above his knees. For a moment, he wondered if the Bermuda shorts Mae Beth had bought him were a good idea.

A.Y.'s voice brought him back to the subject. "I agree with Gerald. We don't want to have to deal with Reverend Pickens and Bessie every year. It'd be better if there was a way we could just let them sing, but not have any other Negro groups."

"What about soloists?" Kenneth Adams asked.

"Soloists, too," A.Y. said. "I just don't want a bunch of fuss every time we have the Singing Convention. Everything's been rocking along just fine until this year, and then Bessie and her preacher had to try to change things. They didn't need changing."

Kenneth and Gerald were nodding their heads, agreeing with A.Y. Stumpy almost did, but a stray thought wandered through his mind. Somebody thought they needed changing or none of this would have happened. Stumpy had known Bessie most of his life. He had employed her almost all his married life, and he knew she didn't have a selfish bone in her body, and so far as pride went, she was proud of the same things he was proud of—raising his children right, paying his bills on time, doing what he could to help other people. If somebody like Bessie was willing to try to change things, was it so obvious that nothing needed changing? On the other hand, that wasn't an argument that he wanted to get into with A.Y., Gerald, and Kenneth. Maybe there was another way.

"Doesn't much matter now," he said, "whether they needed changing or not. They've been changed."

Kenneth started to say something, but Stumpy went on. "Yeah, I know. It's my fault. I had my reasons. And I'll come up with a way to fix it so that we don't turn the Singing Convention into the Negro Gospel Convention. But you're just going to have to give me a day or two to figure it out." He took several long gulps of his tea and sat the glass down on the wooden picnic table. "I've got to go, now. Mae Beth'll have dinner on the table." As he turned and walked away, he could feel the eyes of all three men on his back.

As he walked home, he wanted to be mad at Mae Beth. But he couldn't. Like him, she was doing what she thought was right. He guessed Bessie was, too. Everybody was trying to do right, and they had created a big mess that he was in the middle of. The one person he couldn't figure out was the Pentecostal preacher. He didn't seem to have a dog in this fight, but he jumped right in the middle of it, and he probably knew that about half the people that would be in his church tomorrow didn't agree with him. Three or four of them were probably members of Claymore Thomas's bunch. At his age, Reverend McLamb probably didn't need any more trouble than he already had, but he had stood up to Claymore Thomas, and if Claymore Thomas wasn't much to stand up to, the people in his church who were going to start talking about him behind his back might be.

Stumpy Fowler knew why he liked being a CPA so much. Numbers were nice and neat. Life, especially if you tried to figure out what was right, was messy.

20

It only took Stumpy two days to figure out how to satisfy all the conditions of the Sing eligibility, but it was a miserable two days. On Sunday, as he sat in church trying to listen to the preacher talk about Paul on the road to Damascus, but all he could think about was how to keep Bessie and her choir in the Singing Convention and keep everybody else who looked like her out of it. That night, he tossed and turned and when he went to sleep he had dreams of ledgers filled with numbers that wouldn't add up, a sure sign that he was anxious about something.

But by midday Monday, he went to A.Y.'s office, ready to lay out his plan. After exchanging "good mornings" with Gladys, he went into A.Y.'s office. As usual, A.Y. was behind a stack of files, his sleeves rolled up, the very image of a busy lawyer. He looked up as Stumpy walked in.

"You got it figured out?" A.Y. asked.

"Yeah. Good morning to you, too."

"Okay. Good morning. Now, you got it figured out?"

Stumpy took a seat in the chair across the desk from A.Y., nodding his head. "I think I've got something that'll take care of all the problems we talked about and won't make us look too dumb."

"That'd be good. Is it going to keep Bessie off our backs next year?"

"Yes. If we do what I'm proposing, Bessie's choir will get to sing, but there won't be any other negro groups or soloists in the competition. The deal's this. Any choir in River Falls is automatically accepted. Because this is a River Falls event. Anybody else gets in by invitation. They do that in sports events all the time. No reason why we can't. We'll just be careful who we invite."

"You think that'd work?"

"I think so. Or we could just do what the constitution and by-laws say, and let anybody in who applies and pays the entry fee."

A.Y.'s eyebrows shot up. "You don't really want to do that, do you?"

Stumpy scratched his chin. "As a matter of fact, I do. But I think we took a step this year, and maybe later we can take another step, but I don't want to kill the Sing doing it. I guess since Bessie has worked for my family for a lot of years I may be biased, but since we started wrangling about all this, I've been thinking. I'd a whole lot rather have Bessie and Horace as neighbors than a lot of white people I know. I mean, she's practically raised Li'l, and she's cooked about every meal I've eaten for close to twenty years. She's been about as close a friend to Mae Beth as anybody could be. All that, and we're in an uproar because she wants to sing a song at the Singing Convention. That doesn't make a lot of sense to me."

"I guess it's the principle of the thing," A.Y. said. "You just don't mess around with tradition, and one of our traditions is that the Singing Convention is for white people, and if the Negroes want to have a Singing Convention, they can have one of their own. I don't have anything in the world against that. In fact, I don't have anything against much of anything, but I really don't like the fuss that comes with trying to change things."

"I understand that, but sometimes you've got to put up with some fuss. Maybe Virginia's never explained it to you like Mae Beth did to me."

A.Y. chuckled. "No, but one day she might, and I expect I'd do the same thing you did. Just write what you said up as an Amendment to the constitution, and I'll call a meeting to get it passed. Just make sure it doesn't get all over town before we get to vote on it."

21

As she came through the door, Bessie was pulling the long pin from her hat and getting it off. She hurried into the bedroom to put the hat back in its box, then back to the kitchen. She had to get the chicken on the table and warm up the vegetables before Reverend Pickens got there. She figured she had a few minutes because the Reverend always had to stand around and talk to the people after church. Horace had stayed behind to walk Reverend Pickens to their house, although she couldn't figure out why. As many times as he had put his knees under their table, she thought the Reverend could find it by himself. It wasn't her turn to feed the preacher and his wife but about twice a year, maybe not even that often, but every time it seemed like she was in such a rush.

She had set the table before she went to church. The best china—plates with big flowers in the middle of them and tall tea glasses that matched them—made a nice-looking table, she thought. In a minute, there would be a big platter of fried chicken right in the middle of the table and bowls of butter beans, Crowder peas, potato salad, and a dish of mixed pickles, bell pepper, radishes, and sliced tomatoes. In the kitchen, there was a big fresh coconut cake that she had cooked the night before. Bessie bustled between the kitchen and the dining room, putting food on the table, straightening the knives and forks, and making sure that the napkins lined up at each place. By the time she heard Horace and the Pickens's coming up on the porch, she had everything where it was supposed to be. She looked in the mirror to make sure her hair was still in place and went to the front door. Horace was just opening it for Reverend and Mrs. Pickens.

"Do come in, Reverend. Come on back with me, Agnes, and we'll pour the tea. Everything is right ready."

Compared to Bessie, Agnes Pickens was a small woman; so small in fact, it seemed like in any part of her you could see there were bones sticking out. On her wrists and hands. At her ankles. It almost looked like God had forgotten to put the flesh on Agnes when He was making her in His image. But it was known throughout the church that Agnes, one of the sweetest people you'd want to meet, could be hard to deal with if she heard you criticize Amos. Since their children had grown up and gone to college, protecting and taking care of Amos Pickens had been her job, and she did it well.

Horace went to the head of the table, and Reverend Pickens sat down at the other end. The two women sat at the sides and waited for Horace to say the blessing. He looked at Bessie, then at the food on the table. He reached out, took Bessie's hand in one of his big hands and Agnes' in the other, bowed his head and prayed.

"Lord God, you made everything, and you gave us plenty of it. We thank you for all that you've done for us and for this good food we're about to eat. Amen."

As soon as they had opened their eyes, Bessie started passing the plates of food around, offering them first to the preacher. Nothing was said as they loaded their plates with the food and began to eat. Reverend Pickens paused in his eating, holding a fried chicken breast in his hand.

"Mighty good chicken, Bessie," he said. "As usual."

Bessie smiled and nodded. She was known for her fried chicken, but it always made her feel good for Horace or somebody to say something good about it.

For a few minutes, that was the extent of their conversation. Finally, Bessie broke the silence.

"Reverend, I want to thank you for what you did with the Singing Convention Committee. I know there were those in the church that didn't agree with it."

The preacher smiled, picked up his napkin, and wiped the grease from the chicken from around his mouth. "Yes, there were some," he said. "And I heard an earful from Leola, but I think most of the people are glad the choir's going to sing. We're mighty proud of our choir."

"Wonder what other folks think about?" Horace asked. His low voice was, as usual, very quiet, but everyone turned toward him. Horace just kept eating.

"What other folks?" Bessie asked. She had been feeling really good with all Reverend Pickens's complements, but Horace's comment changed her feeling immediately. His question couldn't have a good answer, at least as far as he was concerned.

"Mostly the white folks," Horace said. "I figure if anybody's going to make a fuss, it'd be the white folks. But I s'pose I could be wrong."

Reverend Amos looked at him. "We usually know pretty well what the white people are thinking, I guess. Almost all the people in the church work for them, and a lot of them work in their homes. In fact, I wonder what they would think if they knew just how much we did know about their going-ons."

He put down the piece of chicken he was finishing off and thought for a minute.

"Leola works for the Pollards, and although she'd rather chew her tongue off than admit what we did was right, the fact that she hasn't shown up at my house with another bunch of stories makes me think Mr. Pollard has accepted it."

Bessie agreed. "And the Fowlers, they think it's a fine thing. Of course, Mr. Stumpy took some convincing, but everybody there seems to think it's time we got to sing."

Horace slowly chewed the chicken, his eyes cast down on his plate. Finally, he swallowed. "Uh huh," he said. That's Mr. Pollard and Mr. Fowler. They're good people. But what about Claymore Thomas and all his gang? He was sure having a lot to say at the meeting that night."

"That's just a lot of talk," Reverend Amos said. "We haven't had anything happening with the Klan around here in twenty years or more. They just try to make some noise. I don't think Claymore Thomas is anything to worry about."

"Uh huh," Horace said, and reached for another piece of chicken.

* * *

Stumpy Fowler sat at the dinner table wondering whether he could get away with, unbuttoning the top button of his trousers. Every time he did, Mae Beth had something to say about how he was eating too much and was going to get fat. Then she cooked these big Sunday dinners. Mae Beth had always done the Sunday cooking because Bessie had her choir and church to do, and it let her remind Stumpy that he had indeed married a fine cook. Today she had fixed a beef roast, mashed potatoes and gravy, garden peas with little pearl onions in them, and a congealed salad. And Stumpy had eaten well. Li'l had a couple of servings then asked to be excused to go over to Billy Royce's, so Stumpy and Mae Beth just sat there sipping their iced tea.

"Is everything okay with the Singing Committee now?" Mae Beth asked. She had asked Stumpy that several times since he had told her what he had had to do to get the votes he needed. He supposed it was her way of showing that she cared about what it had cost him.

"Yeah. I took them a plan that pretty much prevents any other Negro choirs or other groups from participating except for Sister Bessie's. I don't know if that was the right thing to do or not, but it calmed everybody down."

Mae Beth looked at him over the rim of her glass. "Why don't you think it was the right thing to do?"

"I don't know that it wasn't. It's just that since I've thought about it, I can't figure out why we can't just let in anybody who wants to sing. I don't know why we have to keep anybody out."

Even with her hands and the glass in front of her mouth, Stumpy could tell that Mae Beth was smiling. He could tell it from her eyes. She put the glass down, got up and walked around the table, and kissed him on top of his head.

"You're a good man, Stumpy Fowler. And you even think some. That's more than I would be willing to admit about most men." She pecked him again on top of his head and picked up some of the dishes to take back into the kitch-en. But she didn't get away before Stumpy ran his hand down her hip and applied a proprietary pat. He watched her walk away. For all the years they had been married, he still liked to watch her walk, either coming toward him or going away.

22

On the first Monday in June, the first thing Li'l thought about when he woke up was not about not going to school or even his birthday, but that it was the day before he was going to get his learner's permit. He lay in bed thinking about it.

Finally, he got out of bed and went into the bathroom. In the dim light, he studied his face, looking for some sign of a beard. He looked hard at each side, then on his cheeks near his sideburns. The barber had said that when they started shaving under the sideburns and at the nape of the neck, it would make him have to start to shave earlier, but that had been two years ago, and he still saw no sign of facial hair. He lifted his arm and looked at his armpit. There was no hair there either. He turned on the other bathroom light and looked again, but no matter how bright the light was, his face and body were as hairless as they had always been. He washed his face and his neck and under his arms. Then he went back to his room to dress.

He heard the back door close, and when he got to the

kitchen, he could see Bessie at the clothesline, hanging out the clothes. He got a box of cereal from the panty, added the sugar and milk, and sat down at the kitchen table. He wondered what he was going to do with the rest of the day. It wasn't like a Saturday. During school, when Saturday came, he had a full day of things to do he had thought of during the week, and Sunday was full enough, what with Sunday School and church and BYPU. But this Monday had sneaked up on him. The first real day out of school, and he didn't know what to do with it. He stared at the cereal in the bowl as if he were trying to read the flakes to get an idea for his near future.

"I see you finally got up. I guess it feels good to sleep late on a Monday for a change." His mother came into the kitchen, carrying an arm full of sheets. She threw them on the floor beside the washing machine.

"Are you sure you don't want to have some of your friends over tonight for a cookout or something?" she said. "I can't imagine why you don't want to have some sort of celebration for your sixteenth birthday."

"No, it's okay. I've already had fifteen other birthdays. We don't need to do anything for this one."

"Okay. I won't make you have a party if you don't want one," she said and went to their bedrooms.

After he finished his cereal, he rinsed out the bowl, put it in the sink, and went back to his room. He lay down on the bed, staring at the ceiling, trying to visualize how it would be when he got his driver's license. Li'l sighed, and reached over to the bedside table for his driver's manual. He could always read through it one more time.

* * *

Sweat rolled down Otha Forster's face and dripped on the dirt floor of the tobacco barn, just missing Claymore Thomas' hand as he drew a map in the dirt. Otha still didn't understand why Claymore thought they needed a map. All four of the men there knew where Bessie Williams lived, except maybe Aaron Smelt, and he wasn't going to be driving a car anyway. Otha pulled out his handkerchief and wiped the sweat. He looked at Jim Turnage to see how he was taking it. But Jim, as usual, was just squatting there, watching Claymore draw in the dirt. Otha wondered if any of them was much better off than Aaron. Maybe he just showed it more. Finally, he decided somebody ought to say something.

"You're not going to take Bessie out of her house at night," he said. "Horace would break anybody in half that tries to get into his house."

Claymore stopped drawing and looked up at Otha.

"You afraid of one nigger?" he said.

Otha stood up and walked away. If he had to tell the truth, he'd say "yes." He didn't figure that any of the four of them, or maybe all four of them together could take on Horace Williams. Claymore did have a way of making things seem a whole lot simpler than they really were. Three or four of them were just going to waltz into Bessie's house, stuff her into a truck, and take her away. Somehow that didn't seem likely. They didn't even know if Horace kept a gun in the house. Could be they'd waltz into Bessie's house and get their fool heads blown off. He finally turned back around to Claymore.

"Not a matter of being afraid," he said. "It's a matter of being smart. There's no reason we have to go in their house, and there's no good reason to have to face up to Horace."

"So you think you got a better idea," Claymore said, his tone indicating that since it wasn't his idea, he couldn't see how it could be better.

"Maybe," Otha said. "Bessie walks home from the Fowler place every night. I've seen her sometime when I was going into town. Might be easier to grab her then."

Junior looked from Claymore to Otha. Otha thought he saw a flicker of understanding on Jim's face.

"It's still light when she goes home," Claymore said. "I've been watching her. You're talking about grabbing her in broad daylight. That's not real smart."

Otha thought about it. It was full light at six o'clock or so when Bessie would be walking home, and there were a lot of people on the street. Maybe it wasn't such a good idea. But, then, neither was breaking into her house.

Jim spoke up for the first time.

"What time does she go to work?"

The four men looked at each other. Then Otha, Jim, and Aaron looked at Claymore. He shook his head.

"I didn't watch her in the morning. Just in the evening."

"I'd bet it's way before seven," Jim said. "She probably fixes breakfast for the Fowlers."

Otha nodded his head. If they were going to go through with this fool thing, it'd be a lot better to do it in the early morning than in the late afternoon, and either one would be better than breaking into Horace Williams' house in the middle of the night.

"Wouldn't take but a couple of days to find out," he said. "I'll look out for her. I don't sleep that late anyway."

Otha noticed that Claymore started to say something, then stopped. He figured Claymore was going to say that he should be the one to watch for Bessie, but evidently Claymore didn't want to get up that early. That was fine with Otha. If he was going to put ten to twenty years of his life on the line, he'd rather do his own planning.

Claymore stood up, hitched up his pants, and looked around at the other three as if he were reviewing an army. "Okay, then," he said, "Otha'll scout this out tomorrow and the next day, and we'll meet back here Thursday night so we can pick Bessie up Friday morning."

The four men ducked out of the low tobacco barn door. Aaron went with Jim; Claymore — without another word — got into his car and left. Otha stood, one foot on the running board of his pickup, wondering just what he had gotten himself into. Two years ago, or maybe even a year ago, he wouldn't have thought much about it. He had been going to Klan meetings and rallies with his dad since before he was a teenager. He accepted that God had put white people here to keep things in order and black people to haul water and carry wood like it said in the Bible, just like God had put the white people in America and had them chase the Indians off. That had been bred into him by his daddy and granddaddy.

But a lifetime of working in the fields beside coloreds had begun to crack his creed. As best he could tell, they weren't a lot different from him. They worked hard, cared for their families, and did the best they could to get through the day with little education and not a lot of hope of anything really changing. The only real difference between the whites and the coloreds in the tobacco field was that when they brought water, the whites drank out of the jar and the coloreds had to drink out of a glass. To Otha, that wasn't enough of a difference to make any difference.

He pulled the pack of Camels out of his shirt pocket and knocked one out against his knuckles. He snapped the lighter and drew in the smoke, all the way to the bottom of his lungs. As he blew the smoke out through his nose, he stared at the stars and the moon. They looked just like they did when he was just a shirt-tailed kid, but it seemed like everything else was changing. Life was a lot easier when you didn't think about things. You just got up in the morning and did what you had to do. But it didn't seem like that anymore. He kept questioning things that used to be certain.

Otha got into his truck and headed home. He had to get up early in the morning to spy on Bessie.

* * *

Bessie Williams was washing the dishes and humming one old spiritual after another. Behind her humming, she could hear the Bethany A.M.E. choir singing. It was a wonderful sound, and she smiled as she put the plates into the drain rack. She was going to have to decide which one of their songs they would do at the Singing Convention, but she wasn't really worried. Any of them would be beautiful and a blessing.

She looked over her shoulder at Horace sitting in the big overstuffed chair in the living room, reading the newspaper. The smile faded from her face; Horace wasn't nearly as happy about the choir singing as she was. He said he was glad, but Bessie could tell there was something different under what he said. She knew it wasn't that he was worried about what the white people thought; Horace had had to deal with that all his life. Since he was a teenager, Horace had had a hard time keeping a low profile. There weren't many men as tall as Horace in River Falls, and probably none as strong. When he was younger, white bucks, sometimes with too much to drink in them, would yell things at him, trying to get him stirred up, but Horace knew that if he hurt one of those white boys for any reason, he'd be in trouble — and probably his family, too. So Horace just went on about his business. That was one of the things that Bessie had admired about him; he was his own man, no matter what was happening around him.

She wished he wouldn't worry so much. The Singing Convention was this Sunday. They'd have their chance on the stage, and win or lose, it would be a wonderful thing. Then the world would get back to the way it used to be, because, as Horace always said, "things don't change much around here."

Bessie put the last dish in the drain and dried her hands on the dishtowel. She decided that tonight she'd just let them sit in the drain and dry themselves. She felt the need to read her Bible and think about things.

23

Even at six o'clock in the morning, the air was heavy and sticky. Otha Forster, staring out of the windshield of his truck, felt a single drop of sweat running slowly down the side of his face. He didn't bother to wipe it off. He knew it wouldn't do much good. You wipe the sticky wet off your face, and before you put your handkerchief back in your pocket, it's back again. It was just going to get worse in July and August.

Otha knew that some people went to the beach or to the mountains to get away from the heat and humidity for a while, but mostly those people weren't farmers. If you were a farmer, especially one trying to scratch a living out of fifty acres with a two-acre tobacco allotment, you didn't go anywhere for a week but back to the field. Otha didn't particularly resent it; it had been that way all his life, and it had been the same with his daddy and granddaddy. That was just part of being a farmer.

He stared down Disciples Street through the windshield of the truck. He couldn't help wondering what he was doing here. If they did manage to get Bessie and hold her somewhere until the Sing was over on Sunday, they would still have to let her go, and when they did, she'd make a lot of trouble for all of them. Claymore kept saying if they had on their robes and hoods when they were around her, she wouldn't know who they were, but Otha knew that most of the people in River Falls could name everybody who owned a Klan robe. Wasn't much that everybody didn't know in River Falls.

Otha saw Bessie's screen door open. He sat up in the truck, ready to start it and follow Bessie to the Fowlers. But he saw that it wasn't Bessie coming out. It was Horace. Otha knew Horace had to be close to sixty, but watching him from two blocks away, you'd never know it. He took the steps down from the front porch two at the time, went out the gate, and walked toward downtown with a swing in his step. Otha made a mental note that Horace left before Bessie did. That might help. At least they wouldn't have to fight Horace.

A few minutes later, Bessie came out. Otha noticed she didn't stop to lock the front door, but that wasn't unusual. He didn't lock his front door when he left home either. She stopped for a minute in the yard, pulling a leaf or something from one of her flowers. She took another minute or two to look around, then she went out the gate and started walking down the street in the same direction Horace had gone. Otha looked at his watch. It was almost 6:50, so he figured that Bessie was going to be at the Fowlers by seven o'clock. He watched her walk to the end of the block and turn left toward Main Street. He started the truck and slowly drove down the street. He guessed he ought to follow her to make sure, but it didn't take much thinking to figure that she was going to cut over to Main Street, turn left again, and walk up the block to the Fowler's house. If they were going to grab her, it would have to be before she got to Main Street, and probably after she turned off Disciples Street. If any of her neighbors saw what was happening, they might try to do something about it.

Otha pulled down to the street where Bessie had turned and looked on either side. There were only two blocks between Disciples Street and Main Street. Just the other side of Oak Street, about halfway between Oak and Main Street there was an alley that ran behind some of the houses. As best Otha could tell, this was about the only place they could grab Bessie without being right in front of somebody's house. At this time of the morning, probably nobody would be watching the alley.

Otha decided he had seen enough. He turned left on Main Street and drove back home.

* * *

Stumpy Fowler wasn't looking forward to going downtown this morning. In the weeks since the committee meeting, every day had brought at least one and sometimes three or four unpleasant conversations with people he thought were his friends. Most of them started with something like, "I don't have anything against Negroes," and went on to why Negroes shouldn't be in the Singing Convention. A couple of them had asked him directly whey he would get involved in such a thing, and at first, he tried to tell them that he thought that it was the right thing to do, but abstract concepts like right and wrong didn't seem to have much effect on the people he was talking to. Finally, he said that he just couldn't see why anybody who lived in River Falls couldn't compete in the Singing Convention. That's all there was to it, and evidently some people agreed with him because the motion had passed. That didn't seem to convince anybody either, but it saved a lot of conversation about right and wrong.

Stumpy noticed that Li'l hadn't said anything about it one way or another. Stumpy wasn't sure whether that was because Li'l was upset with him for bringing this kind of attention to the family or just because it didn't matter a lot to him. He had been more interested in getting his driver's license.

He sat there, deep in the realization that he didn't really know where anything was going — the Singing Convention, his own business, his son as he took giant steps into adulthood. Li'l was still asleep, one of the last days he'd get to sleep in before tobacco season started, and he'd be picked up by Mr. Cross before light to go to the fields. Mae Beth was already stirring around in another part of the house, getting started on her day. He felt lonely sitting there, missing the calm he always had at that time of the morning.

He was still sitting at the kitchen table making his list when Bessie came in the back door.

"Mornin', Mr. Stumpy." she said. She checked to see if Stumpy's coffee cup was empty, then went over and pulled an apron out of the pantry. "Sure is a beautiful day today."

Stumpy took a sip of the coffee and nodded. Most mornings he had difficulty keeping up with Bessie's up-beat attitude. For years, she had greeted him with, "This is the day the Lord has made. Let us rejoice and be glad." But she finally quit when it became evident that his grunted "uh-huh" was as much as he was going to do at that time of the morning.

"You having any excitement over your way, Bessie?" Stumpy asked, tearing his list from the pad and slipping it in his pocket.

Bessie shook her head. "No, sir. About the only excitement we're having is getting the choir ready for the singing convention. Everybody's real excited about that. We're practicing on Wednesday nights like we usually do, then we're practicing on Saturday. We're about to be ready."

"I'm sure your choir'll do fine, Bessie. I just hope nobody spoils it for you."

"I think Claymore Thomas and those people have about given up," Bessie said. "When your committee voted to let us sing, there wasn't a lot more they could do."

Stumpy wasn't so sure of that. He couldn't imagine Claymore and his buddies being all that concerned with the democratic process, but he had to admit they had been really quiet since the committee meeting.

"What does Horace think about that?"

She smiled, her white teeth brightly white against her dark skin. "Oh, that old man worries too much. He wanted to walk me over here this morning, afraid somebody would try to do something to me."

"I think Horace is just being smart, Bessie. I think you should let him walk you over here and home, or let me come pick you up in the car."

"That'd just be a lot of trouble for everybody. I've been walking over here 'bout every day for almost twenty years, and I don't think we need to change that because of the likes of Claymore Thomas."

Stumpy started to say something, but he had long since learned that arguing with Bessie was a lot like punching a pillow. You felt like you were doing something, but when you looked, you could see you hadn't even made a dent. She just stood there with her smile, and generally agreed with anything you said, then went and did whatever she thought she ought to do. Saying anything more would just be a waste of breath.

"Okay, Bessie, but you know I'll be glad to come get you in the morning and take you home at night. It won't take me but a couple of minutes, and it'd make Horace and me feel better."

Bessie nodded. "When these old legs get to where they can't walk from here to Disciples Street, I'll sure take you up on that, Mr. Stumpy. I do appreciate the offer." She went off to start her day.

* * *

Promptly at two o'clock, Li'l walked into Stumpy's office, ready to go take the written test for his learner's permit. He carried the ragged copy of the North Carolina's driver's manual, just in case he had to read something one last time before taking the test. Stumpy looked up as he walked in, and looked at his watch.

"Right on time," Stumpy said. He was actually surprised that Li'l hadn't shown up early.

They walked down the street and turned the corner toward City Hall. Every Tuesday afternoon, the courtroom became the license examining center and usually there were four or five people there getting their learner's permit or driver's license. The examiner had been coming to River Falls for more than ten years and knew most of the people in town. He was related to some of them.

"Afternoon, Stumpy," he said as they walked into the courtroom. There wasn't anybody else there, and the examiner was sitting back at what was usually the defense table, reading the newspaper.

"Afternoon, Fred. Li'l thinks it's time for him to get his learner's permit. I guess you can tell whether it really is or not."

"I can do that. You ready for the test, Li'l?"

Li'l nodded. Stumpy smiled, wondering what would have happened if Li'l had told the examiner he already knew how to drive. But he figured Fred had been dealing with sixteen-year-old boys too long to worry about it. He took a seat in the jury box while Fred pulled papers from various stacks on the table and putting them in order.

"Just fill out the first page of this, Li'l. Be sure to use

your legal name on it. Then answer the questions on these next two pages and bring it back to me when you finish."

Li'l took the papers over to the prosecution table, sat down, and started writing. Stumpy sat there, staring at him, wondering how in the world Li'l had grown up so much, so quickly. In Li'l's scrunched up face, Stumpy could still see something of the eight-year-old boy in short pants trying to put the chain back on his bicycle. But mostly, all the little boy that Stumpy had been so proud of was gone. He was still proud of Li'l, especially when he showed the kind of character he had in the schoolyard, but it was a different feeling, almost man to man, instead of father to son. It hadn't bothered him when Li'l had gotten taller than he was; Stumpy had been dealing with people taller than he was most of his life. And it hadn't really bothered him when he found Li'l was doing some things that he didn't tell them about. He'd come home smelling like most of a pack of cigarettes, and Stumpy and Mae Beth had talked about it. Mae Beth's view was that if all Li'l did was smoke some cigarettes with Billy Royce, they'd turn a blind eye to it. But knowing Li'l was about to get his driver's license ground on Stumpy. It wasn't that he feared that Li'l would go away; it was that he could.

It only took Li'l about fifteen minutes to go through the questions and fill out the rest of the form. He took the papers back to Fred and stood beside him while he went through the questions, checking them off. Then Fred checked the form.

"You scored 100% on the test, Li'l," he said. "You must have about memorized the driver's manual."

"I guess so," Li'l said.

"Well, get your dad to sign this and give me $10 and you'll be legally permitted to drive with an adult in the car. I'm sure Stumpy'll take care of being the adult, at least for a while."

"Yeah, it'll be a while before I'm going to be willing to let the Oldsmobile out of my sight, I guess." Stumpy said. He walked over and patted Li'l on the shoulder. Since you made a hundred, I guess you've learned all about driving. Now we'll have to see if you can learn to drive."

"I imagine you've already been getting some practice, haven't you, Li'l?" Fred said, grinning. Li'l didn't respond. Fred turned back to Stumpy. "That's why God made dirt roads."

Stumpy signed the permit form, and Li'l pulled ten dollars from his pocket.

"Okay, Li'l" Fred said, tearing one part of a two-part form from a pad. "Keep this with you anytime you're driving. Make sure you have an adult in the front seat with you. And be sure and follow all those laws and rules you learned about."

"Yes, sir. I will," Li'l said. To Stumpy he suddenly sounded like a little boy again, even though his voice was a full octave lower.

As they walked down the steps back to the street, Stumpy asked Li'l what he thought of the whole business.

"It was a lot easier than I thought it would be," Li'l said. "I was afraid I wouldn't pass it, much less make a hundred on it. I stayed awake worrying about it last night."

It crossed Stumpy's mind that his staying awake and worrying was just starting.

* * *

Claymore Thomas was wishing he had talked to Otha already. He stood at the edge of his tobacco field watching Roscoe Allen Tart's big car barreling down the dirt two-lane track from the road, leaving a plume of dust in its wake. Three or four cuss words had run through Claymore's mind before he got to that thought; if he had talked to Otha, he would have had something to say to Roscoe. As it was, Roscoe was going to beat him like a dog.

Damn folks who won't leave their fields long enough to tell somebody what's going on, Claymore thought. He and Otha were having to meet at night because Otha kept saying he couldn't spare the time from his fields. Claymore watched the car drive through the yard and slide to a stop just beyond the edge of the field. Another five feet and Roscoe would have taken out a half dozen tobacco plants, Claymore thought. The door flung open, and Roscoe stomped across the dry dirt, coming straight toward Claymore. He started talking before he got within ten feet of Claymore.

"You were going to take care of those niggers. There's nothing to worry about. You had it all under control. Damn it, if you'd had WW Two under control we'd all be talking German now."

He stopped right in front of Claymore's face, looking like he was about to spit. Claymore started to say something, but before he could figure out what to say, Roscoe had started again.

"If Ferd was still alive, none of this would have ever happened. He knew how to deal with niggers. That man had some backbone."

He leaned even closer to Claymore, so close Claymore could feel the heat coming off his face. Finally, Claymore couldn't take it anymore. He turned and walked away, leaving Roscoe talking to his back. He picked up the water bottle again, opening it and taking a long swallow. Roscoe had run out of steam and was just standing there snorting. Slowly, Claymore put the bottle on the ground.

"I said I'd take care of it," Claymore said softly, trying to give voice to a confidence he didn't really feel. "There's nothing I can do in a committee meeting, short of dragging a bunch of people out and horse whipping them, and they're all white. But there's something I can do outside of the meeting."

He turned to face Roscoe and saw that he had the Grand Dragon's attention.

"Bessie Williams is behind all this. And if Bessie Williams ain't at the Sing, the nigger choir won't be able to sing. Ain't none of them got the grit to get up there without her. And she won't be there."

"Where's she going to be?"

"She'll be out in the country. Resting."

Roscoe's eyes widened. "You planning to kill that nigger?" he asked. The way he asked it, Claymore couldn't tell whether he thought that would be a good idea or not.

"Don't need to."

"Well, what are you going to do?"

Claymore let the question hang there, enjoying the fact

that for once he had the upper hand on Roscoe. Claymore knew what he was going to do, or at least he was acting like it, and Roscoe didn't.

"Just need to keep her out of sight for a couple of days," he said. "We're going to grab her Friday morning. I've got my best man watching her when she goes to work in the mornings. We grab her, hold her until Sunday night, then take her and let her loose somewhere."

"You think that bunch won't sing if she's not there?"

"I know they won't. They won't know what happened to Bessie, and they sure won't want it happening to them."

When Roscoe finally said something, it sounded more like a low buzz than a sentence. Claymore had to work to understand what he had said.

"That's just the sort of half-assed thing I'd expect from somebody like you. You start something and don't have the guts to finish it. What do you expect that nigger to do when you turn her loose? Go back to picking cotton and singing about massa in the cold, cold ground? The first thing she'll do is go to the law and finger every one of you. They may even come after me."

Roscoe stepped closer to Claymore. "And I ain't having any of that. You get that woman. You make sure she don't ever show up at the Sing. Or anywhere else. You understand what I mean?"

Claymore wasn't sure that he did. He had never thought of killing Bessie. Or anybody else. But Roscoe knew more about this kind of thing than he did. He just nodded his head, afraid to say anything.

"All right. Take care of it. And if you don't take care of it, don't let me find you. You'll be real sorry."

Roscoe turned and stomped back to his big car, leaving Claymore to figure out how he would kill Bessie.

* * *

A.Y. Pollard sat in his little office in the back of the house. It was almost dark, the only light being a weak pool shining from the goose-necked desk lamp. He really didn't need much light. He wasn't reading anything. He wasn't even looking at anything. He wasn't even thinking. He was just worrying.

When he had first come into the little room, he was worrying about what would happen if word got out about him and Emil. Then he wondered why it had never gotten out before. He and Emil had been seeing each other for years, since they both graduated from college, but they had been careful. A lot of people wondered about Emil. He had never married, and he had his prissy ways, but most people thought he was odd, not queer. As far as he knew, nobody had ever suspected A.Y. was anything other than a loving family man. He was married. He liked to hunt and was a good shot. He had played football in high school, on the same team with Stumpy, Al, and the others. Nobody knew but him and Emil. And now Stumpy.

With the thought of Stumpy, A.Y.'s worries moved from himself to the Singing Convention. He didn't know what kind of mess was going to happen when that Negro choir got on the stage Sunday. How many people would get up and leave? How many would try to shout them down, destroying the beauty of a tradition that was nearly 30 years old? And all this happening while A.Y. was supposed to be in charge. He leaned back in the old desk chair. For the only time in his life, A.Y. wished he smoked. This was the kind of situation where people usually smoked, filling up the ashtray to show time was passing.

I've never really failed at anything, he thought, except my marriage. He laughed a soft, embarrassed laugh when he realized just how big that exception was. He and Virginia had gotten off to a good start, for almost a year. The next two years weren't really bad; he had just figured that the honeymoon was over. After that, they appeared to be married to everybody else in River Falls, even to the twins, but each of them knew they weren't really married. And that failure hurt A.Y. almost every day, not so much because of his pride, but because he had brought a lovely woman to River Falls and being married to him had turned her into a sad, angry, bitter alcoholic. The wasted life was what made him saddest. And the fact he couldn't do anything about it.

He wondered if he ought to work on his opening remarks for the Singing Convention. Then he decided that the remarks could wait. He wasn't through worrying.

24

Stumpy and Mae Beth slipped into one of the back rows of the sanctuary. Stumpy looked around. It didn't look much like a church at all. There was no stained glass. The pulpit was white and plain, and the rail that separated the choir loft from the pulpit was just plain wood, painted white.

There were about thirty people scattered around the room, and Bessie and her choir were at the front. He recognized Levon Lassiter sitting at the piano. Levon worked for Mr. Stewart at the feed mill. He recognized two or three others in the choir. It bothered him a little that there was anywhere he could go in River Falls and not recognize most of the people. It also made him a little uncomfortable, like he was among strangers. He wondered if he should have insisted that he and Mae Beth come to the church and hear the choir.

"You can hear them Sunday," Mae Beth had said.

"I just want to hear them. With all the fuss this has kicked up, I'd like to know what they sound like."

"You heard them when they sang downtown. Didn't that satisfy your curiosity?"

"I don't think that was the best of circumstances. People were throwing things."

Finally, Mae Beth had agreed to go, although she said they probably shouldn't show up without talking to Bessie about it. Since Bessie was already gone for the day and would soon be at the church, they couldn't do that, so they just drove up to the church.

Now that they were there, Stumpy thought it would have been better just to listen to Mae Beth. He could hear Bessie talking to the choir.

"We're going to sing *It Is Well with my Soul*," she said, pointing to a stack of music on the choir rail. There was a mumbling in the choir that mixed with the rustling of the paper as they passed it down the rows. Then a man in the back row said, "Ain't that awfully white?"

"Not a matter of white. Or colored. This is God's music, and what we're going to do we'll do to the glory of God."

"I thought you said that we're going to win this thing." It was a female voice. Bessie didn't look up. She just stared at the music.

"That, too," she said. "But let's don't get so messed up with trying to win that we forget why we sing this music. It's going to be a Sunday just like every other Sunday."

Several people nodded. A few almost laughed.

With small motions of her hand, Bessie counted off four beats and the piano came in.

Stumpy didn't know Levon played the piano. That surprised him, but the way Levon played amazed him. As he played the introduction he whispered the notes, shaping them so it sounded like each one wanted to cry.

When the four-measure introduction was over, Bessie brought in the choir, very softly. The chords were wide and rich, and every eye was on Bessie's hand and the small calm motions she made.

When peace, like a river, attendeth my way,
When sorrows like sea billows roll;
When peace, like a river, attendeth my way,
When sorrows like sea billows roll;
Whatever my lot, Thou has taught me to say,
It is well, it is well, with my soul.

There was just a hint of silence at the end of the verse and a very soft gasp as the choir took a breath to go into the chorus.

It is well, with my soul,
It is well, with my soul,
It is well, it is well, with my soul.

Stumpy felt tears come to his eyes. This was the song they sang at his daddy's funeral, but he didn't remember it being sung with the kind of feeling he was hearing now.

The piece had four verses, and the volume built almost imperceptibly from one verse to the next, until they got to the final verse. At the end of the refrain before the fourth verse, the choir held the last word, and Levon, crashing the keys with both hands, built chords from the very bottom of the piano to the top, then the choir, full throated and joyous, entered into the final verse.

And Lord, haste the day when my faith shall be sight,

To Bessie, the twenty people up there sounded like a

heavenly choir. It was the kind of sound that made you expect a shining shaft of light to come through the church ceiling, illuminating the choir like a host of angels.

The clouds be rolled back as a scroll;

Then Levon began building huge block chords, and the choir sang with a near fierceness.

The trump shall resound, and the Lord shall descend,
Even so,

Then suddenly it was quiet again, and the choir slowly, quietly, and reverently sang the last words.

It is well with my soul.

Stumpy wiped a tear from the corner of his eye. He felt like the old hymn was worth more than a sermon. He started clapping, but Mae Beth put her hand on his and stopped him. He noticed that nobody else in the church was applauding. There was absolute silence. At the sound of the single clap, Bessie had turned around and saw them. She said something to the choir that he couldn't hear and started walking back toward them. Stumpy stood up.

"That was beautiful, Bessie. It's one of my favorite hymns, and I've never heard it sung so good."

"Thank you, Mr. Stumpy. I'm surprised to see you here, but you and Miss Mae Beth are surely welcome."

"Arthur wanted to hear the choir," Mae Beth said, grinning. "I guess he wanted to make sure it was worth a picture window."

Stumpy shot a look at Mae Beth, but then he noticed that Bessie was smiling, too. There was something they shared he would never understand.

"So, Mr. Stumpy, was it? Was it worth a picture window?"

"I'd say so, Bessie. And when I die, I'd like for your choir to sing it at my funeral just like that."

"Figuring that I'm a lot older than you, I doubt I'll be around to do that. But if I am, I'd be honored. Now I got to get these folks back to practicing. We still got a service on Sunday, even if it is Singing Sunday, and we don't want to slight our real service. Y'all are welcome to stay and listen, if you want to."

Stumpy nodded. "Thank you, Bessie. I think we'd like to." He felt a lot more comfortable than he had when he came in. He was able to just sit back and listen to the choir.

25

It was the gray time between night and day, but the air was already heavy and warm. Otha wondered if there wasn't a place a man could farm that didn't get so miserable in the summer, but he figured if there was, it probably got miserable in the winter, and that would be worse. He felt a little silly sitting in the pickup in his Klan robe. It made it even hotter, but Claymore had insisted they all wear their robes. He wanted them to wear their hoods, too, but Otha pointed out that four men in hoods sitting in an alley that time of morning might look a little strange. Otha looked over at Claymore, sitting on the driver's side, leaning against the doorpost with his eyes shut. He heard Aaron Smelt and Jim Turnage moving around in the back of the pickup. And he wondered what he was doing.

"What time did you say she got by here?" Claymore said.

"About quarter to seven. I guess she's getting to the Fowler's before seven."

Claymore looked at his watch. "Ought to be by here any minute then. You know what to do?"

"Yeah. I know what to do. I just don't know why you brought Aaron. If anybody can screw this up, he can."

"He's just along for the ride. Jim'll take care of that part. You just be sure you take care of yours."

Otha turned and stared out the window. Jim was supposed to jump out of the bed of the pickup behind Bessie and throw the tow bag over her head. Otha was to tie her hands and push her into the cab of the pickup. Since Bessie weighed at least as much as he did and was a good deal wider, he figured pushing her into the pickup might be a problem.

He saw Claymore look at his watch again. Otha just wished Bessie would come on and let them get this over with. He still thought it was a bad idea, but it would be a worse one if there wasn't somebody there to make sure Claymore didn't do something to hurt Bessie. He just breathed in some more of the warm, damp air and waited.

It was only a few minutes later when they saw Bessie walking along the street, her head up, her purse tucked under her arm. Claymore waited until she had passed the mouth of the alley, then he cranked the pickup. The starter was loud, like a screeching bird, and when the motor caught he could hear the throb of the exhaust. Otha wondered how Bessie couldn't hear that. But when Claymore pulled the pickup out of the alley and onto the street, Bessie was still walking, looking straight ahead. Claymore rapped on the back window. Otha looked over his shoulder and saw Jim Turnage gathering up the tow sack, getting ready to jump over the side of the pickup. As they got closer to Bessie, Claymore slowed down. Jim Turnage climbed from the pickup bed to the running board, and jumped, running up behind Bessie. At the sound of the footsteps, she started to turn, but Jim had already thrown the bag over her head and wrapped his arms around her body, pinning her arms to her side.

Claymore stopped the truck, and Otha stepped out. He had a length of rope with a slipknot at the end. He grabbed her hands and slipped the rope over them. Then he looped it over her wrist and tied it off. Inside the tow sack, Bessie was yelling, but it was muffled, and in less than a minute they were trying to stuff her into the cab of the pickup. Aaron Smelt had jumped out of the pickup bed and was running around, trying to find a place to push Bessie. Finally, Otha got behind her, pushed her off balance, and while she was trying not to fall, shoved her into the truck. He pushed her to the middle and climbed in. Jim and Aaron climbed into the back.

There was no sound in the truck except for Bessie's muffled voice saying they had better take that dirty bag off her head and turn her loose. When nobody answered, she finally quit talking, and the two men and the woman with the bag on her head rode out into the country to a two-lane path that led to a tobacco barn and an abandoned sharecropper's shack. Claymore pulled the pickup in front of the shack. The four men got out of the truck, leaving Bessie sitting in the front seat. They put on their pointed hoods.

"Get her out," he said.

Otha got out of the truck and appraised the situation. Bessie was sitting in the middle of the pickup seat, blindfolded, with her hands tied in front of her. She looked like more than two or three of them could move.

"How we going to get her out of there?" Aaron asked. Like Otha, he was impressed with Bessie's size. Otha was also impressed that it didn't seem to bother her a lot that she was wearing a bag on her head and had her hands tied. She just sat quietly on the seat, apparently staring straight ahead.

"No way we're going to carry her," Jim said.

"No way," agreed Aaron.

"Just step back," Otha said. He put his foot on the running board of the pickup and leaned in. "Sister Bessie, would you mind sliding this way?"

"Yes, I would," she said. "Especially with this dirty bag over my head. I don't want to go sliding if I don't know where I'm sliding to."

"Well, if you would, just slide over this way, and I'll make sure you don't slide off the seat.

She just sat there, staring straight ahead through the tow sack.

"Sister Bessie, we can't take that sack off your head until we get inside. So the sooner we get inside, the sooner we can get it off and untie your hands.

After a moment, Bessie began to slide to her right, slowly, like a glacier cutting a new valley in the earth. Otha just stood there and waited. When Sister Bessie reached the edge of the pickup seat, Otha took her arm.

"Okay, Sister Bessie. Now you need to step down a little bit, just down to the running board."

Bessie edged her leg over the side of the seat and felt for

the running board with her foot. When she found it, Otha moved back a step.

"Now, step down again."

Bessie stepped down to the ground. Otha turned toward the door, and they started walking toward the shack.

When they got to the steps that hung off the sagging front porch, he told Bessie to step up and he guided her into the shack.

"Sit her down over there," Claymore said.

Otha pulled the chair away from the wall and started untying Bessie's hands.

"What are you doing?" Claymore demanded.

"Untying her. We're here. She don't need to be tied up." By the time he had finished saying it, he had untied the ropes around Bessie's hands, so there wasn't much use in Claymore telling him not to do it. Then he lifted the bag from her head. Bessie blinked a few times and looked around the one-room shack.

"'Bout what I would expect," she said. "Don't nobody round here know how to use a broom and a dust rag?"

"You be quiet, girl," Claymore said. "You just sit here quiet, and you won't get hurt."

Bessie's gaze turned slowly toward Claymore like a large cannon finding its target. The way she looked at him, Otha thought she must be able to see right through the hood, right through those little eyes, and right into his brain cavity. She stood up and turned to face him.

"Girl?" she said. "*Girl?* I was cooking and cleaning and taking care of good white children while you were still messing your diapers, Claymore Thomas."

She turned to the next one. "And you, Aaron Smelt. I thought you knew better than this. I know you ain't too smart, but I thought you were a good person anyway. Guess that shows that I can be wrong."

Then she turned and faced Otha. "And you, Mr. Forster. When your baby was sick, your wife called Miss Mae Beth when she couldn't get the doctor, and we went out to your house and took care of her 'til the doctor came. And this is the way you repay a kindness. Grabbing somebody and sticking a bag on their head and tying them up. Shame on you."

"You be quiet, girl," Claymore said. "You don't know us. We're not from around here."

Bessie turned back to Claymore, a little bit of a smile on her face.

"I guess I could wish that that was so, Claymore Thomas. But I know it ain't. You're from around here. Everybody on Disciple Street knows you from around here, and if it won't for the trouble you kick up sometimes, it'd be funny. We know about your meetings, and we know about the signs you put up, and that cross you tried to burn in our yard."

She stood there staring at Claymore with her hands on her hips.

"Yes, suh. We know you."

Claymore turned around and stomped out the door. Jim Turnage and Aaron Smelt looked at each other, at Otha, then turned and followed him out, leaving Otha with Bessie. She turned to him.

"Mr. Forster, I know you to be a good man. I just don't know what you're doing messed up in something like this."

Otha couldn't think of an answer, so he suggested that Bessie make herself as comfortable as she could, and walked out of the shack, pulling the door to behind him. He found Claymore talking to Aaron and Jim. They all had their hoods off. Claymore turned to Otha as he walked up.

"I'll take you by your truck on the way home. Jim and Aaron are going to stay here and watch the nigger. I'll come back tonight and relieve them."

"When do you need me to come back?" Otha asked.

"I don't think you need to. We'll be able to handle it. You've done enough."

Otha nodded and walked with Claymore to the pickup.

"She knows who we are," he said.

"Don't matter," Claymore said. "Ain't going to be a problem. Let's get home and get some breakfast."

* * *

It hadn't worried Stumpy that Bessie wasn't there when he left for work; in fact, he hardly thought about it. He had his list of things that needed to be done, and he knew that Bessie had sometimes been late to work, usually because she had stopped off to get breakfast for one of her neighbors who was sick. However, when Mae Beth called him at 9:30 to tell him that Bessie still wasn't there, he decided he needed to walk down to the cotton yard to speak with Horace. Horace said that she was about to leave for work when he left. She should have been there by seven o'clock. So Stumpy walked over to city hall to speak with Earl.

"You really think somebody grabbed Bessie?" Earl asked, his face scrunched up and one hand scratching his red hair.

"I don't think 'somebody' did it. I think Claymore Thomas kidnapped Bessie, and I'm worried about what he might do with her."

Earl shook his head. "I think Claymore's bark is a whole lot worse than his bite. All he's done so far is hold those meetings and make speeches."

"And try to burn a cross in Bessie's front yard."

Earl snorted. "From what I hear, they came closer to torching one of the kluxers than they did burning the cross."

"Still, it could be that Claymore would get desperate enough to do something like this. He's not going to look real good when Bessie and her choir gets on the stage Sunday."

"Well, you could be right. I don't think you are, but if you are, it could be bad for Bessie. I guess we need to go look for her. I'll send Albert over to talk to her neighbors. Maybe one of them saw something."

"We probably should check the route that Bessie walked to work. Just to make sure she didn't trip and break something or have a heart attack."

By the time Li'l got out of bed, his mother had talked to Stumpy again and to several of the neighbors. None of them had seen Bessie. She told him about Bessie's disappearance while he ate his corn flakes. He could tell she was already upset, and he guessed if they didn't find her soon, she was going to get more upset.

"Daddy thinks she's been kidnapped?"

Mae Beth nodded. "I can't believe anybody, even Claymore Thomas, would do something like that, but your daddy is convinced that he did. Just to keep Bessie's choir from singing on Sunday."

"Couldn't they sing without Bessie?"

"They could, but I doubt they would."

"What can I do to help?"

"I don't know, Arthur. Your daddy and Earl and Horace are out talking to anybody that might have seen anything. Wait until your daddy comes home and ask him. I need to make some more phone calls."

Li'l decided to go down town and find out what everybody was saying. He went to the barbershop, both drug stores, and ended up at the Canteen. All he learned was that everybody was talking about the Singing Convention on Sunday except for those who were talking about the fact that Carl Cagle had somehow sprained his back and couldn't get out of bed. He was even going to have to miss his television program Saturday night. On his way home, he stopped by Billy Royce's house, but Billy Royce said he had been hanging around the house all day and hadn't even heard that Bessie was gone. Li'l walked back home, not knowing any more about where Bessie was than when he left.

* * *

Stumpy, Earl, and Horace had been up and down Disciples Street, and Stumpy had knocked on every door along the side street and Main Street, but nobody had seen Bessie or anything unusual. Several people did advance some theories about what had happened.

Mavis Whittington pursed her lips and nodded her head several times. "I guess she was just ashamed of what she's done and left town. I guess that's the best you could expect."

Edna Penny figured that somebody from the negrah section had taken her because she was stirring up such a fuss and the right thinking negrahs knew that if there was a fuss they would be the losers.

A few people expressed concern about what had happened to Bessie.

Earl dropped Horace by his house and then took Stumpy home. They had run out of places to look for the time being.

"I'll check by with the Sheriff and see what he found out," Earl said. "And I think I'll swing by Claymore's place to see if he knows anything."

"You want me to come with you?" Stumpy asked, thinking how nice it would be if Claymore resisted arrest.

But Earl shook his head. "I'm just going to make a neighborly visit. Technically, it's out of my jurisdiction, but the sheriff and I have an understanding. I'll be fine."

Stumpy said he'd make some more phone calls. He didn't think that somebody like Bessie could just vanish.

* * *

Otha had spent the day in the field, but he couldn't get his mind off Bessie and what Claymore had meant when he said it didn't matter that she knew who they were. The more he thought about it, the more he was convinced Claymore had changed the plan and was going to do something to Bessie, maybe even kill her. As soon as he finished dinner, he told his wife that he was going to see Claymore about some Klan business. It only took him about twenty minutes to get to the sharecropper shack.

Jim Turnage and Aaron Smelt were sitting on the porch, leaning against the square porch posts with their feet swinging. Otha was relieved; nothing had happened, or they wouldn't have been sitting out there looking so bored.

"Hello, boys," he said, as he walked up to the porch. "What's going on?"

Jim Turnage just shook his head. "Not a damn thing. The nigger woman's in there. We're out here, and Claymore told us to stay here until he got back. I wish he'd get on back here, so I could go home. I'm getting hungry."

"So Claymore's going to do guard duty all night? By himself?"

"I guess," Turnage said. "He just told us to stay here until he got back."

"I'm going in to check on the prisoner," Otha said, walking up the steps. He saw Jim Turnage look at Aaron, then shrug his shoulders. He opened the door and went in.

Even in the dull light he could tell the shack was a whole lot cleaner now than it was when he had left. The old lopsided eating table had been dusted off and a couple of chairs had been pulled up to it. A brush broom stood in the corner; Otha figured that was the reason the floor looked so much cleaner. Bessie was sitting in a chair against the wall with her hands in her lap and her eyes closed. It looked like she was praying.

"You okay, Sister Bessie?"

She opened her eyes and looked at him.

"Well, Mr. Forster. You didn't wear your sheet and little pointy hood."

"Didn't figure there was much need since you seem to see through hoods."

Bessie grunted a deep laugh. "Ain't much these old eyes don't see. Like, I saw you wasn't like them others. And you ain't."

"I don't know, Sister Bessie. I may be a lot more like them than you'd think. Or that'd I'd want to believe. The problem I got is that I'm afraid something is going to happen to you, and that wasn't what I signed up for."

She looked at him straight in the eyes, as if she was trying to see in his brain.

"Mr. Forster, why does it bother you for me and my choir to sing in the Singing Convention? Since that's what all this is about, I'd like to know."

He turned his head away from her.

"I don't know. I guess it's because that's not the way it's been done. Lord, you know I'm grateful for what you and Mrs. Fowler did for Maggie. She might have died if y'all hadn't been there. But what you're trying to do changes something. I don't know how important it is, but it seems important."

Bessie nodded. "So you're scared of what's going to happen if we really change something, even something like the Sing."

Otha started to tell her that he wasn't scared of anything, that he had faced down Germans in the Battle of the Bulge, and that he'd kept shooting Germans while the shells were throwing dirt all over him. But he didn't say anything. The Germans seemed like they were a long time ago, and they were just trying to kill him. He had a feeling a change like this one was trying to take his life. He pulled one of the chairs from the eating table over beside Bessie and sat down.

"Maybe you're right. Maybe I am just scared because if anything changes, I don't know what it's going to be like. So I'd like for things to stay like they are."

"Then why are you here?" Bessie asked quietly.

"Because I think Claymore plans to hurt you, maybe real bad, and I can't be a part of that."

"All you have to do is walk back out the door and go home. Then whatever Claymore Thomas does is up to him. It's not on you."

"I don't see it that way. I helped get you here. Now I need to help you get out of here before he gets back."

"And how we going to do that? Them two are sitting out on the porch, and Lord knows I can't outrun them. And I don't think you can out fight both of them."

Otha got up and walked around the little room. The

windows on the front were mostly boarded up. In the back corner, there was a door that opened onto the path that probably led to the outhouse, but it looked like it had been nailed shut. Beside it was a window with a couple of old boards nailed over it. Otha tried the door, but it didn't give. Then he tried the boards on the windows. They seemed to be held by only a few nails, and those not very big. He pushed on one of the boards. It moved out, the nail squeaking as it pulled away from the window frame. He stopped and listened, but there was no sound from the front porch. Carefully, he brought the plank back in through the window and put it on the floor. He thought a moment, then picked it up and handed it to Bessie.

"Take this and stand over by the door. If anybody comes in while I'm working on the window, hit 'em with it. And be sure to hit 'em with the edge. If you hit 'em with the flat part, it won't do anything."

Bessie walked over to the door and took a couple of practice swings with the board. When she was satisfied, she looked at Otha and nodded. He went back to work on the window board. This one was more stubborn. He stood up on the chair and put his shoulder against one side of it. He felt the board give a little. He pushed it again with his shoulder, and he heard the nail squeak. It sounded like some kind of monster waking up. He looked at the door. Bessie was standing there holding the board, but there was no sound from the porch. He finished pulling that side of the board out and let it swing down toward the ground. Otha got down from the chair, motioning Bessie to come over to him.

"You think you can get out that window?" he asked.

She looked at it for a minute.

"Ain't much of a window, is it?" she said. "I may be bigger than it is."

"I think we better try. Just get up on the chair and climb through the window, I'll keep an eye on the door."

Bessie nodded and handed the board to Otha. She climbed up on the chair, gingerly, like she was afraid that the chair that had held Otha might collapse under her weight. It took her two or three tries before she found a way to start putting her body through the window. She had one leg hiked over the window sill, her head and shoulders scrunched down, and an arm holding on to the top of the window. Otha watched while her body seemed to seep through the window with the leg that was on the inside sliding up. She turned loose of the top of the window and suddenly all of her disappeared. He heard a dull thud as Bessie fell into the soft dirt behind the house. He listened for some movement from the porch, figuring that those two must be either asleep or wandering around in the front yard. He put the board down and stepped up on the chair, ducking his head and shoulders through the window. He slid out and felt his foot touch the ground. He stopped and looked around.

It was nearly dark, even darker in the back of the house under the trees than in the front. He could barely make out Bessie's form standing in the edge of the yard near the outhouse.

"Can you drive?" he asked.

"Never did," she said.

"Then we got to figure a way for me to get to my truck and for you to get in it."

Bessie looked at the outhouse. "Maybe I could tell that Turnage fellow that I had to go to the outhouse. I bet they'd both come around here. Then you could get your truck?"

Otha smiled. "That's an idea, Sister Bessie, but there are a couple of things wrong with it. One is that you'd have to climb back inside that window. The other is that you'd be back here with those two while I was in the front with the truck. No, there has to be something better."

Otha crouched on the ground for a minute, his chin in his hand. Bessie kept watching the house. Finally, Otha stood up.

"Okay, I have an idea, and if those two are as dumb as I think they are, it'll probably work." He pointed to the edge of the house away from them. "You go and hide over there. I'm going to go get them and bring them around this way. When they come back here, you go get in the truck. I'll come back and we'll take off."

Bessie nodded and headed to the far corner of the house, keeping in the tree shadows. When she had gotten there, Otha walked around the side of the house. He stopped at the corner, stooped low, and peered around to the front yard. Jim and Aaron were standing in the middle of the front yard, smoking. He stood up, took a deep breath, and ran into the front yard.

"She's gone. You dummies let that nigger get away," he yelled.

Jim Turnage turned around. "What do you mean, she got away?" he said. "And how come you ain't in the house?"

Otha stopped in front of them.

"She wasn't in there when I went in. She'd climbed out a window. I went out the window to see if I could find her. She went down into the woods, and when I couldn't find her, I came back here. We better find her before Claymore gets here. He'll have your ass for letting her get away."

The two men just stood there, their jaws dropped. Otha figured they were thinking harder about what Claymore was going to do to them than finding Bessie.

"Let's get going. We'll find her and get her back here before Claymore shows up."

He grabbed Jim Turnage's arm and started pulling him to the back of the house. Aaron followed. When they got to the edge of the woods behind the house, Otha pointed Turnage in one direction and Aaron Smelt in another.

"And I'll go that way. As big as she is, she ain't gone far. Let's get in there and find her."

He took off running to the edge of the woods, looking over his shoulder to see if the other two were moving. He got into the shadows of the trees and stopped, leaning up against one of the big oaks and listening to Jim Turnage and Aaron Smelt crashing through the woods. After a minute, he crept out of the woods and went around to the front of the house. Bessie was sitting in the pickup.

"Let's get out of here. Claymore was supposed to be back already."

"I heard what you said about me being big."

Otha looked at her and was surprised to find that she was smiling.

"Well, it's the truth," she said. "God just decided this world needed a lot of me."

Otha started the truck, threw it in gear, and headed up the two-lane path. He had almost made it to the road when he saw that he was nose to nose with Claymore's truck. Two men jumped out of the back and Claymore and another man got out of the cab. They ran up to Otha's truck and yanked the doors open, pulling him out of one side and Bessie out the other.

"Where the hell you think you're going, Otha?" Claymore said, standing right in front of Otha. Otha noticed that Claymore didn't have his robe and hood on. Neither did the other men.

"I'm going to take Sister Bessie home and hope that she'll forget this mess, Claymore. I ain't about to go to jail for kidnapping." He looked at the other men. He didn't know any of them. They just stood there with their faces set, grim, like they had already decided they had a job to do and were just about to do it. "Or murder."

"Otha, Otha, Otha," Claymore said, beginning to pace back and forth the way he did when he was giving a speech. "I knew you thought too much, but I never figured you for a streak of yellow. You ought to know that we can't let this nigger go now. She knows who we are. And these boys have come over from Oak Grove to help us out. If you'd just stayed home tonight, we'd had her over in Oak Grove and nobody would have ever heard from her again." He stopped and walked back up to Otha. "Now you've screwed that up. Now I've got to decide what to do with you. I don't guess I could trust you just to keep your mouth shut, could I."

"I imagine you could," Bessie said. "I made him try to get me out of there. He didn't want to."

Claymore snorted.

"You made him. How did you make him? You threaten to sit on him or something?" He let out a big laugh and the other men looked at each other and joined in.

Otha shook his head.

"I don't guess you can count on much of anything from me, Claymore. You told me nobody was going to get hurt with this mess, and you lied to me. I ain't for killing anybody, and if you are, I guess you're going to have to kill me, too."

He just stood there and looked Claymore right in the eyes. For a long minute, Claymore didn't move. Finally, one of the Oak Grove men asked if they were going to do this or not. He said he didn't plan to stand out there all night watching them two stare at each other.

"Shut up," Claymore growled, still looking at Otha. "The plan's got to be changed, and I've got to have some time to think this through."

"Well, we goin' do this tonight, or we not?" the Oak Grove man said. The others mumbled about wanting to get this over with.

Claymore shook his head. "Not tonight. You boys take my truck and go on home. I'm going to stay here with Otha and the nigger and figure out how to get rid of them. But before you leave, get them back to the house and tie them up. And tie them up good. I don't want to be chasing them through the woods tonight."

The men nodded, and one of them pulled a coil of rope from the back of Claymore's pickup.

Claymore grabbed one of the Oak Grove men by the arm. "While they're doing that, would you see if you can find those two idiots I left here guarding her."

The men grabbed Otha and Bessie and pulled them back to the house, not saying anything to either one of them. Otha saw Claymore get into Otha's truck and back it up to the yard. He figured his truck would be in somebody's pond by tomorrow night.

It didn't take the men but a few minutes to shove Otha and Bessie into the straight chairs and tie them up. Otha felt the rough rope cutting into his wrists and ankles, and he knew it must be worse for Bessie. The men checked the ropes again and went out the front door. Otha could hear them talking on the front porch.

"You a brave man, Mr. Forster," Bessie said.

"I don't know, Sister Bessie. Maybe just dumb. Dumb to be here in the first place. Dumb to come back. But I don't guess it makes a whole lot of difference now."

"Well, I think we ought to pray. Lord knows we ain't got much else to do right now."

Otha looked at her. She had her head down and her eyes shut, her lips were moving, but no sound was coming out.

He bowed his head.

26

Li'l was having trouble identifying the sound. He was dreaming it was the dead school bell that had suddenly come to life, but he finally recognized it was the telephone. He heard his daddy talking, then he heard him talking to his mother. Li'l got out of bed and went into the kitchen.

"Did they find out anything about Bessie?" he asked.

Stumpy shook his head.

"That was Earl. He's been out all night, but all he found out was that some of the kluxers weren't home last night. But that doesn't prove anything."

"What are you going to do?" Li'l asked.

"Earl's going to pick me up and Horace, and we're going to go look in some other places." He rubbed his forehead with his hand. "I don't know where we're going to look or why we're going to look there. She could be about any-where."

"Can I go with you?"

"I don't think so. Earl didn't even want Horace and me to go with him because he's afraid that if he does find Bessie somebody might get hurt, but I talked him into it. I don't think I could do that again."

Li'l nodded and went back into his room to get dressed. He sat down on the edge of the bed, trying to think of something he could do to help. The idea of Bessie being hurt cut into him as much as if it had been his own daddy or mother. Bessie was a part of the family, and he ought to be doing something to find her and save her. He thought about what Mike Hammer might do, but that didn't help. Mostly Mike Hammer found a beautiful woman and somehow solved the crime while he made love to the woman. Then he thought about Joe Friday and his partner. They went around asking questions, getting the facts, but he knew that Earl had already talked to about everybody there was to talk to. In the movies, they sometimes did stakeouts where they just sat and waited for something to happen. That didn't seem like it would do a lot of good either, but it might be better than doing nothing at all.

Li'l got dressed and went back into the kitchen. His mother was just about to walk out the back door.

"Get you some breakfast, and I'll be back in an hour or so," she said. "I'm going over to help Mable get her mother's stuff ready to move. She's going to have to move in with them."

Li'l pulled the cereal box out of the pantry, fixed it with some milk and sugar and sat down at the table. He stared at the cereal, wondering where he could go that might turn up something that would help find Bessie. But the only place he could think of was the Thomas place. Somebody might be coming or going there that could help. But that was out in the country, further than he could go on his bicycle. He sat there for a few minutes trying to think of something else to do, but his mind kept going back to the Thomas' place. His daddy was gone with Earl, and his mother was going to be at Mabel Jackson's for a while, probably a lot more than an hour or two. And the car was in the garage. And he had his learner's permit, which really didn't matter much since he was supposed to have an adult with him whenever he drove somewhere. But he decided that getting caught driving when he wasn't supposed to was better than sitting around the house doing nothing, and if he did help find Bessie it would be worth it.

He got the spare set of car keys out of the drawer in the kitchen and went out to the garage, being careful to prop the garage doors wide open. That was usually his job when he and his daddy went somewhere anyway. Stumpy didn't want the doors to swing into the car and scratch it. He got into the car and cranked it. He shifted it into reverse, then looked over his shoulder. Suddenly, it struck him; he'd never backed the car out of the garage. They'd practiced backing when they were driving on the dirt roads, but there was plenty of space between the road and the ditch. There didn't seem to be any space at all between the car and the rough wood doors of the garage. He turned the car off and got out. From outside the car, it seemed like there was at least a foot to spare. He got back in the car and cranked it again. Looking over his shoulder, he eased the car back slowly, watching the small space between the fin on the Oldsmobile and the garage door. Twice he stopped the car, staring over his shoulder, trying to decide if the space had gotten larger or smaller, and if it had gotten larger, what had happened to the space on the other side. It was several minutes before he saw the edge of the garage door come even with him. Now the car was out, and all he had to do was back out of the driveway.

By the time Main Street became Highway 55, Li'l was comfortable again. It was just like when he and his daddy had gone out for driving lessons. He watched the speedometer, making sure he didn't go over fifty-five, and he kept both hands on the wheel. He just hoped he didn't meet Stumpy and Earl while he was going out to Claymore Thomas'. He wondered if they had the same idea he did, and if they did, should he be more afraid of Earl, who could give him a ticket and keep him from getting his license or his daddy, who could ground him forever.

When he got to The Crossroads, Li'l carefully gave a hand signal and turned down the smaller road toward the Thomas'. Now he had to decide how he was going to do the stakeout. By the time he reached the two-lane path that went down to the Thomas house, he had decided the best thing to do was drive down the road, then sneak back to where he could get a good view of the driveway, hoping sooner or later somebody would come out.

About a hundred yards further, he found a dirt road. He pulled down the dirt road and over to the shoulder. He got out and started walking back to where he could see the path leading to the Thomas's, staying in the shadow of the trees so he couldn't be seen. He sat down behind a tree and peered around, waiting for something to happen.

He'd only been there a few minutes when the big

flies found him and started buzzing around his head. He flicked them away and wiped his face on the sleeve of his shirt. He hadn't thought about what he was going to do if nobody came out. How long would he stay there? What would happen if somebody did come out and see him sitting there staring at their driveway? He began to wonder if the whole thing had been a bad idea. If it was a good idea, why wasn't Earl already here? He was just about to give up and go back home when he saw the nose of a car stop at the end of the driveway. Then the car pulled onto the road, turning away from where Li'l was sitting. It was Petey, and he was heading toward The Crossroads.

Li'l ran back to the car and jumped in, wishing he had thought to turn it around when he got there. As he pulled back out onto the paved road, he could see that Petey was already out of sight. Li'l mashed the accelerator, watching the speedometer pass sixty-five. It was almost to seventy when he saw Petey's car down the road. Li'l slowed down and trailed Petey until he saw him stop at the general store. Li'l pulled over to the shoulder of the road and waited, hoping that Petey hadn't gone to the store just to get a loaf of bread for his mother. In a few minutes, he saw Petey's car pull away from the general store, heading away from his house. Li'l followed him. He felt like he was beginning to get the hang of this.

Petey drove about five miles down the highway, then turned off onto a county road. Li'l couldn't ever remember being here before, so he started noticing landmarks. He passed a small white church on the right. The sign out front said Elevation Baptist Church. Then he passed a pond. Petey had turned off just beyond the pond, so Li'l pulled up to the edge of the path and got out. It was a two-track dirt path, probably heading down to somebody's house. He decided it wouldn't be smart to drive down the path and maybe come nose to nose with Petey or his daddy, so he got back in the car and pulled it down the road and parked, making sure the Oldsmobile was hidden from the road. Then he went back to the path. On one side there was young corn, but not tall enough to provide any cover. On the other side of the path it was mostly woods, so he went that way.

He didn't have to go far before he saw the sharecropper shack, and two men were standing out in the yard. Petey was getting some things out of his car, two paper bags. One of the men walked over and took a bag from Petey. He pulled out something, took the wrapper off it and started eating. He handed the bag to the other man. *So Petey brought breakfast.* Then Claymore Thomas walked out on the porch and said something to one of the men. The man went into the shack.

Li'l crouched in the weeds, trying to decide what he'd really found. There was Claymore Thomas and some of his friends. There was Petey. But did that mean that Bessie was in the house. Li'l wanted to believe it did. That would mean they could rescue Bessie. And it would mean his daddy probably wouldn't be so mad that he had taken the car. But he didn't know if there was anything or anybody in the house. Very quietly he went back into the woods and worked his way around to the back of the house. Every time he stepped on a stick it sounded like a gunshot and made him jump. Once, he dropped to the ground to keep from being seen and found himself almost on top of a big clump of poison ivy. But finally, he could see the back of the house with a window with the boards knocked out of it.

Checking to see that none of the men were walking around in the back yard, he ran up to the back of the house. He stood on his tiptoes to peer into the window. Inside one man was leaning against the wall chewing on something that looked like a Honey Bun, and two people were sitting in chairs. From their shapes, Li'l could tell that one of them was Bessie, and from the way they were sitting, it looked like they were tied up. He could hear Claymore talking in the front yard of the house. Li'l ran back to the cover of the trees and made his way back to the car.

He jumped in the car, cranked it and started down the narrow paved road. The fence posts on the side of the road seemed to be flying by. He looked at the speedometer, and it said that he was doing seventy, but he decided it didn't matter. The only thing that mattered now was finding Earl and his daddy. He turned back onto the road to River Falls, thinking he would go to the police station, and they could call Earl on the radio.

About two miles from River Falls he saw a familiar black and white car heading toward him. He started blowing the horn, but the car drove right past him.

In the police car, Stumpy was looking at a county map, trying to find places that looked like a likely hideout, but since he didn't know anything about hideouts, he hadn't found anything. Horace was hunched in the back seat staring first out the right window and then out of the left. Suddenly Earl said, "Don't that look like your car?"

Stumpy looked up just as the police car met and passed the Oldsmobile. He saw Li'l blowing the horn and waving at them. The first thing he thought was "get both hands back on the steering wheel."

"It is my car. Li'l driving it. Turn around," Stumpy said.

The police car wheeled around. The Oldsmobile had stopped just down the road and Li'l was piling out of it and running toward them.

Earl pulled up beside them, and Li'l grabbed onto the windowsill.

"I found them," he gasped. "They're at an old shack down beyond that Baptist church. Elevation Baptist Church. They've got Bessie and somebody else tied up there."

"Who's got them?" Earl asked.

"It's Claymore Thomas. He's there with two other men and Petey. Petey just took them some food."

Stumpy started to say something, but decided this was police business and he'd let Earl do the talking. Earl stared straight ahead, chewing on his lower lip.

"That's probably good," he said. "If the boy took food to them, they probably don't plan to leave right away. I better get down there. Can you show me where this place is, Li'l?"

Li'l nodded. Stumpy got out of the police car.

"I'll follow you in my car," he told Earl.

"Y'all better leave this to me, Stumpy. They might want to get mean since they're going to get charged with kidnapping."

"I think I need to help out, Mr. Earl," Horace said. "They got my wife down there, and I can't be doing nothing."

Earl looked at Horace, then at Stumpy.

"Okay," he said, "but if they try to get rough, remember I'm the one who's got a gun."

Stumpy trotted back down the road to his car. The two cars turned around and headed up the highway.

As he followed the police car, Stumpy tried to sort out his feelings about Li'l and the car. He had done a real good thing by finding Bessie, but he did it by breaking the law and not following what he knew Stumpy's orders would be. Once this was over, they were going to have to talk about this, but right now, Stumpy didn't know what he was going to say.

Before he figured it out, the police car pulled over to the shoulder of the road, and Stumpy pulled up behind it. Earl got out of the police car. He opened the back door and Horace got out. Stumpy started to get out of his car when Earl waved him back.

"We're going to drive down there," Earl said. "In fact, we're going to turn on the lights and the siren, and try to make them think the whole damn state police has come to get them. And I want Horace to ride with you. I got an idea that he's going to want to get out in a hurry, and you can't open the back doors on my car from the inside. Y'all just try not to get yourself killed or hurt or something."

Earl turned around and walked back to his car. Horace started to get into the back seat, but Stumpy waved him into the front seat.

"Do you think they hurt Bessie," Horace said softly.

"I hope not," Stumpy said.

Earl pulled out and pointed the nose of the police car straight down the path. Then he turned on the lights and siren and went crashing down as fast as he could navigate the little two-track path. Stumpy pulled the Oldsmobile straight in behind them, and they both slid into the front yard of the shack.

Stumpy saw Claymore Thomas and Petey and another man in the yard. Then he saw another man come out of the house onto the porch. Earl jumped out of the police car yelling that they were all under arrest. The three men in the yard ran toward the house. Claymore and Petey ran into the house. The other two turned around on the porch just in time to see Horace charging at them, screaming. He jumped up on the porch, slamming into one man. The other one took a swing at Horace's head. The punch connected, but didn't slow the big black man down. He swung his left arm around in a huge arc and the forearm caught the white man in the neck, just under the chin, lifting him off his feet and slamming him into the wall. He slid slowly down the wall, as if somebody had pulled the plug and all the consciousness just leaked out of him.

Just as Horace ran into the house, Stumpy heard a crash behind the house.

"They've gone out the window," Li'l yelled, taking off around the house. Stumpy ran after him. As they rounded the corner of the house they saw Claymore and Petey running toward the woods, fighting the tall weeds that kept tripping them up.

"You get the boy," Stumpy called. "I'll get Claymore."

Running over the clear ground in the back yard, they were catching up with Claymore and Petey, but then they felt the weeds grabbing at their legs. They both kept running as hard as they could. Then Stumpy heard Li'l yelling.

"Petey, you're just a chicken shit coward. You'd run away from anything."

Petey stopped and turned. Claymore yelled for him to get moving, but Petey was standing there, trying to get the smirk back on his face.

"Ain't nobody afraid of you, Li'l," he said, just as Li'l barreled into him, throwing his whole body across Petey's chest. Li'l rolled over and punched Petey in the face as hard as he could.

"You leave my boy alone," Claymore yelled. He looked at Petey on the ground. Then he looked at the safety of the woods. His feet seemed to be nailed to the ground, at least until Stumpy grabbed him by his shirt, yanking Claymore almost nose to nose with him. Stumpy drew back his fist, enjoying the thought of planting it right in Claymore's face, but he saw the terror in Claymore's eyes. He just threw the man down on the ground.

"You aren't even worth hitting," he said. Claymore just lay there, his face down on his arm, his shoulders heaving. It took Stumpy a minute to figure out that Claymore Thomas was crying. Stumpy looked around and saw Petey Thomas was crying, too. Tears were running down his face and blood was running out of his nose. Li'l was sitting on him, breathing hard. But he had quit hitting Petey.

"Let's take these back up to Earl," Stumpy said, grabbing Claymore by the shirt collar and dragging him to his feet. Li'l got up and pulled Petey up after him. Petey was trying to wipe his tears and blood away with the sleeve of his shirt.

When they got around to the front of the house, the two men who had been on the porch were sitting there, handcuffed together, their heads down. Bessie was in the yard, Horace's arm around her shoulders. Otha Forster leaned against the police car, talking to Earl. Earl saw them coming around the house and walked over, pulling another pair of handcuffs from his belt. He grabbed Claymore's wrist and slapped one of the handcuffs on it. He put the other one on Petey's wrist. Petey winced as they tightened down.

"Wasn't much of a fight, was it?" Stumpy said.

"Nah, not after Horace took out those two on the front porch. I think they got in one punch and Horace got two. Got one of these kluxers with each punch. How'd you do?" He looked at Petey trying to wipe the blood of his face.

"Not even that good. I just couldn't bring myself to punch old Claymore. That was more dignity than he deserved. I think Petey fell down and Li'l's fist fell down on top of him, or something like that."

"Whatever happened, it's all right. Bessie's just fine. Said that she and Otha talked a lot, and that he's a brave man for trying to save her."

"What does Otha say?"

"That he's a brave man for trying to save her, or maybe dumb. I don't know. Bessie won't say that he was one of those who grabbed her, and Otha just says he knew about it and tried to help her. I get the feeling he's saying what Bessie told him to say. I don't care."

"What'll we do with these?" Stumpy asked. "I don't think we have enough room to take them into town."

"I've got that figured out. Otha's pickup is over yonder, so we're going to dump these four in the back, and tie them up with some of that rope they used on Bessie. Otha'll drive and I'll ride along behind them. If anybody tries to do anything funny, I'll just shoot 'em."

"You ever really shot anybody," Stumpy asked, grinning.

"Nope, but this could be a right good time to start. You take Bessie and Horace home and make sure she's okay. She seems fine to me, a whole lot better off than those bozos who grabbed her."

"You think Otha'll really take them in. I heard he had more than a casual connection with them."

"I think so. I don't think he wants to have anything else to do with that bunch. Besides, Claymore'd rather go to jail than to go home to Ruby. I bet he prays he never gets out."

"I'll take Bessie and Horace home."

Earl grinned. "And what are you going to do about your juvenile delinquent? You know, driving without a license and all that."

"I don't know. I'll probably give him a good talking to, but I'm going to have a hard time doing it with a straight face. You should have seen the way he lit into Petey Thomas. I'm a peaceable man, but it still made me proud."

Earl nodded. "Just tell him that if I catch him out without a driver's license, I'll be duty bound to enforce the law. That might make him think a couple of times before he does it again."

Earl walked over and checked the ropes on the Klansmen, and went back to the police car. Then he waved to Otha and the pickup and the black and white started up the two-track path.

Stumpy turned and held the car door open for Bessie. She smiled.

"Much obliged, Mr. Stumpy."

27

Before noon, the news of Bessie's rescue had gone all over town with the usual accuracy of the small-town grapevine. Various accounts had Earl Holland and Stumpy Fowler engaged in a shootout with Claymore Thomas and the Klansmen and the SBI storming the sharecropper shack after investigating Claymore Thomas for years. One account, circulating on Disciple Street, had Bessie marching the four men out of the shack into Earl Holland's custody by the force of will and the grace of God. However, a few people, like A.Y. Pollard, took the trouble to talk to Earl Holland and get an outline of what happened. Earl asked him if he was going to represent Claymore. All A.Y. said was that he hadn't been asked to, and Earl didn't ask any more questions.

Stumpy had allowed himself about an hour to finish dealing with Bessie's kidnapping. He took Bessie and Horace by their house, then took Li'l home, and told Mae Beth what had happened. Then he put the Oldsmobile in the garage and walked to his office. He pulled out his list from yesterday, and made him a new one. Then he started to work.

He'd already crossed two items off his list when he heard a shuffling at the door to his office. He looked up and A.Y. Pollard was standing there, leaning a little against the doorframe. His face looked like it was sagging. In fact, his whole body looked like it was sagging.

"If you'd have closed your door, I could have knocked," A.Y. said.

"Don't need to knock. Just come on in."

A.Y. came in and flopped into the chair opposite Stumpy. He squirmed around a bit as if he was trying to find a comfortable spot.

"I don't know whether to thank you or not. My life'd been a whole lot easier if you'd just let Bessie sit out there a while," he said after he had finished squirming.

Stumpy leaned back in his chair. "I don't think they were going to let her sit there long. According to Otha, Claymore had brought in some boys from Oak Grove to get rid of her."

A.Y.'s big frame squirmed in the wooden chair. He had a sour look on his face. "Hell of a thing to do over a spot in the Singing Convention."

"Yeah. I guess it was just the principal of the thing. But I'm pretty sure that Claymore would have had her killed. He couldn't really do much else after he had grabbed her like that. She says she knew who they were even before they took the blindfold off her. It's a good thing we found her, even if it does complicate your life. What's Earl going to do with Claymore and his boys?"

"He's got 'em in jail right now, talking about having them transferred somewhere else since he doesn't have the manpower to keep a guard on them. I guess he's worried about some of their buddies trying to get them out. I don't think they've figured out exactly what they're going to charge them with yet. I told Earl that kidnapping and aggravated assault might be a good start. Sort of a pity he didn't take her into South Carolina. Then it'd be a federal case."

Stumpy shook his head. "If he'd taken her into South Carolina, we probably wouldn't have found her in time, and Claymore could have killed her."

A.Y. pursed his lips, nodded his head, and let out a long sigh.

"You're right. It's still a mess, but you're right." He shifted himself around in his chair. "And that brings up another subject. We need a new judge. Seems that Carl Cagle sprained his back somehow, said he did it lifting a box of beans. Anyhow, he can't get out of bed, so he's not going to be judging the Singing competition. I thought you might do that, seeing that you're some sort of hero and all."

"You know I don't know one note from another. I may be the worst person in town to try to judge somebody's singing."

"Could be," A.Y. said, "but we still got to have another judge."

Stumpy thought a minute.

"You know, this could solve a problem for me." he said slowly. "I've been wanting to do something for Li'l because he was the one who actually found Bessie, but I haven't because he went speeding off down the road on my car with no license. Maybe if you let him be a judge, he could get some recognition and I could still be the disapproving parent."

"He's pretty young," A.Y. said. "We've never had a judge that wasn't a grown-up."

"Nothing in the bylaws that says a judge has to be a grown-up. In fact, best I remember, about the only qualification is that they'd be able to show up."

"Yeah. I forgot. You're the expert on the bylaws."

"Come on, A.Y. Get over it. We didn't have any good reason not to let Bessie's choir sing. We did the right thing. You know that."

A.Y. Pollard stood up, staring down at Stumpy. "You may be right, Stumpy. I just wish you could have been right when I wasn't in charge. Okay, tell Li'l that we want him to be a judge, and I'll tell the other judges."

He turned to leave, then turned back, a small smile in the corners of his mouth.

"You think since you rescued Bessie she might be grateful enough to pull out of the Singing Convention, I mean, if you ask her to?"

Stumpy laughed, a short bark.

"No, she wouldn't. After what she's been through, she's not about to stop now. And I wouldn't want to be the one that asked her. She shouldn't have needed rescuing in the first place."

"Yeah, well, it was a thought," A.Y. said. When he left, Stumpy thought he was walking like an old man, an old man who was carrying a big load on his shoulders. Stumpy was glad he wasn't carrying anything like the burdens A.Y. Pollard was having to carry.

That evening, when he got home, Stumpy found Mae Beth and Li'l sitting in the living room waiting for him. He could hear Bessie in the kitchen, occasionally rattling a pan or a plate. Stumpy wondered why Bessie was still in the kitchen. Usually, she had gone home by the time he got there. He looked first at Mae Beth and then at Li'l, but neither of them moved or said anything.

"What's up?" he asked, finally. "You two look like you have something on your mind."

Mae Beth smiled.

"I just want you to know that I have never been so proud of you or Arthur, Jr. as I am right now."

She walked over to him and hugged him.

"I always knew you were a good man, Arthur Fowler, but you proved it beyond anything you had to do. And you just did it because it was the right thing to do."

She hugged him tighter.

"And I love you for it."

Stumpy stood there, wondering what he was supposed to say. He couldn't think of anything, so he just hugged Mae Beth back. She loosened her grip on Stumpy and looked up at his face.

"I've already told Arthur how proud of I was of him..."

"Even though he's a lawbreaker?" Stumpy said.

"Well, maybe not that part, but the way it came out."

"I'm just glad he didn't wreck the car or run into somebody." Stumpy looked over Mae Beth's shoulder at Li'l. He didn't seem to be real worried about Stumpy being mad at him. He was grinning. Finally, Stumpy smiled back at him. The fact was, Li'l had done what he thought he had to do, and he did it knowing he could get into trouble, but finding Bessie had been more important than what could happen to him. Stumpy couldn't help feeling proud of what Li'l had done.

"We're going to have company for dinner," Mae Beth said.

Stumpy pulled back, his eyebrows raised in a question.

"Bessie and Horace," Mae Beth said. "We're going to celebrate her being rescued."

Stumpy felt his arms stiffen around Mae Beth. He couldn't think of Bessie or even Horace as company, and he was having trouble thinking of sitting down at the dinner table with them. He knew when he wasn't there, Bessie and Mae Beth often had a sandwich together, and sometimes even when Li'l was there. But Bessie had always found something else to do when Stumpy was home at noon. It was different from the way things were usually done.

"I don't know how you can call Bessie company when I can hear her cooking dinner," he said, finally. He decided he had been through too many things in the last few days that weren't the way things were usually done to worry about somebody like Bessie and Horace sharing a meal with them.

"I told her I'd cook it," Mae Beth said, "but she wouldn't have it. She's been at it most of the afternoon."

It was just a few minutes later when they heard Horace at the back door. Stumpy got up from his chair and went to the kitchen and held the door open for Horace.

"Evenin', Mr. Stumpy," he said as he came in. He stood just inside the doorway, looking at Bessie. It occurred to

Stumpy that Horace didn't know whether he should come all the way in or not. Stumpy held out his hand, and Horace shook it.

"Come on in the living room, Horace. The ladies'll have dinner ready in a few minutes," he said. He motioned Horace into the living room. With the slightest hesitation, Horace went in, spoke to Li'l and sat down. They watched the news on television until dinner was ready.

28

The second Sunday in June was hot and humid, just like it always was, except for the two or three times it had actually rained. There were people in the Singing Grove by seven o'clock, even though the competition didn't start until nine. The Boy Scouts were already out on their corners in their olive uniforms with gold-colored neckerchiefs and silver whistles hanging from gold lanyards. The vendors were setting their booths up along the street, and cars were pouring in from the north, south, east, and west. Although he didn't have anything official to do, Stumpy was among the early arrivals. He went to one of the benches on the edge of the grove and sat down, watching the families as they claimed space on the benches or spread blankets up near the oak trees. As he watched the people get ready to listen, he whispered a prayer that the day would go smoothly and that what he had done wouldn't cause a fight or bring an end to the Sing.

He sat there for a while, wondering just what this day was going to be like. Soon he'd need to go back home to get ready for Sunday school and Church. Every Sing Sunday, the attendance at the Baptist Church dropped by nearly half; some of the people were at the Sing, but most of them just didn't want to get out of their houses into the crowds. Stumpy walked back through the grove, stopping occasionally to pick up a candy wrapper or a drink bottle and take it to the trashcan. At the edge of the grove he turned around and looked at the stage. It was important to Stumpy that he could stand in the same spot and see the same stage next year, knowing on that Sunday people would be singing their gospel music and competing for the tall trophies. He stood there staring at the stage, wondering how as things change they can still endure. He felt sure they could. He just didn't know how.

* * *

Although Li'l had been awake since before six, he didn't get out of bed until nearly eight o'clock. He didn't want to seem like he was nervous or excited; he wanted to make it look like being a judge at the Singing Convention was just an everyday thing. But he didn't believe that himself. He put on his blue seersucker suit, white shirt, and blue tie, had a bowl of cereal, and left for the Singing Grove. He was supposed to be there before nine o'clock.

When he got there, Mrs. Evers was sitting in one of the folding chairs at the left side of the stage, a large pink hat with purple flowers on her head. She was talking, loudly, with Mrs. Turner. Li'l looked around for the other judges, not wanting to get involved in the conversation between Mrs. Evers and Mrs. Turner.

"You must be the new Carl Cagle."

Li'l looked around. The man looked like he was in his late twenties. Like Li'l, he had on a suit and tie, but to Li'l, it looked like he wore it much more comfortably. His blond hair was perfectly in place. The man stuck his hand out.

"I'm Stanfield Turner. This is my third year of doing this, and it doesn't hurt real bad."

Li'l shook the man's hand. "Li'l Fowler. I really don't know what I'm doing here."

"Don't worry about it. Most of the judges don't. See that man over there." He pointed to a tall gray-haired man standing under one of the big oaks with about a half-dozen men, most of them in overalls. "That's Congressman Tyler. He's been a judge here forever, just because he's a Congressman. Doesn't usually have much to say about anything, except 'they sounded real good.' And he says that even when they sound like a train wreck."

He gestured to the two ladies in the chairs. "Mrs. Evers is pretty good; she knows something about music, but dear old Mrs. Turner can't even hear it. Usually it's Mrs. Evers and me, and everybody else goes along with it."

"That sounds easy enough," Li'l said, relieved that somebody had told him how this worked.

"I didn't say that's what you ought to do. Just listen to the singers. You'll hear some that you know are really good, even if you don't know why you know that. And you'll hear some that you know aren't all that good. Just listen, and when we talk about it, say what you think. Might be a good thing to have a new perspective here. And relax. This is a singing convention, not an execution. If you're wrong, nobody's going to die. Let's go get us a chair. It's going to be a long day."

They walked over and sat down in two chairs away from the ladies. Li'l looked at all the people gathering in the singing grove and wondered if it was really as easy as Mr. Turner said.

* * *

In church that morning, Stumpy listened to the choir with a new attention. It wasn't a big choir, about twenty people, and he didn't know if it was good or not. After hearing Bessie's choir, he thought it sounded sort of listless, but since he didn't know one note from another, he didn't know if that was a problem or not. He looked from one face to the next, and almost every face was wearing a smile as they sang about God, every face except for Mr. Rector, who probably hadn't smiled a dozen times in his nearly 80 years. As they sang about the Balm in Giliad, Stumpy tried to find the differences between the Baptist Choir and the A.M.E. Choir, and he felt relieved that except for their color he couldn't find any real differences. He kept thinking about it as the young pastor labored through his sermon. Stumpy thought about Li'l, who was at the grove judging the competition. It gave him a strange feeling to think of his son in a position of responsibility. But he had to admit that Li'l acted grown up, and in a lot of ways, he was. Stumpy took Mae Beth's hand and tried to hear what the preacher was saying.

As they walked back to their house for dinner, Stumpy and Mae Beth talked about things that didn't matter much. How nice the Willis' yard was looking this year. That the Johnson's had just had their big, two-story house painted. Finally, Mae Beth brought up the Sing.

"Are you going to hear the choirs this afternoon?" she asked.

"I plan to. You?"

They walked along for a minute before she answered.

"I want to, and I guess I will. But I worry about something happening when Bessie's choir gets up there. Somebody could throw something, or they could scream at her. I don't want anything bad to happen."

Stumpy took her hand again, and they walked along, hand-in-hand. It occurred to Stumpy it was probably a good thing that Li'l wasn't with them. He might have thought it strange that his parents were holding hands in public. It was what Mae Beth called "a public display of affection," and told Li'l he shouldn't do.

"There might be some booing," he said. "I don't know, but I imagine Bessie figured on that when she started all this. I don't think Earl will let anything really bad happen. These are mostly good folks who behave themselves."

Mae Beth nodded and squeezed his hand.

After they ate, they walked down to the Singing Grove. Now the traffic was backed up at almost every corner as the Boy Scouts tried to maintain some order. Stumpy noticed that one Scout had the idea of letting one car go from one direction, then letting one go from the other direction. The farmers sat at the wheel of their cars and pickups and glared at the twelve-year-old, but they stopped when he held up his hand. Stumpy waved to some people he knew, and he and Mae Beth found a place to stand under one of the oak trees. They could see Li'l, dressed in his Sunday coat and tie sitting at the left side of the stage with the other judges. He was taller than the women judges and almost as tall as the men. He was staring intently at the family group that was singing, his pencil poised over the note pad. Stumpy nudged Mae Beth and pointed to him.

Stumpy figured there were probably ten thousand people in and around the grove, about usual for a Sing Sunday. Little children ran after each other between the benches and around the trees, and Stumpy saw a teenaged couple trying to keep the trunk of the big oak between them and what must have been her parents as they stared into each other's faces. The big speakers in the trees carried the sound beyond the grove and into the streets.

"So far, so good."

Stumpy turned around and saw A.Y Pollard standing behind him. Mae Beth turned and smiled at him.

"You know, for a fair-sized man, you sure do walk quiet," Stumpy said.

"Part of being a lawyer. Maintaining the element of surprise," A.Y. said, smiling. "I don't guess we'll know just how this day's going until after the choirs sing, and that's the last part of the program."

"Didn't seem to hurt attendance a whole lot," Stumpy said. "Of course, some of these people could be here just out of curiosity. Wonder if any of the folks from Disciple Street are going to show up."

"I wouldn't be surprised. Earl has a place over there he's going to suggest they go. Wouldn't be the first time they came to hear the music."

Finally, the choirs came on. The first two were from Methodist churches, one in River Falls and one from out of town. They got up and sang, received some applause, and left the stage. These choirs and some others like them came every year, but never made much of an impression.

Then, the River Falls Baptist Church choir took the stage. They looked a little strange to Stumpy without their gold robes; they all had on white shirts and black skirts or pants. Stumpy had heard that the new preacher suggested they save their robes for the church services. There was some grumbling among the choir members, but they had decided black and white was just as good.

They started singing, and the first thing Stumpy noticed was they were singing "It Is Well with my Soul," the same hymn that Bessie and her choir had practiced Wednesday night, and as far as Stumpy could tell, they were doing a good job. It was a big sound from the twenty people, and they seemed to start and stop just like they were supposed to. Stumpy asked Mae Beth how they were doing, and she said they were a lot better than the other choirs. They received loud applause when they finished.

When the Baptist choir left the stage, Bessie, in her white dress, led her choir on. They arranged themselves on the risers, an expanse of gold with dark faces above maroon stoles. The crowd was murmuring, but there was no yelling. Stumpy saw one family get up and, after taking a pointed look at the stage, leave, but mostly they sat, waiting, wanting to know what the Negro choir was going to sound like. There was more murmuring when they started and the crowd recognized they were singing the same old hymn that the Baptists had sung. Then it stopped, and the only sound Stumpy could hear was the choir. When they finished, most of the crowd applauded; in fact, the applause sounded about as loud as it had for the Baptists. Stumpy was beginning to believe the day was going to be all right after all. They had all sung, and nobody had started a fight, or even yelled or booed. He could feel himself smiling as Bessie and her choir left the stage.

Stumpy looked at a small group of Negroes congregated at the side of the grove. They had come just in time to hear the choirs, and now they, like everybody else, were waiting to hear the decision of the judges. Usually the head judge announced the winner within a minute or two of the end of the competition, but the minutes wore on without an announcement. Somebody came over and said something to A.Y., and he started up to the stage. Stumpy wondered if one of the judges or somebody else had come up with a way to disqualify Bessie even after she sang. He could see A.Y. talking to the head judge. A.Y. was nodding and shaking his head. Stumpy couldn't imagine what they were saying except that it had to be about the choirs. Finally, A.Y. nodded his head again and left the judges. He took one of the microphones to the front of the stage and motioned for the crowd to be quiet.

"Folks, we've got a first at this Singing Convention. In twenty-nine years, we have never had a tie, but today, it seems like we do. The River Falls Baptist Choir and the Bethel A.M.E. Choir are tied for first place." He looked over at the judges. "Or at least that's the best our judges can do. Since we only have one first place choir trophy, we can't have a tie. We've decided the only thing to do is have each one of the choirs sing again and see if we can't get a winner. Since the Baptist Choir has had a chance to catch their breath, we're going to let them sing first. If you folks will come back up to the stage, we'll get started."

Stumpy saw several people dressed in white tops and black bottoms get up from benches around the park and head for the stage. In just a few minutes they were up there, the director huddled with the piano player trying to decide what they would sing, leafing through the black folders that each choir member carried. Finally, they must have agreed on something because the pianist sat down, opened her folder up and smoothed out the pages. The director got the choir's attention and raised her hands. The pianist sat still, her hands over the keys. Then she ran them softly from the bottom to the top. Then she brought both hands down, hard, and the choir sang:

There is power

The pianist played another grand chord, this one louder and broader than the first. And the choir sang:

There is power

Then they were off, with more energy and enthusiasm than Stumpy had ever heard them sing. They testified loudly and in harmony to the power in the blood of the Lamb. The piano player was leaning low over the keyboard, not looking at the music at all, the best Stumpy could tell, ringing out notes that wove all around the choir. Stumpy looked at the crowd. Their feet were tapping, their heads were bobbing, and a few were even clapping, softly since clapping with the music wasn't something they usually did in the Singing Grove. Stumpy couldn't help but feel proud of his church choir. He looked at Mae Beth, and she was smiling, nodding her head in time with the music. The choir sang four verses, each with more joy than the one before it, and by the time they got to the end, it seemed to Stumpy they had wrung every bit of emotion out of the crowd they could have. Bessie's choir was good, but he couldn't imagine how it could connect with the crowd any better than that.

When the choir finished, the applause was louder than it had been all day. Some people were on their feet clapping. The Baptist choir left the stage and the crowd settled down, waiting to see what the A.M.E. choir could do that would be better than that. It seemed like the stage was empty for a long time. Then Bessie came up from the right side, followed by her choir. They shuffled around on the risers getting in position. Bessie looked at them, and motioned for one or two of them to move slightly. Then she turned around to face the crowd. Stumpy heard what sounded like a single piano note.

If you want to go to heaven, come along, come along

It was Bessie's voice, but it was more than Bessie's voice. It rang out through the speakers in the trees like an angel summoning all the people to heaven.

Then the piano came in, an explosion of notes that seemed to lift the choir as they joined Bessie. The choir began to sway and clap as they sang, and Stumpy saw people in the crowd begin to sway and some of them began to clap. By the time they got to the second verse, the choir was clapping their hands and stomping their feet, reaching out with their voices to the mostly white crowd in front of them. And it looked like the crowd was reaching back, transformed from a bunch of farmers and farmers' wives who got up tired in the morning and went to bed tired at night to passengers on some train going to heaven where they wouldn't ever have to be tired again. With each verse, the choir's sound grew more expansive, wrapping them in the invitation. Then suddenly it stopped. And there was Bessie's voice again, soft, mellow:

For to try on your long white robe

She left the soft low note hanging in the air for a long time, standing still with her hands clasped up under her chin. Then she dropped her hands and the choir behind her sang a soft chord that lay in the air and gradually disappeared. There was nothing in the grove but quiet, and Stumpy wondered if the crowd was going to just get up and leave or something. Then somebody started clapping, and others joined in. The applause grew, and there were people getting to their feet, still clapping. Stumpy saw one old man, raw boned, in his best overalls and straw hat, stop clapping long enough to wipe a tear from his cheek. The applause lasted a long time, but finally everybody sat down and quit clapping. The choir just stood there.

Stumpy saw A.Y. talking to the judges again. Finally, he

went over and picked up the trophy. He came out to the front of the stage.

"Folks, the judges tell me that it was a really tough decision, but they have come up with a winner. This year's winning choir is the Bethel A.M.E. choir, directed by Bessie Williams."

"Mrs. Bessie Williams," Stumpy muttered under his breath.

The crowd applauded, not as loudly as before. The spirit had dissipated, and it was dawning on the crowd that the Negro choir had won. Stumpy looked around to see if anybody was going to boo or throw something, but nobody did. The Negroes at the edge of the grove continued to applaud loudly, but as best Stumpy could tell, it was over. He and Mae Beth started making their way toward the stage. He could see Bessie holding the big trophy, tears running down her face. Choir members were crowded around her, hugging her and patting her on the shoulder. The director of the Baptist choir came up and spoke to her. Bessie smiled and said something back. They came up to the edge of the stage where Li'l was standing. He grinned at them and jumped down.

"How did you do, son?" Stumpy asked.

"I guess I did all right. I just sort of listened to what the other judges were saying, and I tried to vote for the one I thought was best."

"It was probably good for Bessie that you were a judge," Stumpy said.

Li'l shook his head. "I didn't vote when the choirs sang. Since I was a member of the Baptist Church and Bessie works for us, I thought I just shouldn't vote. But Bessie didn't really need my vote anyway. Her choir won by two votes."

Stumpy waved at Bessie, and she waved back. He, and Mae Beth, and Li'l started walking home, picking their way through the people streaming out of the Singing Grove. The day had gone well. There'd be another Singing Convention next year, and there was no telling what was going to happen between now and then. Stumpy didn't worry about it. He just walked home with his family.

29

FROM THE RIVER FALLS CURRENT
Thursday, October 11, 1956

Three Local Men Convicted of Assault Receive Suspended Sentences

Claymore Thomas, James G. Turnage, and Aaron Smelt pled guilty to Simple Assault charges in Superior Court Tuesday. They were charged in the assault of a local Negro woman.

According to County Attorney H. Canley Johnson, the plea was the result of an agreement between his office and the defendants' attorney, George Connelly. The three had originally been charged with kidnapping, false imprisonment, and aggravated assault, but Johnson said the plea bargain would save the county taxpayers thousands of dollars in trial costs.

On accepting the plea, Judge Addison Henry sentenced each of the men to one year in the county jail, but suspended the sentence, saying he thought the pain and suffering brought on their families by their actions had been sufficient punishment.

CPSIA information can be obtained
at www.ICGtesting.com
Printed in the USA
BVHW07s1605081018
529574BV00007B/1278/P